A HOSTILE PLACE

Also by John Fullerton

FICTION
The Monkey House

NON-FICTION
The Soviet Occupation of Afghanistan

JOHN FULLERTON

A HOSTILE PLACE

MACMILLAN

First published 2003 by Macmillan
an imprint of Pan Macmillan Ltd
Pan Macmillan, 20 New Wharf Road, London N1 9RR
Basingstoke and Oxford
Associated companies throughout the world
www.panmacmillan.com

ISBN 1 4050 2119 5 (HB)
ISBN 1 4050 3376 2 (TPB)

1 3 5 7 9 8 6 4 2

A CIP catalogue record for this book is available from
the British Library.

Typeset by SetSystems Ltd, Saffron Walden, Essex
Printed and bound in Great Britain by
Mackays of Chatham plc, Chatham, Kent

In memory of Abdul Haq, a guerrilla commander and friend who was murdered because he remained true to himself and could not be bought.

AUTHOR'S NOTE

A Hostile Place was inspired by actual events and some personal experience. But it is a work of fiction; all portrayals of military and paramilitary forces, intelligence officers, their agents, Afghans and their friends and relatives as well as Taliban and al-Qaeda leaders and fighters are imaginary.

ONE

DECEMBER, 2001

I was alive. I had no right to be.

My people were dead, and I should have been, too.

The enemy staunched the bleeding. He bound my wounds. He gave me bread and tea, refilling my cup and offering me a smoke, the enemy commander lighting the cigarette himself and putting it between my lips because I couldn't keep the fingers of my one good hand still enough to hold it.

I felt stupid in my helplessness. Angry. Like a child. I could barely talk. I gritted my teeth and tried to swallow my groans. Jesus, it hurt. I was given a mattress, a blanket and a cushion, and a place was cleared for me near my captors' fire. They stared. Their friends came to look, craning their necks. Every painful move I made, every gesture, every expression, every grunt, was noted. They kept up a running commentary, as if I was in the news. I was something of an exhibition, a novelty. I felt a little better when I told myself they surely could not intend to execute me after treating me so well.

All the same, I was surprised they didn't.

I steeled myself as best I could, determined to die well if it happened, to stifle my fear, not to whimper, not to show weakness.

I knew how it was done. It could be quick, merciful – a bullet in the head while kneeling in the dust, sucking on one of their boiled sweets or muttering the Lord's Prayer. What-ever palliative helped. That would have been my preference. Or it could be slow, a coward's death. They would cut a man's

1

hamstrings and throw their knives to the children and watch the soon-to-die try to crawl away from his tormentors, wriggling under the blades, his pleas for mercy drowned by contemptuous laughter.

A thief's death, providing some entertainment.

I showed them what I needed. I demonstrated by gesture how to help with the dressings I carried. I used a shaving mirror so I could see the back wound. I flinched at the sight of it. It was so deep it scared me. God almighty, the jagged RPG fragment was still in there somewhere. They watched me closely, learning from me until I lost consciousness again. I had far better equipment than they had, but they didn't take it from me, except my weapons. They turned everything over in their hands and passed all I had from one man to the next. They discussed all that I carried, but they took nothing. It went back into my Bergen, all of it, even the prismatic compass, my little shortwave radio receiver and the GSM satphone. I did not make the mistake of offering them my paper money or the gold sovereigns sewn into my clothing.

They found those, too, but their leader told them to leave well alone.

They even left me my boots.

I'm not sure I would have in their place.

My comrades were mostly dead. Their mothers would never look upon their sons again, boys barely half my age. Yet I slept well that night, the painkillers giving me the untroubled rest my captors sorely needed and which I did not deserve.

What kind of people were my enemies? They were poor and illiterate. Their natural lives were short, half that of my own people. They looked upon death in battle as something to be wished for, as conferring honour on the soul of the deceased and enhancing the reputation of the family. Life without faith meant little to them, had no value. Compared to me and my kind they had nothing, or next to nothing. Nothing, yet they gave what little they had: bread and tea and cigarettes and a dry, warm place to sleep. They were gentle, courteous, even solicitous in their rough way. In that sense they had everything my kind lacked, and it was we who had nothing of value. It was a matter of perspective.

My enemies might be poor and ignorant, but they did not hate. That was the strangest thing after what we had done to them.

I really did not understand.

I was in shock.

That was the first day.

They shook me awake before dawn.

My first thought through the fog of pain: I am still alive.

They had to help me onto my feet. I wasn't thinking clearly. I resented their hands on me. I resented my uselessness. I swore at them with every filthy word I knew. I batted at them with my right hand (my left was worse than useless) but they took no notice of the foreign man-child's silliness. They laughed at my obscenities, making a joke of the pantomime. I was the source of amusement in their TV-free, monotone world. They gripped my legs and pushed my feet into my boots, but left the laces undone. They got me upright. I blacked out with the pain. When I returned to my senses they had my blanket around me and three of them half-carried, half-propelled me outside.

Fuck your mothers, I screamed at them.

Fuck you all.

The cold wind slashed at us in the darkness. The only ones warm enough not to feel it were the grave-diggers.

They were burying the dead, theirs and ours, together, side by side, in a row. Perhaps they were going to bury me.

3

No coffins, no cremation, but bodies in contact with the earth.

They looked at me. They waited for my response. I nodded, raised my torn hands to my chest. Their rite could do no harm. Who knows? It might do some good. My companions were buried with their heads and right sides towards Mecca, the prayers said aloud over their remains as they were lifted down into the deep earth, no distinction made between friend and foe.

'O God, pardon this dead person; lo, Thou art the Most Forgiving, the Most Merciful.'

Equal in the sight of a God I didn't acknowledge.

I prayed with my enemies, running my right hand – my left hurt too badly – over my face in a washing motion.

Curly. Philippe. Andy.

Felix, my best friend. Was he among them? I couldn't see him. Maybe he'd got away, slithered into a hole, nursing his injuries. God, I hoped so, but I didn't see how. The bodies were white as marble, their blood sponged away, their torn, waxy flesh wrapped in muslin like a newborn's swaddling clothes.

I am ashamed of it now, but I cried as the soil was shovelled back, the graves filled, the stones heaped up, the grave markers planted, long poles with gaudy cloths for the martyred, the *shahuda*, the men fallen in war.

Our glorious dead.

'To God we belong, and to God we will return.'

My mates.

Women in black appeared. They cried out, prostrating themselves on the graves of their menfolk, tearing at their clothes.

I don't think anyone saw my tears.

Loneliness and guilt.

*

They had to move. Safety lay in ceaseless movement. They could not lie up to rest, not even for a single morning. They had to keep going. They could not sleep in the same place twice. Our side had made sure of that with constant air patrols. They could not leave me behind, not with strangers. Word of my presence in the village would spread quickly if it had not already done so. They had to take me with them, or kill me. It was a simple choice, and I know what I would have done in their place – without a moment's hesitation. Expediency suggested the last was the most efficient way to eliminate the problem of the injured prisoner, but their code would not permit it. *Pashtunwali*, they called it.

My Bergen was strapped to a mule. So were the mattress and blanket I had used the previous night. They improvised a saddle out of the blanket, and I was lifted onto the animal's back. No attempt was made to bind my arms or legs, or tie me in any way to my mount. A youth – a teenager in the West but a man in this world – was the beast's minder, perhaps its owner, and his duty lay in ensuring it kept up and did not stray. He said no word to me. He didn't even look at me. His indifference was in contrast to the curiosity I aroused in my captors. His diffidence hinted at a message I could not yet decipher. He showed no sign of suffering from the cold despite his threadbare *chalwar kameez*. His hands and sandalled feet were large, calloused and ingrained with dirt like any peasant's. He carried a stick, no other weapon, and the expression on his grubby face was one of pride, a sense of being every bit as equal as the fighters around us.

He walked in silence behind the mule and slightly to one side.

I made no attempt to talk to him or ingratiate myself.

We would meet again. I do not know how I knew.

*

5

He, or his father or elder brother, might have been contracted to provide this service as far as our next destination (wherever that was) and to return with his mule to his village when it was accomplished. Perhaps it was a commercial arrangement. He was deliberately keeping himself aloof, distant from this war party of ours. That interested me. Was he of a different tribe? Did he resent these travellers who had passed through his village and slept under his roof? Was there enmity, and if so, of what kind? Was he a royalist, perhaps? Did he resent his family's need for money? Or was he merely frightened, and working hard to keep his fear concealed?

If so, I knew just how he felt.

I was not immune. I was scared, too.

Our journey was likely to be long, and I thought that perhaps I could turn this silent youth to my advantage in some way.

We headed north-east. At least I thought so. The leader used the lie of the land, staying below the crests of hills, keeping off roads and tracks and using paths only when he felt he had to for fear of unmarked minefields. He used shadow, shunned light when he could. He used the ground to space his fighters, shifting men and weapons from one high point to another. He had the presence of mind to form overlapping fields of fire on the hoof, to guard natural passes or funnels and to cover dead ground with his weapons before it could be cleared on foot. As a commander he was a natural. I admired him for it. I recognized in him that rare affinity for landscape without the benefit of map or compass. He was a preacher, but I told myself he must surely have inherited the genetic predisposition of a farmer from his forebears.

I heard his voice, saw his shadow pass by and witnessed the effect of his orders, and I wondered who he was.

I watched the sun rise, marked its warm embrace shifting on my bruised body like a compass needle. By my reckoning we had crossed into Oruzgan by breakfast time, and by noon we had crossed the road to Tirin Kot, the provincial capital, making the move in three rushes. My crossing was more a panicky trot, provoked by my escort's shoving his stick up the unfortunate beast's anus. By then two squads had been deployed north and south, their weapons trained up and down the 'highway' where it turned almost ninety degrees around the base of a stony hill of blue-black volcanic dust. The perfect site for an ambush, or to counter someone else's, and my grenades had been distributed among the rest of the men, sited by the commander in a gully below the road.

His men were lucky to have him.

I fell twice that morning, passing out on both occasions. The worst of my wounds reopened, and I bled heavily before they could be closed again with fresh dressings. The hot sun, the loss of blood and my fatigue made me delirious. I found myself talking to myself, crying out, even laughing. I was seeing things. I was in a taxi in Pimlico at one point, the windows all misted up. It was night and raining hard. Then I was enjoying a bath by candlelight with a strange woman with red hair.

It was obvious to everyone I was weakening, slowing the group down, and in my moments of lucidity I could tell from their looks and mutterings it was a matter of concern. I was a burden to them, and a troublesome one, no longer simply an amusing distraction.

Even I could smell my blood and pus.

Just how far would the honour code of the Pashtuns be allowed to override common sense?

I knew what I had to have. Rest and a plasma drip.

The sweet green tea helped. I kept emptying the glass, using a finger to get at the sugar at the bottom, and my captors kept refilling it as hospitality demanded. The bread filled my belly, but what we all needed was protein and vitamins. Eggs, meat, fruit – but there was little chance of that without heading for a town, and I knew that wasn't on the cards. Not with me around. I was their secret.

Their leader came over and looked at me. He bent down to get a better look at his captive. I peered back at him. For a moment we stared at each other. When it finally sank in I opened my mouth to speak, but there was no sound.

I wasn't sure what I'd have done if I hadn't been so weak.

Part of me wanted to jump up and hug him with sheer relief. Yes, gratitude even. Gratitude for a face I knew. Gratitude for being kept alive.

Another part of me wanted to tear his miserable heart out.

If he had one.

In revenge for Curly, Philippe and Andy.

I wanted to ask about Felix, but my tongue was too swollen to function.

Despite his beard, the sun and windburn, the dirt and the greasy turban, I knew who he was.

What he was.

Abdur Rahman was London's man. And here he was, the notorious Taliban commander, killing London's men.

His was a filthy game.

What did they care back at MI6? The SIS buggers at Vauxhall Cross minded not at all. Not as long as Abdur Rahman worked at his cover by doing what he was so good at, namely evading bounty hunters like me, and from time to time turning the tables on his pursuers and teaching us all a lesson.

Yesterday it had been us. Today it might be Royal Marines and tomorrow the 101st Airborne.

Abdur Rahman knew I knew, but he gave no sign. He just moved away again, out of my field of vision.

It wasn't simply *Pashtunwali* that was keeping me alive. It was Abdur Rahman. The question was why, and I had no answer.

I lay on my front and slept.

The next four hours were torture. Every step the mule took was agony. The spasms of pain were like lashes from a steel whip. Always the same place, and nothing I could do to stop it.

Between each spasm, I had to struggle to stay awake.

We halted again at dusk. I fell off the mule all by myself, and the pain made me retch.

I needed a shit.

Afghans aren't British soldiers. They don't dig two holes, one for rubbish, one for a latrine. Too poor to have rubbish, they use the slope of a hill for the latter, a gully perhaps, at a discreet distance from their camp. They use stones held in their left hands to clean themselves, not tissue paper. It's no wonder so many of them have hepatitis B.

My left hand was twice its normal size and oozing blood.

I had trouble explaining what I meant to do. In the end I had to point at my arse and blow a loud and long raspberry.

Merriment briefly erupted in Abdur Rahman's camp.

Two fighters helped me over the ridge and sat me down, none too gently. They made raspberry noises, too, signalling I could go ahead. They walked off a few paces, keeping their backs turned, as I loosened the cord on my baggy Afghan trousers and tried to keep the tails of my long Afghan shirt clear.

It was never easy with two hands at the best of times, but with the thumb on my left hand almost severed and a hole in my back it was almost impossible. I groaned aloud, and this time I didn't care if my minders heard me.

I knew Oruzgan from the map. It was big. Mountainous. Few roads, even fewer passable by a wheeled or tracked vehicle. In winter – it was December and winter had us in its grasp – it snowed on high ground, and the tracks became treacherous and slippery. Tirin Kot was the only town worthy of the name. Villages were few. Unlike much of south-western Afghanistan, still in the grip of a four-year-long drought, there was water. Where there was water there was food. The province was sparsely populated. A man could live in Oruzgan for years without anyone knowing he was there. As long as he could stay fit and healthy, he could survive in the wild for extended periods without making contact with any village.

It was perfect territory for fugitives.

Perfect for the guerrilla.

Perfect for holding a foreign prisoner.

Was I to be ransomed? Held hostage for the prisoners held by the Americans at Guantanamo?

If that was the case, it was unrealistic. I was British, not a US national. They'd got the wrong man, and I didn't want to think about they'd do when they learned of their mistake.

Abdur Rahman knew. Of course he did. He must.

So why did I still live?

What was it that I had that was so important to Abdur Rahman?

I would have plenty of time to think about it. For a long while thinking would be all I could do, and the answer would gradually begin to take shape.

But in my delirium that second night, I thought Felix had come to see me. I talked to him and grasped his hand. It was good to talk to him again. I missed him. I missed all our boys. Jesus, I did. So I talked pretty much non-stop.

'I'll be with you soon, my Russian friend. Keep a long thumb of pepper vodka for me, you devil. You thought you'd have it all to yourself. didn't you, Christ on the cross, but I'll be along very shortly, you old commie, just you see if I won't. We'll hit the nightspots and I'll get myself that blow job I've been promising myself. Here's to you, Comrade Zotov. Here's to all you ex-Red Army bastards.'

I was sure I was dying, but for Felix's sake I wanted to be

cheerful. I hummed the opening bars of the 'Red Flag'. The mention of martyrs, the certainty its lines evoked among a previous generation, seemed apposite. I sang a verse in my best imitation of Chelyapin, and we laughed uproariously, cynical by virtue of hindsight.

> The people's flag is deepest red
> It shrouded oft our martyred dead;
> And ere their limbs grew stiff and cold
> Their hearts' blood dyed its every fold.

Right on.

Only it wasn't Felix's hand I held, but a Velcro tab on my torn sleeping bag.

I had never been so afraid of dying.

Pathetic, really.

TWO

I was lying on metal. It was like a cold shower, shocking at first, then puzzling. I had to piece it together by physical sensation, mostly by feel and sound. Apparently they had placed my cotton mattress down on its surface, and then carried me from the mud house to whatever it was and placed me face down. They were careful. They knew I was very weak. There was lots of the usual shouting and I could hear Abdur Rahman's voice giving orders, and that was somehow reassuring. I felt the corrugated metal surface with my fingers, and the cold reached me through the mattress. My eyes were open, but I couldn't see more than a rim of sky.

It was dark, but whether morning or night I couldn't tell.

The stars were brilliant, but there was no moon.

Morning, possibly, around 3 or 4 a.m.

There was a lot of excited talk. Other men climbed onto whatever it was I was lying on, clutching their weapons. I heard them clearing their Kalashnikovs, putting them on safe before clambering up and squatting next to me, hawking up phlegm and turning their heads and spitting. I could smell them: dirty feet and mutton fat. They were Afghans all right.

Someone gave me a cigarette. It seemed to amuse them to light a cigarette, then put it between my lips and watch me smoke it. Sometimes it was a sweet or a piece of bread. Not that I wasn't grateful. I was.

I don't know if I finished that particular cigarette or not. Perhaps I've simply forgotten, but what I remember next was the movement: a shuddering, sliding sensation. A bit like being in a small boat in a choppy sea. There was the stench of diesel. I could hear an engine chugging away somewhere in front and felt the vibration of it in my belly. I was lying on the floor of a trailer, I realized, and in front of me was the tractor. We went downhill. I tried to steady myself, but it didn't work. I slid about, helplessly, until my escorts placed their feet on the mattress and anchored me to one spot.

When the sun rose the track improved. The tractor stopped briefly, and I was given water. Men left, others arrived. There was more talk. Something prickly and scratchy was placed around me. I realized it was brushwood, a dried weed used for firewood. They piled it high like a stockade around me, and the tractor coughed into life once more.

My back was a dull ache that throbbed away, but it was not so bad I could not sleep.

Abdur Rahman had to weigh the risk of keeping me with him, or sending me to Tirin Kot where I might survive with better care.

Either way, it was a risk.

If I did pull through, I might also reveal his presence in the area. What I didn't know then was that Abdur Rahman had decided to use me as bait to mount another operation, and that he reasoned it was all a matter of timing. My arrival in Tirin Kot was set to follow the action he had planned, so my intelligence – if indeed I was capable of passing it on to the military in my weakened state – would in any event have been overtaken by events.

My blood-soaked dressings had already been used to lay a trail. So had my shirt and trousers. I knew none of this. Once everything else had been prepared, Abdur Rahman had used the tractor to partly recharge the battery of my GSM satphone before sending me off down the track.

He made one call, using the last number on the handset's memory.

He told me later he said only one word, over and over again.

'Help.'

Then he left the phone, still on, where he knew they would find it, along with my radio, my compass, my sleeping bag and the Bergen – in full view, the satphone connected to the Indian Ocean geostationary satellite at 180 degrees, or due south.

He used sixteen empty yellow casings from defused or exploded bomblets from US cluster bombs to deny ground. He took them from a satchel, scattering the two kinds – anti-personnel and anti-tank – where he believed his enemies would try to form a defensive position to cover a withdrawal to their waiting aircraft.

A couple of seconds' hesitation would be enough.

Then he fed his men with their first hot meal in a week – scrambled egg, onion and tomato – and showed them their positions, a half-circle of shell scrapes among the rocks and scrub.

He left the back door tantalizingly open.

His foes would only see the bomblets when they were almost on top of them, and Abdur Rahman had a two-man crew manning an RPK light machine gun sighted on the spot, set for enfilading fire at knee height from a distance of eighty feet.

Three men in foxholes and armed with RPG launchers covered the open ground where Abdur Rahman felt sure the rescuers would try to land a Chinook or Puma. They were told to fire at the tail rotor once the aircraft was on the ground, and not a moment before.

Abdur Rahman had drawn us to him deliberately, then hit us where we least expected it. We had lost our entire patrol strength of twelve for his two men killed and four wounded.

He was about to do the same thing again, with greater elaboration, only three days later and thirty-seven kilometres away in an adjacent province.

All he had to do now was sit tight and wait for the first aircraft to appear. In the event, he did not have to wait long.

But trundling slowly to Tirin Kot hidden in the brush-wood, I knew none of this.

The rest of it wasn't real. It didn't seem real. I was out of it for most of the time. I remember being on a gurney, the slap of feet on lino, being pushed, doors slamming. Shouts. Machines. Corridors, bright lights, gloved hands, tubes in my mouth and nose, fighting for breath, trying to break free from the restraints on my arms and legs. Faces peering at me, talking to me. There was always the smell, a chemical smell, a smell of disinfectant trying and failing to overpower the stench of body fluids.

There was pain, too. Sharp pain, dull pain, but always pain. A long overland journey. The smell of dust, needles going into my arm. Someone in a white coat asking me – in English, of all things – to count.

Count up to ten.

Lie still now. Relax. You're gonna be fine. Count.

Up to ten.

What's your name, son?

I think I got to seven.

My name? My name is . . .

There was a great deal of movement. I thought it was a plane, but it could have been a ship. It was full of metallic echo, the squawk of radio, a thunder of engines, the clatter of boots, wind and salt in my face. Cold air. Night. The stench of high-octane fuel. American accents, faces on a television screen, laughter. Food in a tube. Food on a fork.

White sheets.

Orange juice through a straw.

Sit up. Try. There. I'll fix the pillows.

Thanks, nurse.

Better? Be a good boy, now, and eat your dinner.

Thirsty?

You bet.

Someone wants to talk to you. Here you are, sir.

Hello?

A familiar voice.

My kids.

When you coming home, Daddy?

Soon, baby. Very soon.

It's been ages, Dad.

Had it?

Love you. Love you lots. Love you so much.

Same here, sweetheart. Same here.

'You got a visitor, man.'

I hadn't had a visitor before. I had no idea who it might be. I was in the prison wing of the US military hospital in Dhahran, Saudi Arabia. Don't ask why. I had no idea. I had no radio, no newspaper. I had little sense of time. I must have been there for weeks. Since the operation on my back I could already walk without help. I could raise both arms above my head, though it still hurt. The dressings had come off, revealing a large and purple scab that looked to me like the profile of a turnip, starting just below my left shoulder blade with the root running down to my waist. There was a big indented place where they'd grafted some skin on from my inner thigh. It looked pretty ugly. They told me I had lost some muscle and a little bone from my ribs, and I would feel stiff for some time, but I would be fit enough for active service in a matter of weeks, provided I did my two hours of physiotherapy every morning. All I had to do was work at it, get back into shape and I could serve my country again.

Yessir.

Great stuff. That's the spirit, Thomas.

Just what I wanted to hear.

When I told the African-American doctor I was a civilian and suggested what he and the rest of the US armed forces might want to do with the active service bit, he just smiled.

'That so?' he said in his slow voice. 'Then what are you doing in here?'

'Wish to hell I knew, doc.'

I was British, I told him. Didn't I sound it?

He gave me that look again.

I'd not been charged with any crime.

They all say that, his expression said.

I asked the MP who my visitors were.

'A man and a woman,' he said.

That stopped me in my tracks.

'What woman?' I asked.

'Just keep moving, buddy, and you'll find out soon enough.'

I wore pale blue prison pyjamas and matching blue slippers. Everything was two sizes too big, deliberately so. I still had to be frisked, then my handcuffs unlocked, the manacles on my ankles and finally the chain joining hands and feet released.

'Who is it?' I asked the MP sergeant, a tall thin man with a pimply face from Georgia named Gregson. He was unlocking the cuffs. Another MP had squatted down and was freeing my legs. A third watched from a safe distance, holding an electric cattle prod at the ready just in case I decided to throw my teddy in a corner for the hell of it.

'Why, Mr Morgan, sir. Didn't anyone tell you?' Gregson

showed me his yellow teeth, leaned across and pushed open the door.

'No, sergeant, they didn't.'

I rubbed my wrists.

'That's too bad,' said Sergeant Gregson.

He gave me a nudge in the back that made me wince and I stepped past him into the artificial light, one hand holding up my pants.

I was the only prisoner. The man and the woman, sitting silently side by side at one of the tables, were the only visitors. An MP stood at ease at either end of the room, each armed with nightstick and 9 mm pistol. The room was very bright and without shadow, and I could hear the hum of the air conditioning. A one-way glass panel from waist height to ceiling ran the length of the room behind me, and I felt sure Gregson was watching.

I felt like a battery hen.

My visitors did not get up.

'My name's Quilty,' said the man. I pulled out a moulded plastic chair and sat down at a slight angle so I could keep my eye on the nearest MP. 'I'm from the consulate here in Dhahran,' he added.

I didn't look at the man who called himself Quilty. I looked at the woman. She was about my own age, maybe two or three years younger. She wore a cream silk blouse and a long red skirt – the long sleeves and the generous cut of skirt concessions to the sensibilities of our Saudi hosts. Her blonde hair was cut in a neat bob. She had little make-up, just a dab of lipstick and perhaps moisturizer and some eyeliner. She didn't need anything more. She had large blue eyes, a pert nose, a perfect bow of a mouth. She didn't blink at all, and didn't seem to mind me staring.

After a regime of boiled cabbage, she smelled wonderful.

'Mathilde is your legal representative,' Quilty said.

'A lawyer,' I said, still looking at Mathilde.

I was sure no one present believed it.

'Should you need one,' said Quilty.

So far Mathilde hadn't said a word.

Quilty took a small Nagra tape recorder out of his pocket and placed it on the table.

'You don't mind?' he said.

'I don't know,' I said. 'I might. It depends.'

I didn't like Quilty. I don't know why. I'd never seen him before. He wore glasses, and his hair was carefully combed across his forehead. His skin was unhealthy, as if he ate all the wrong stuff and never went out of doors. His neck spilled over his collar. He looked like one of those school swots who was hopeless at football. He wore a lightweight linen jacket and what looked to me like a university tie. I was sure he was very, very clever, and that he had nothing to do with the Dhahran consulate, if there ever was such a thing.

'How are you feeling, Thomas?'

Mathilde's voice was low, soft.

'Stiff,' I said, adding: 'My back, I mean. The operation—'

'Would you like to leave this place?'

I looked at her the way the doctor had looked at me.

Mathilde leaned forward.

'I mean today, Thomas. Now. There's an RAF VC-10 flight at 8.30 tonight to Brize Norton. Or Air France from Riyadh at 23.30. It gets into London at 05.30 GMT.'

I had decided to play along with their little game, whatever it was, but this was absurd. 'What do you think, Mathilde? I think the Riyadh flight would be nicer, don't you? Specially with a stopover in Paris for a little shopping.'

I gave her a broad smile to make sure she understood I thought she was talking balls.

Quilty interrupted.

'We need to check a few things first, Morgan, if you don't mind. Just to establish the facts.'

Morgan. Not Mr Morgan. Just Morgan. The officer class

was reasserting itself, re-establishing its authority over the lower orders. Know your place was the message. Other ranks over there, officers and gentlefolk this side. I did mind, but there wasn't much I could do. Clearly I was going to have to defend Washington's notion of civilization whether I wanted to or not.

'Sure,' I said. 'Why not.'

'You are Thomas Paul Morgan. Born Pilton, Edinburgh, January 17, 1961.'

He looked at me.

'Correct,' I said.

West Pilton. Inchgarvie. Hard by the gasworks. There were two ways to get on in life if you were born in West Pilton, though I doubted Quilty knew it. You either joined the Army, or you took up crime as a full-time career. Unemployment was twice the rate for the rest of the city, and the city's was bad enough. My brother-in-law (my ex-brother-in-law, that is) was sent down for eight to twelve for armed robbery with aggravated assault. I had taken the only alternative, the Queen's shilling.

Quilty was reading from his notes.

'You signed up for the British Army Junior Leaders' course aged fifteen. That was in 1976.' He adjusted his glasses. 'At seventeen you were accepted into the Parachute Regiment. You first saw active service in Belfast aged eighteen at the rank of corporal. You had a note of commendation attached to your record following your initial six-month tour, but you lost a stripe because of a pub brawl in Aldershot you initiated. According to your file you were detached for special duties for ten months in 1981. You deployed to the Falklands with the Second Battalion the following year, aged twenty. You had your second stripe back. You were mentioned in dispatches.'

I nodded. So far so good.

'You bought yourself out of the Army in 1983. By this time you were a sergeant.'

'Yes.'

'May I ask why?'

'Why what?'

'Why you left.'

They were both looking at me.

'It's a long time ago.'

Quilty looked pained. 'Please.'

'Look. You train for something, and if you're lucky, you get to practise it. Afterwards it's an anticlimax. Peacetime soldiering can be bloody dull after people have been trying very hard to kill you, and you them.'

The truth of it was that I had been scared most of the time, but once I got back home all I could think about was going back, or finding myself another war.

'You found it hard to settle in Civvy Street.'

Too bloody right, and I was far from alone in that. A job as a milkman or postman didn't really suit me.

Mathilde said: 'You tried the Strathclyde Police.'

It hadn't worked out. Too much paperwork, too much bull.

'You re-enlisted,' she said. 'In 1986, aged twenty-five.'

'I did.'

'The Royal Military Police.'

'I thought it might be interesting.'

Quilty's turn again.

'You were stationed in Germany for two years.'

'I was. Osnabrück.'

'You studied Russian.'

'Yes.'

'To A level.'

'My only A level.'

Mathilde smiled. She was all understanding and light.

'You went back to Northern Ireland.'

'I didn't ask to go, if that's what you mean.'

'No,' Quilty said. 'You didn't volunteer.'

'Look, what's this got to do with—'

Quilty held up a hand.

'Please—'

Mathilde stepped in again.

'As a reward for undercover work in the province – the details of which are still classified – you were offered the chance to travel abroad as a member of an RMP close protection team. By now you were a staff sergeant. This was—'

'1990,' Quilty said, referring to his notebook.

'You were twenty-nine,' Mathilde said. 'You had qualified as a small-arms specialist.'

I didn't say anything.

'You went to Beirut as Lebanon's civil war was ending.'

'I did, yes.'

'There were twelve of you, responsible for the security of the diplomatic staff. The ambassador, the military attaché and the political counsellor. Everyone else had been withdrawn.'

'Correct.'

'Then Kabul. There was a civil war there, too. Remember?'

Belatedly I realized where this was leading.

'You do remember, don't you?'

Quilty again. Acting stern. His schoolmaster act.

'I remember.'

'Do you recall what happened in Kabul in 1992, Morgan?'

Mathilde was nodding at me, urging me to speak.

'We evacuated the embassy staff.'

'April '92.'

I nodded. April 15.

'What else?'

'What do you mean?' I looked from Mathilde to Quilty and back again. I shrugged despite the stiffness.

I knew perfectly well what they meant, but I was damned if they'd get it that easily.

Quilty put his hand in his pocket.

'Perhaps this will jog your memory, Morgan.'

He placed the object carefully in the centre of the table.

It was a spoon. A big tureen spoon. Beautiful lines, like a boat. Georgian. Solid silver. Heavy. 'G Rex' on the handle. Of course I recognized it. It was mine. Well. Not quite mine. Not legally mine.

Quilty leaned back. He looked up at the ceiling.

He was enjoying this, the smug shit.

'It comes from a 188-piece set, circa 1779. Solid silver. Georgian, of course. You had to keep one piece, didn't you? A memento, in the shed at the bottom of your garden. In your toolbox. A silly thing to do, Morgan, for a bright fellow like you. I was surprised, frankly. So was your ex-wife when Special Branch showed her the search warrant. There was also gold and silver plate in the Kabul mission, and some very fine antique crystal glassware. Also rare Meissen. All told, four trunks were buried under the azaleas in the grounds of the ambassador's residence, the contents carefully packed in greased paper. I'm told it was at the dead of night, too. Quite a party. You supervised it. You were in charge, sergeant major. You chose the spot, and you helped with the digging.'

Sergeant major.

Mathilde was looking down at her hands. The nail varnish was pink, and matched the lipstick.

I said, 'They were rhododendrons.'

Quilty sighed. 'Morgan, azaleas are a type of rhododendron.'

'Is that right? You've taught me something, Mr Quilty.'

Mathilde took up the story.

'You went back, Thomas. You waited. Four years. God, I do admire your patience. You hired a mate of yours, Zotov. A Russian. Like you, an ex-soldier and Afghan vet. A former Dutch marine, Kessler – nicknamed Curly – was another member of your team. Philippe Baz, a French national of Lebanese origin with special forces experience, was the third member. You went back when the Taliban took control. That would have been '96. You retrieved the lot, didn't you? Split it between you. Equal shares. Paid off the mortgage on your Victorian terrace in north Lambeth, paid the kids' school fees and of course with the divorce . . .'

They had left out a couple of names.

Abdur Rahman, for starters.

That's how we'd met, Abdur and I. His cut had been for keeping the Taliban sweet and off our backs. Only I had no idea he'd been doubled and was working for Quilty's people back then. Not until he dropped us in the shit – once he'd taken his share, of course.

Bastard.

'I'm not saying a thing,' I said.

'Thomas—' Mathilde looked up.

'Interview's over,' I said. 'Thanks for coming. A real pleasure. Much appreciated.' I gave Mathilde my coldest smile. 'Best of luck.'

So this was why I'd been kept alive, why Abdur Rahman had sent me out on a trailer to Tirin Kot, why the US military had evacuated me from their airbase at Kandahar to surgery on one of their warships in the Arabian Sea and then on to a prison hospital in Dhahran. London had a job for me. Quilty wanted to drag me back into the business.

It had to be very important to go to all this trouble and expense. It had to be special. I couldn't work out the timing. Maybe it had been three or four weeks, even as much as a couple of months, since we'd been hit by Abdur Rahman's men.

It felt like years.

I pushed the chair back and got up.

'We're offering you a deal,' Mathilde said, looking up at me. There was something in those eyes of hers. Amusement, perhaps, or irony. I really wasn't sure.

'A deal? What kind of a deal?'

The nearest MP was watching me. He held the truncheon

across his body with both hands. I could tell he would have liked a chance to use it on me, but I really wasn't in the mood.

'Immunity from prosecution,' Mathilde said in a stage whisper. 'You walk out of here a free man, Thomas. No charges. And you can keep the spoon.'

'The alternative?'

Quilty cleared his throat.

'Extradition, Morgan. Pending that you will be held in a Saudi jail. Then Belmarsh on remand until your trial. Could be as long as two years before you come up before the beak while they collect witness statements. That's a long time in a maximum security prison without privileges. After all, they can't be sure Kabul was the only mission you decided to rip off. If convicted, as I am sure you would be, you'd be looking at seven to ten years with good behaviour.'

They would never take no for an answer.

'What does my lawyer have to say?'

Mathilde opened her mouth, but Quilty spoke first.

'We've got a job for you, Morgan.'

I felt my gut turn.

'We? What kind of job?'

'It plays to your strengths,' Mathilde said sweetly, those unblinking eyes on me again.

'Go on.'

'Let's put it this way, Morgan,' Quilty said. 'You took something that belonged to us. Now we want something you've got.'

'Which is?'

Whatever it was, I knew it was the same thing that had made Abdur Rahman so concerned about my welfare in Oruzgan.

Mathilde leaned forward. 'How exactly did you get that stuff out of Kabul and across the border, Thomas?'

So that was it.

They wanted directions.

'Buy a map,' I said. 'The Americans produce wonderful aerial maps.'

I knew it wasn't on any map. So did they. It was in my mind. Contours, escarpments, valleys, ridges, peaks, tracks, streams, river beds, desert. All of that – printed on my brain, as clear and as fresh as if it was only yesterday.

Quilty and Mathilde exchanged glances. Quilty said: 'You'll have to talk to Abdur Rahman.'

'Abdur Rahman?' This was too much. The name stuck in my throat and I started to choke. My coughing fit made my back hurt again.

'You've got to be fucking joking,' I said, wiping my eyes and accepting a glass of water from Mathilde.

Quilty looked embarrassed, as if he found the whole thing unsavoury and beneath his dignity as one of HM's servants.

'Abdur Rahman wants you. Says you're the man he needs for what we have in mind. Says he won't do it without you.'

I tried to play dumb.

'He's a Taliban commander, for Christ's sake. Their best.'

'Was, Morgan. Was a Taliban commander. Still the best no doubt, but he's with us now. He's part of the coalition against terrorism. He's asking for you. That's why we're here, Morgan. To ask on his behalf if you will play along. If you do agree to his proposition, we'll drop all charges relating to the Kabul embassy. You can keep your house, of course – and the spoon – and the kids can stay at their independent schools. Alleyn's for the boy, isn't it, and Godolphin and Latymer for the girl?'

Bastard know-all.

He pushed the silver spoon over to me.

'Agree? Agree to what? To do what?'

'Talk to him, that's all we ask,' Mathilde said.

'You don't understand, do you? I was a bounty hunter,' I said. I was shouting. 'For fuck's sake, don't you get it? I was hunting al-Qaeda and Taliban for hard cash. For money. A

26

cabinet minister was worth 100,000 bucks tax-free, dead or alive, and for reasons of personal safety that meant dead. Understand? Do you? A dead al-Qaeda fighter was worth four grand, the Americans paid thirty K for a commander. We were scalp hunters, for Christ's sake. Do you understand? We didn't take fucking prisoners. Abdur Rahman, he's—'

Quilty wasn't put out in the least by my outburst.

'He's what? A man of honour? Too proud to deal with someone like you? Is that what you were going to say? That he despises your kind? Maybe he does, Morgan. But he's got to live, too. He's certainly not doing it for free. He's looking at the kind of money that will make him a real player. For Abdur Rahman it's not just a matter of paying off a mortgage or buying his kids a decent education or sending his wife off on a weekend in Milan for the summer sales. He's an ambitious man. He's got dreams, big dreams.'

It wasn't what I meant.

'He's killed a lot of people. Our people. You don't give a toss, though, do you? As long as he has what you call access, as long as he turns in reports on his buddies in the Taliban and al-Qaeda . . .'

'So have you, Morgan. Killed, I mean.'

'For God, Queen and Country.'

Quilty's mouth turned down at the corners. He didn't have much of a sense of humour and he certainly didn't like mine.

'I don't believe it,' I said. 'You're lying, Quilty.'

I was pleased to see his ears turn crimson.

'Talk to him, Morgan.'

I finished the water and put the glass down. I looked round the room. The MPs hadn't moved.

'Will you talk to him, Thomas?'

It was Mathilde's sweet talk again.

All tea and sympathy.

She said: 'Abdur Rahman says you owe him.'

'For what?'

'He said you'd know what he meant.'

Cheeky sod.

'Well, Thomas?'

'Okay,' I said. 'I'll talk to him.'

That queasy feeling in the pit of my stomach I always felt before the start of a new operation was back. It gave me sweaty palms and I wiped my hands on my prison pants.

The fear made the pulse hammer away in my throat.

I didn't want to believe it.

Not even when Quilty produced the release forms from his black leather briefcase. Not when Gregson returned my wristwatch and a wad of dirty 1,000-rupee notes and when Mathilde gave me a farewell peck on my cheek and I got a lungful of her favourite scent, Remember Me. Not until I was sitting on the back seat of an embassy Jaguar in Riyadh on my way to the airport with a shave and a clean shirt and an Air France ticket for a business-class window seat in one hand and a brand new passport in my own name in the other.

I really was going home.

It was easy. All they said I had to do was talk to that shit Abdur Rahman. Nothing to it, I told myself.

THREE

He'd given up the turban. But he was wearing a pale-yellow Kandahari-style shirt, ending well below his knees and with all the fine, hand-worked embroidery one might expect across his barrel chest. Round neck, no collar, two buttons to one side. A pale-grey waistcoat. A thick, tweedy *potu* or shawl of the same colour was thrown casually across his left shoulder, a concession to the tawdry British winter.

'Not bad, English,' Abdur Rahman said, looking round at the foyer of Italian marble.

'It's okay,' I said, trying to free myself from a bear hug. It was the back-slapping, rib-squeezing part I was afraid of. I was still feeling fragile, but I managed to pull away.

'You're recovered, English?'

He looked at my left hand. It was healing nicely, and the doctors said it would be as good as new in a matter of weeks.

'Pretty much.'

'Thank God.'

'Yes, thank him by all means.'

'No hard feelings.'

'None I can't handle, Abdur.'

We were both on our best behaviour.

I had been booked into the Hotel St Oswald's in Victoria, and a nondescript navy-blue Mondeo with a uniformed driver had dropped me off there the previous morning after picking me up from Heathrow. St Oswald's described itself as discreet and intimate and I should have realized that meant the single rooms were the size of small shoeboxes.

Blahnik shoeboxes.

I asked Abdur Rahman where he was staying.

'The Savoy.'

'Fuck you,' I said. 'And I bet it's a suite.'

'Of course, English. Naturally. I am a guest of Her Majesty's Foreign and Commonwealth Office.'

He was still pumping my right hand.

'I'm not English. I'm Scots born and bred,' I said.

'With a name like Morgan?'

I already knew a fair amount about Abdur Rahman, and Mathilde had filled in some of the blank spaces.

He had gone to school in Dulwich. His Trinidad-born parents still lived on Brixton Hill. He had taken a first in psychology at Goldsmiths'. Somewhere in between, around the age of twenty, he had converted, changing his name from Trevor Winston Dickinson to Abdur Rahman. He looked a lot cleaner and more relaxed than he had in Oruzgan. He had the scrubbed, shiny look of a man enjoying his leisure. He had put on weight. His beard had been trimmed well below the Taliban minimum of eight centimetres, but there was more white in it than I remembered.

I led the way into the dining room and asked the Polish waitress for orange juice, a croissant and a double espresso.

Abdur Rahman was content with Earl Grey and two lumps of sugar.

'You wanted to talk to me,' I said.

'I wanted to see you,' he said. 'We can talk later.'

'Later?'

'They haven't told you?'

'Told me what?'

'You're going on a refresher course. Hostile environments. Nice place in the countryside, all mod cons. You'll like it. Teamwork, all that male bonding and rugged outdoor stuff you enjoy so much. We'll talk properly when it's over.'

'I don't know what you're on about.'

'They must have told you something, English.'

'I wish you'd stop calling me that. You're more English than I am, for God's sake.'

He touched a forefinger to his lips.

'Don't tell them.'

I dropped my voice too, imitating his stage whisper. 'All right. I won't. As long as you tell me what the fuck's going on, Trevor, because no one else has.'

He put his cup down.

'I've got a car waiting. I said I'd take you. We can talk on the way. Okay?'

'Fine.' I finished the coffee.

'First, I've a surprise for you, English. I think you'll be pleased.'

Trevor Dickinson alias Abdur Rahman was smiling at something or someone behind me.

I tried to turn, but a heavy hand fell on my shoulder. It pinned me down in my chair.

'Zdrasvitye.'

I knew that voice. But I told myself I was imagining it. I tried to twist round, but couldn't. It hurt too much. He must have come from the kitchen or the heads, because I was sitting facing the door that led into the dining room from reception, and he would have stood out among the American tourists.

'Hello, Thomas.'

It was the ghost of a man I thought had been killed with the rest of our freelance team in Oruzgan. A ghost named Felix Zotov.

Hampshire is spectacular in winter. The great oaks were naked, their muscular branches reaching up in supplication to a menacingly low sky of tattered grey. The fields were iron-bound with ice, the grass bleached and salted with rinds of frost. Vicious volleys of sleet swept the open fields. It was magnificent in an appalling sort of way. Until the first bang, swiftly followed by a second detonation, then the sound of grown men screaming.

Joseph took off at once, legs pounding, heading for the hedgerow up ahead. Yannis was hard on his heels. Headbangers, the two of them. I held back, and I could tell Felix was thinking the same thing I was. There was no cover for fifty metres in any direction. There could be mines underfoot, and the hedgerow might conceal tripwires and Bouncing Betties and only God knew what else. It wasn't looking good.

We settled into a steady jog, following in the others' footsteps.

'Watch your feet.'
　　'Jesus, get me out of here.'
　　'Check his back.'
　　'For crying out aloud, get me out.'
　　'Butterfly mine – two o'clock.'
　　'Got it.'
　　'Can you get up?'
　　'Help me lift him.'
　　'Right.'
　　'Fucking hell, watch it.'
　　'Claymore, birch, 10 o'clock.'
　　'Get me out.
　　'Ready?'
　　'Got his legs.'
　　'That's it.'
　　'His back's clear.'
　　'Help me.'
　　'Mind the tape.'

'Keep still, damn you.'
'I'm dying.'
'Tripwire. See it?'
'You're okay.'
'I'm fucking dying.'
'Bollocks. You're fine.'
'Got a light, anyone?'
'WATCH YOUR FEET.'

I was paired off with Joseph Gerber for the first exercise of the afternoon.

It was all very realistic. A man had shot himself in the thigh with a 9 mm Browning Highpower, and was going into shock. I kicked the automatic out of the way and talked the gunshot victim down and stopped him rolling about and shouting. He was shivering and I gave him my coat. Joseph found the entry and exit wounds, and applied pressure, but it clearly wasn't going to be enough. It was a real bleeder, the stuff shooting up like a geyser. In reality Joseph would have had to cut down to the vein and tie it off, something he'd been trained to do as a paramedic. In practice all he could do was talk his way through it for the benefit of the instructors and fellow students, and I helped with the dressings, but it was like trying to soak up the Atlantic with a sponge. By the time we'd finished we had five dressings on his leg, one piled on top of the other, and still it was coming through.

It was our turn to watch. This time the glass roof of a conservatory had collapsed on a handyman while he was painting it. There was glass embedded in his head, more in his shoulder and a huge slice of it in one arm. The make-up was really very well done. Felix talked to the instructor playing the role, reassured him, persuaded him to get up and move out from the structure in case more of the roof came down on the three of them. There was a lot of exposed muscle and bone.

Yannis had the task of closing the wounds and stemming the bleeding without driving the glass deeper, and without doing serious damage to the blood vessels.

It was one thing to learn how to dress wounds in a classroom, another entirely to do so in practice, even if we all knew the lavish amounts of blood being thrown about consisted only of dyed water.

The last was a team job, a three-car pile-up.

Joseph and Yannis sprang forward, racing each other to reach a VW hatchback belching smoke and flame, a woman slumped against the wheel and apparently unconscious. Once again the instructors were the actors in our little drama. Felix approached car number two, a Ford Fiesta. Its driver was fighting drunk, weaving about in the road, clutching a gin bottle and challenging anyone within earshot to a fight. Felix wisely decided to leave well alone. I squatted down on my heels and looked around. Beneath the front end of the third vehicle, a Citroën Xantia, I saw what looked like a bundle. It turned out a passenger in the second car had shot through the windscreen and ended up under the Citroën's front wheels. I won a brownie point for that, but lost it again when my cellphone squawked while trying to wrestle the victim clear.

It was Mathilde, our missing team leader, calling from Gatwick.

In the break I went up to my room and took a shower to get rid of the fake blood and gore. On the face of it, what had happened in the past few weeks was straightforward enough.

In the early 1980s I had volunteered for an undercover job in Afghanistan while the country was under Soviet occupation. Then I'd gone back a decade later, to Kabul this time, as head of the British ambassador's close protection team, and hatched the scheme to solve my financial problems at a stroke. It was a long wait, but when the Taliban came to power and I finally went back to do the job as a civilian, Abdur Rahman had offered me and my people protection – at a price. Instead of helping us, of course, he waited until we had disposed of the loot and paid him off before selling us down the river to the British authorities. No doubt it had greatly improved his credit rating with his handlers at Vauxhall Cross. I hadn't heard of him again until I had started work as a bounty hunter in the wake of the September 11 attacks. His name had come up as a notorious Taliban fugitive with a price on his head. The kind of price people like me would kill for.

In Oruzgan he had decided that attack was the best means of defence against the assorted freelancers and coalition forces snapping at his heels. I couldn't blame him for that. If I'd been in his place I hope I would have had the smarts to have done half as well as he had.

Only he'd been working both sides of the street all along.

Quilty was only interested in what an agent could produce in the way of intelligence, in the access he or she had to the upper echelons of whatever it was they were trying to penetrate. What Abdur Rahman had to do to protect himself, to further his career as a top-line Taliban commander, hadn't mattered. Not to Quilty. Not even if it meant whacking members of Her Majesty's armed forces. It wasn't his concern.

Now it was time for London to cash in the investment they'd made in their man all these years.

For some reason they wanted me. They said it was Abdur, but it was Quilty and his ilk. The only thing I knew for sure was that I knew the route. Whatever it was, I told myself I should be glad. If the Office hadn't wanted me to take part in their little caper, I wouldn't have survived Oruzgan. After using me to leave a trail for his next ambush, Abdur Rahman would have made very certain I wasn't around to tell tales.

We both knew that.

No, there were no hard feelings.

When Mathilde entered the lecture room, the impact was hardly less spectacular than a lightning strike.

Yannis was startled out of his doze, sat up at attention and stared. Joseph dropped his pen and pad on the floor and made a lot of noise scrabbling about trying to pick them up without tumbling off his chair. Felix scowled and gave me a black look. He thought I knew more than they did, and that I was holding out on him.

It simply wasn't true.

They were shocked because it was a woman.

I was shocked by her appearance. The feminine bob had gone. Instead, the blonde hair had been scraped back, almost pasted to her skull and pinned up at the back. Round tortoise-shell glasses masked her blue eyes. She wore no make-up. Her figure was hidden under a drab grey suit. The skirt ended at her knees, and she wore sensible shoes with low heels. Mathilde was playing her sexless, anally retentive Whitehall role to the full.

No jewellery of any kind.

'Thank you, Bill.'

Mathilde nodded to one of the course instructors. The lights dimmed. She waited until Bill had left, having closed the door behind him.

'Gentlemen, the target.'

She stepped aside, pressed something in her left hand, and a face filled the end wall behind her. The face of a man. A smiling face. Serene, gentle, even kindly. Self-deprecating in the certainty of its owner's undoubted faith.

It was hard to imagine him as a killer, a terrorist, a psychopath.

Certainly not the personification of evil, but someone who

liked children and cats, and helped little old ladies with their shopping safely across busy streets.

He was bearded. His eyes were large, almost soulful, and very dark. The mouth, caught in a half smile, was wide. On his head he wore a simple white turban of cotton, not silk.

A dreamer.

'You know this man,' Mathilde was saying. 'You know his name. You know what he is supposed to have done. I have prepared a file on his activities, with copies for each of you. Let me have them back in the morning, please.'

The face vanished, the lights came back on.

'I am Mathilde.'

She faced us, looking at each in turn.

'You can call me Mattie or Mat, or Mother if it helps. Whatever works for you. But remember this. I am your post-man, your travel agent, your quartermaster, your paymaster and your commanding officer. I am always there for you. In case you're in the least confused on the issue of my gender, let me make one thing absolutely clear now to avoid any future misunderstandings. If you need someone to provide hand relief or sit on your face, then you will have to look elsewhere, in your own time, and at your own expense.'

Thoroughly flummoxed, Yannis broke off staring.

'But when it's FUBAR – for those of you not already familiar with the term, it means Fucked Up Beyond All Rec-ognition – I will be there. I am the shoulder you cry on. Not your girlfriend's. Not your wife's. Not your mother's. Not your boyfriend's, either.

'You talk to me about your problems. No one else.'

Felix was looking at me again. I wasn't sure why. Perhaps he guessed. Or maybe he knew, but I didn't see how. We had a past, Mathilde and I, and it was not one I wanted to deal with, not now.

'The terms are these, gentlemen. You will be paid a per diem of twenty sterling in-country. The bank account of your choice will be credited with three thousand five hundred sterling a month in arrears for expenses. Tax free. If the mission is not a success, you or your heirs will keep what's left of both allowances. If you succeed, look on your expenses and per diem as advances deductible against your share – an equal share – of the reward.

'Twenty-five million US dollars, gentlemen; split five ways.'

Mathilde paused.

'Anyone who does not wish to continue with this assignment may leave now. Transport will be provided to the local station.'

She waited on a beat of three. No one moved or spoke.

'Very well. The objective is to eliminate the target, and to retrieve sufficient physical evidence for identification. Preferably the head if you can manage it, otherwise a finger, an ear, urine or blood, even a strand of hair. We need DNA. We need photographic evidence for corroboration. Elimination of the target and returning with insufficient authentication are tantamount to failure. You will have wasted your time and mine. Details are in your folders.' She tapped the maroon covers, a drum roll of varnished fingernails.

'Any questions?'

I drove Mathilde back to Granby Mallett for the 16.10 train to London via Woking. I took a white Transit van smelling of fish, sweat and stale cigarettes from the transport pool of the firm of ex-Royal Marines who ran the courses for aid agencies and news media. That's what we were – a non-governmental organization or NGO, Asia Logistics Relief. ALR even had a blue logo, a dove in a circle of laurels, and we had baseball caps and T-shirts adorned with the motif to prove it. I wondered if anyone believed it.

A call to UN headquarters in Geneva or New York would surely be enough to establish that no one there had ever heard of us – but then the world body was a ponderous, bureaucratic beast and I told myself it could take many calls over several days to establish that we were not what we claimed to be.

'How did I do?'

I was taken aback by the question. It wasn't like Mathilde to share self-doubt with anyone, least of all me.

'Good,' I said. 'You did good.' The words were out of my mouth before I realized just how lame they sounded.

'Did Yannis buy it?'

'Oh, yes. Completely. He was gobsmacked.'

'He's so bloody macho it makes me sick.'

'You hired him. He's a Londoner of Greek origin, and from what he said to me in the bar, I gather he's ex-Royal Navy.'

'What do you make of Gerber?'

'Joseph is another para. Two Para, though long after my time. A team player, but reserved.'

'Not quite the same team in all respects, Thomas.'

'Meaning?'

'He's gay.'

'He doesn't look it or sound it.'

'Nobody does.'

'I wouldn't know.'

'It shouldn't be a problem.'

Then why had she mentioned it?

'Wait till Yannis finds out. They're buddies.'

'I think he knows.'

'You sure?'

'The services have changed since your day, Thomas.'

'I'm sure they have, and no doubt for the better.'

'In any case, Gerber isn't the kind to let his sexuality get in the way of his work. It never did before.'

'Where we're going it may be different.'

She turned in her seat to look at me.

'Meaning?'

I recited the few lines I knew of an Afghan ditty:

> 'There's a boy across the river
> With a bottom like a peach.
> Alas, I cannot swim.'

She punched me on the shoulder. Hard.

'He isn't like that.'

'I bet he's a good swimmer, though.'

'You're impossible.'

'You should know.'

Granby Mallett station was ahead.

Mathilde asked, 'Did you talk to Abdur Rahman?'

'I saw him. He had a driver. I suspect he was Special Branch; at any rate, he probably reports back to Quilty or someone very like him. We couldn't really talk shop.'

'You don't resent him for what he did?'

'You mean the Kabul job? His shopping us to you people – once we'd got the stuff out and given him his cut?'

'Yes.'

'It was a long time ago.'

'And what he did to your friends in Oruzgan?'

'He didn't know it was me. He knew contract headhunters were on his tail, but that was all. It wouldn't be the first time. Bounty hunters are crawling all over southern Afghanistan hunting down his kind for greenbacks. As for me, I didn't know it was his group we were tracking. It wouldn't have made any difference, though. It was just bad luck.'

'And you, Thomas?'

'What about me?'

'You're all right with this.'

'Do I have a choice?'

The picket fence that ran along the platform had once been

white, but vandals had spray-painted its entire surface with lurid graffiti. The ticket office was shut.

Mathilde tried again.

'I meant your family – how are they?'

'They're fine, thanks.'

Meaning, don't pry. It's none of your affair. Not any more.

I stopped the van as close to the station entrance as I could, then leaned across and opened the door.

She put a hand on my arm.

'How do you feel, Thomas?'

'I feel fine. Why?'

'Just asking. It's been a while.'

'It has, yes.'

'Thomas—'

'Looks like more rain, boss.'

I didn't want to open up. I didn't even want to think about it. Emotional stuff always made me run a mile. I was a lot more scared of it than I was of being shot at. Mathilde looked less disappointed than resigned. Men. All the bloody same. I could almost hear her thoughts, or thought I could.

Mathilde climbed out and slammed the door.

I regretted it immediately, but I couldn't help myself.

I still wanted her.

She did not look back.

I wondered if Quilty knew. Or guessed, as Felix had.

When I pulled away from the station yard I looked in the offside rear-view mirror.

Mathilde had gone, and it was raining harder than ever.

The last three days were the best because we were kept busy out of doors. We crawled around the South Downs in gillie suits. We practised walking silently; on our heels on hard ground and on our toes on soft ground. I taught everyone to recognize the hunting cry of the barn owl, a useful signal for

41

falling back on an RV in an emergency. As far as I knew there were no barn owls in Afghanistan, so there was no risk of hearing the real thing, or of an Afghan imitating one. We were driven in a truck to Dorset, where we spent a morning fighting our way through a mock village built for Northern Ireland training defended by a platoon of eager Green Jackets. We spent the last two days on the ranges at Aldershot, and the climax was a twenty-three-hour, twenty-five-mile-long compass march through the Kentish countryside, each of us carrying a dozen bricks in his Bergen.

On the final night in our Hampshire conference centre we had a booze-up with the instructors, but I slipped away for some fresh air, walking across the sodden grass to the half-frozen pond. I stood there, well away from the lights, listening to the night sounds.

I had my books, CDs, a few pictures, my grandmother's antique sideboard, dining room chairs and two knife boxes and a little family silver – including the infamous tureen spoon – in storage.

There wasn't anything else.

Last time I looked I was 613 quid overdrawn.

I'd lost the house. That wasn't strictly true; I had given it away – changing the deed in favour of my wife – to provide some security for the kids. I was determined to keep the lawyers' greedy hands off what I had, and equally determined that my family wouldn't suffer, not in any material sense. I had agreed to give up half my net income, even half of the tiny army pension. The car was in my wife's name, anyway. I was stony broke, in other words. I needed this job. Badly. Like every other crim, I was looking for a short cut to solve all my problems at a stroke.

It was dumb.

But what else could I do to get out of the mess I'd got myself into?

'Was she worth it?'

'God knows.'

'You could have had your pick of the chicks at Metelitsa and no one would have been the wiser, or the sorrier.'

'Not with my overdraft, I couldn't.'

'The Hungry Duck, then.'

'Bottom fishing's not my style, Felix.'

'Fuck your mother, that's not how I remember it.'

'That was Moscow. That was then. We were young and foolish,' I said. 'And single.'

'We were drunk and horny, you mean.'

'That too.'

He'd come through the trees, seen me and stopped behind a weeping willow, then veered left. He thought he had me cold, but I heard him coming and turned to meet him.

'I could tell,' he said. 'Sorry.'

'Apparently.'

There was no point in denying it.

'How did you two meet?'

'It's a long story.'

'I'd like to hear it sometime.'

I didn't answer.

'You always were a legs man, and you always liked them tall. Me, I like 'em well stacked.'

The crux of it was that Mathilde was a member of that admirable but all too rare breed of women who make use of men for their own sexual delight. I had always found that a big turn-on. Or maybe it was because we had shared the illusion that two people could enjoy a sexual relationship shorn of feelings. It wasn't true, of course, and never had been, but it had been good while it lasted.

We had both been running away from ourselves.

Felix was working up to whatever point he wanted to make. I waited.

Felix said, 'She's getting the fifth share, is she?'

'Why do you say that?'

43

'Four of us on the course. Equal shares, she said. So who gets the fifth? Is it her?'

Felix had spotted the connection. It was intuition. But that wasn't what bothered him. He was wondering if the relationship – if that's what it was – would affect the reward and the way it was divvied up. He didn't want me ganging up with the head girl against him. He was trying to work out how it would play, how he would come out of it at the end.

'I hadn't really thought about it,' I said.

'I have,' he said. 'Four into twenty-five million sounds a lot better to me than five into twenty-five million.'

It did, too. If Mathilde wasn't getting her share of the action, it could mean only one thing: that she was official. Felix would want to know that, too.

He said, 'You really think they'll pay up?'

'You don't?'

'I tell you,' Felix said, 'I know what we Russians would have done.'

'Yes?'

'I think they'll make sure we're never in a position to collect. That's what I think. Truly.'

I changed the subject.

'How did you get away, Felix?'

'I didn't.'

I waited.

'They kept me separate, in a room on my own. There was a kid with an AKS rifle. About eighteen, I guess. Maybe you saw him. Didn't say much. He waited until everyone was asleep, just grabbed me by the arm, pulled me away. I had the feeling he'd been told to do it. Orders. The guards weren't around, or they were asleep – or carefully looking the other way. Whatever. Took me out the back, down an alley, pushed me into a hovel two or three doors down. That's it. I stayed low for two days. The kid left. I don't know what happened to him. Maybe he went off with you lot.'

'You didn't buy him off?'

'No. I might have tried if the opportunity had presented itself.'

'What happened then?'

'I emerged from my hole. I had to. I had nothing to eat or drink. The villagers took me to Tirin Kot.'

'That's it?'

'Sure. What happened to you?'

'The commander let me go,' I said. 'I was no use to him. I was slowing him down. Put me in a trailer and had someone take me to Tirin Kot, too. I really thought you were dead. I could swear I saw you, stretched out and ready for burial. Jesus, it was a bad moment, Felix. I really thought you'd bought it.'

'Not me, friend.'

'Curly. Andy. Philippe. They'd had it. We were the only two who survived. All seven Hazara guys were killed, too.'

The Shi'ite Hazaras hated the Sunni Pashtuns for the way they, and the Taliban in particular, had treated their kind.

'We were damn lucky,' Felix said.

It was getting really cold. I started to walk back to the manor house. Felix fell into step beside me. I didn't say anything. I didn't contradict him, but I knew he was wrong. It had nothing to do with luck. It had everything to do with Abdur Rahman.

FOUR

'How long have we been sitting here?' I said. I dropped the rear side window of the Pajero a couple of inches. The air outside smelled of dust and wood smoke. The steady wind from the south was very cold. It had tinted the sky sepia, blotting out the sun with a veil of dirty brown dust.

'A quarter of a century,' Felix said. He was sitting in front, next to the driver. Sher Muhammad. Every now and then a beggar would notice one of us foreigners and tap on Felix's window, or mine, thrusting a mutilated limb at us. I looked away, trying hard not to see. I knew if I did, if I failed to turn off, I wouldn't be able to help myself – whatever cash I carried would be gone in a matter of minutes.

It was the women and children that got to me.

Sher Muhammad shooed them away, insisting the beggars we saw were organized in gangs. I didn't believe him.

Felix said, 'Those guards weren't even born when Daoud launched his coup against his cousin the king in '73, and most of them probably weren't around for the military takeover in '78, either.'

Now King Zahir Shah was back.

The Kandahar governor's gunmen were a ragamuffin bunch. Long-haired, mostly clean-shaven – no doubt a reaction to the former Taliban rulers' insistence on short hair and long beards – their camouflage uniforms, provided by the Americans, were either far too big or far too small. They carried their AK-74s any which way: over their shoulders, slung across

46

their chests, upside down, even dragged along the street. Few had boots, and those who did lacked socks and even laces. They smoked and laughed and the senior pair lounged on plastic deckchairs outside the gates.

Felix was right. These dopeheads wouldn't have been around in '78 when the People's Democratic Party of Afghanistan had launched their pro-Soviet revolution. The pace of change had sparked a backlash among the traditionalists, fuelled by Pakistan's active support for the seven mujahedin parties, and it had been war, invasion, anarchy and yet more war ever since.

'Governor's not back from London,' I said.

'How do you know?'

'When Gul Agha's here those guards have their work cut out keeping back the thousands of people trying to get in to see him. It's a semi-permament riot.'

The letter writers squatting on the pavement looked miserable; there weren't the usual queues of illiterates waiting to dictate their petitions.

One old man waved a small bunch of twigs at me. They were the local version of toothbrushes, a soft wood used to scrape the gums and teeth in idle moments – and there were many idle moments among Kandahar's innumerable unemployed.

'So why are we waiting?'

'Because Abdur Rahman's in there,' I said. 'And we need to catch him when he comes out. I promised I'd be here.'

Felix was getting impatient.

'What's he doing?'

I didn't get a chance to answer. Two four-wheel-drive vehicles, the first with tinted windows and both carrying the national flag of red, green and black, swept past us and up to the gates, kicking up yet more dust. The first hooted twice. The gunmen stood more or less to attention, and several even attempted a clumsy salute as the way was cleared. The second vehicle contained bodyguards, and they exchanged banter with the governor's men as they too entered the compound.

'Who the hell was that?'

'There's a city *shura* meeting today,' I said. 'That was Ahmed Wali Karzai, brother of Hamid Karzai.'

Ahmed Wali held no government post, but he was still an important figure, doling out cash to the impoverished provinces and districts in the south-west. As hereditary leaders of the Popolzai tribe, the Karzais had long been influential. They had lost seventy-two of their number during the Soviet-backed rule of the communists. Their prestige and wealth went a long way – even without Hamid's role as leader of the interim government in Kabul and his close relationship with Washington.

The road outside the governor's house was broad, but no longer than 500 metres, linking two districts of downtown Kandahar. Guards manned both ends. At one they held a chain across the road. At the other they raised or lowered a boom.

Pedestrians moved at will up and down the four-lane avenue, and there were stalls selling fruit and cigarettes on the far side. On Thursdays business was brisk as thousands of people queued to enter the pleasant compound of trees and shrubs opposite. It held a shrine housing the cloak of the Prophet Muhammad, which, legend had it, was made of the wool of the lamb sacrificed by Abraham and was said to have been brought to Kandahar by King Ahmed Shah, the Afghan conqueror of Bokhara and India.

'There he is.'

I leaned forward between the front seats.

'There.'

'That's Abdur Rahman?'

Felix tensed. I should have known what was about to happen, but I didn't think.

Abdur Rahman was on foot, shaking hands with the guard commander.

Sher Muhammad started the car.

I said, 'Let's see what he does.'

'He hasn't spotted us,' Felix said.

'Wait,' I told Sher Muhammad.

The moment he emerged through the gates, Abdur Rahman was joined by three other men. The first – better dressed and younger than his fellows – walked next to Abdur Rahman, the other two fell back. Their *potus* were wrapped around them in such a way that it was obvious they were carrying concealed weapons.

'Who are they?' Felix asked.

'I think the young man is a relative. His face is familiar. The other two are Abdur Rahman's bodyguards.'

'They're carrying, all of them.'

'Sure,' I said. 'A man's wealth is no longer measured in land or horses, but in how many Kalashnikovs he commands.'

'Some things never change. Are you sure that's the same bloke?'

'Oh, yes,' I said.

'I don't recognize him.'

'He was thinner then, and a lot dirtier. We all were.'

'He's coming this way.'

Felix didn't know it, but he was looking at the missing fifth of our $25 million.

Abdur Rahman and Felix looked at each other.

Felix ran the window down.

'Motherfucker.'

I'd almost forgotten the famous Zotov temper.

'Felix—'

Abdur Rahman had stopped short.

Felix was pulling at the door handle, trying to get out. For safety, Sher Muhammad had locked all the doors centrally.

Felix wouldn't wait. He started kicking his door in frenzied frustration, the fingers of his left hand trying to release the lock at the same time.

God alone knew what he thought he was going to do. He wasn't armed. None of us was.

'Felix—'

'Bastard. Fucking murderer.'

The rest was a stream of Russian obscenities.

'Cocksucker—'

'Felix, wait—'

The situation was saved by Abdur Rahman's bodyguards. One dropped his *potu* from his shoulders, revealing a Skorpion, shiny with age. His companion uncovered an AKM rifle.

It was a warning. They weren't particularly mad at us. Just careful in the face of what appeared to be a crazy, apoplectic Russian who couldn't climb out of the front passenger seat of a Toyota.

'Jesus, Felix. Calm down. You'll start another war single-handed, and at two metres I don't rate our chances very highly.'

'Fuck you, Morgan.'

Sher Muhammad was shaking with fright.

I dropped the rest of my window, pushed my head out.

'*Asalaam Aleikum.*'

'*Waleikum Salaam.*'

'*Bakheer . . . ?*'

'*Singye.*'

'*Sterimushi?*'

'*Kheryat?*'

'*Jurey. Singye?*'

We went through the ritual of Pashtun greetings, a circular procession of question and answer that goes round and round until all enquiries about health and well-being have been asked – repeatedly – and satisfactorily answered.

Abdur Rahman's eyes never left Felix, not for a moment.

Cautiously he approached. We shook hands. The body-guards' weapons were still at the ready, but so far no one else had noticed. The toothbrush sellers were still sitting on the pavement, though they would have been directly in the line of fire. The governor's guards were too busy cracking jokes and sharing cigarettes to take an interest. The last thing I needed was to attract attention.

'Let's go,' I said to Abdur Rahman.

'We'll follow, English.'

He was still keeping a wary eye on Felix.

'We've got room,' I said.

I opened my door, making sure my hands were visible to the two bodyguards. They were peering into the vehicle, looking for signs that we might be armed, that it might be a trap.

'This is Khaled,' said Abdur Rahman.

I shook hands with the young man through the open door.

Abdur Rahman turned his head and said something to his bodyguards. The man holding the Czech sub-machine gun dropped the weapon to his side.

'We will follow in my car,' he said.

The second man objected, and Abdur Rahman snapped at him in Pashto. The fellow glowered at us, then shrugged and put up his Kalashnikov, folding the stock and slinging it under his *potu*.

As we drove off, Felix was hunched forward, staring out through the dusty windscreen.

He didn't say another word.

Mathilde had arrived in our absence, along with our equipment, including, to my delight, my bag containing the Barrett 82A2. Felix momentarily forgot his anger at the sight of the briefcase containing his beloved Rampart rifle.

We grinned at each other.

51

I'm sure we both had the same thought: we can start work.

Mathilde was sitting on the couch in the first-floor sitting room, boots up on the low table. She wore combat pants, a fleece, fingerless gloves and, for custom's sake, a black-and-white Palestinian keffiyeh covered her head. Her arms were crossed over her chest.

'It's bloody cold,' were her first words.

'You look like Leila Khaled,' I told her.

'There's only a thirty-year age difference. If not more.'

'I beg your pardon.'

'Which is my room?'

'You're staying?'

'I'm so sorry. Western women do work in Afghanistan, you know. Doctors, nurses, reporters, photographers, aid workers – you might not approve, but that's just tough.'

'I didn't mean that.'

'I have bad news,' she said, getting to her feet and shaking hands with Felix. 'Joseph Gerber got as far as Karachi, checked out of his hotel the next morning – and vanished.'

Felix looked at me. He said, 'What happened?'

Mathilde answered. 'He was supposed to join you both in Quetta.'

'I know,' I said. 'We waited for him.'

'He never checked in for the flight.'

His room at Quetta's dilapidated Lourdes Hotel had also been booked in advance, but he never checked in there, either. When Yannis, Felix and I assembled outside the local Serena Hotel the following morning for the trip to Chaman on the border, he didn't turn up. We gave him an extra thirty minutes and left without him. It wasn't worth jeopardizing our security arrangements for one straggler.

Not an easy decision, but necessary.

Mathilde said, 'You'll have to do without a paramedic. There's no reason to believe we've been compromised.'

She was putting a brave face on it. He could have been kidnapped. Turned, even. Forty-eight hours had passed, and if Joseph was in the wrong hands and they knew their business, he'd have started to talk by now. I wondered how much he really knew. He knew what the target was. He knew us. He knew enough to make life uncomfortable.

'I'm taking his place,' Mathilde said.

I didn't like it, but I didn't show it. I had no objection to women in combat. Equally, I had no objection to foreign women working in Afghanistan. But we were an assassination squad, a hit team. We faced certain challenges other trades did not. A foreign woman stood out a mile – unless she wore a head-to-toe burka and could speak passable Pashto.

Whether male or female, intelligence officers knew too much, and were too expensively trained, to be risked in the field. It was agents like me who worked the coalface. With luck she would stay safe behind the wire in Kandahar or Kabul.

'You can choose your room,' I said.

'I don't want to have to share.'

'You won't have to. There's plenty of space.'

I didn't ask how she got in with all our gear. I assumed it was through Kandahar airport, using the good offices of the small Canadian contingent rather than the US 101st Airborne. I didn't trust the Americans. Southern Afghanistan was their patch, and I was sure they wouldn't hesitate to screw up our plans given half a chance. To Washington, allies were people who did as they were told. The alternative route was via the British mission in Kabul, but it was a long way by road.

To be honest, there were a couple of other things bothering me. Mathilde was the boss. But I did wonder how she'd shape up. She was no paramedic. The second issue was personal; the last time we'd slept under the same roof it had been in the same bed. Her bed. It was a while ago, but it had also marked the collapse of my marriage. It had been entirely my fault, but that didn't make it any easier.

I had rented the first floor of a house in the Sharinau district the day we arrived in Kandahar. Sher Muhammad, unaware of the true nature of our business, had driven us to the two city hotels deemed appropriate for foreigners. The first was on a busy road close to Herat Gate, and sat in a cesspool of sewage. I didn't look at the rooms, and in any case I was told it was full, and occupied primarily by American journalists. The second was close to the governor's house. It was regarded as more secure, but all manner of people walked in and out, most of them armed, and the rooms had flimsy doors and even flimsier locks, and they were asking $200 a head.

It had been a long and bruising drive from Quetta. Two hours to the smuggling town of Chaman on the Pakistan side of the border. Then, after the Pakistani formalities, over the other side to Spin Boldak, and another three hours along the back-breaking road or what was left of it to the country's second city. The desert would have been a smoother ride – but there were mines, Soviet ones, millions of them, to which the Americans had more recently added their cluster bombs.

En route, every few hundred yards and for many, many miles, sat lone beggars, covered in dust. Old men, women and children mostly. There were the remains of Soviet-built tanks and armoured fighting vehicles. There were gaping holes in the bridges attacked by US aircraft, vast craters in the road itself and straddling it.

We arrived at three in the afternoon. My back was playing up. It felt on fire, as if someone had attacked it with a razor. As for hotels, Felix didn't seem to mind either way. He'd lived in worse shitholes. Yannis shrugged. He was tired. He declared he would get his head down wherever we were.

I decided to look further. Sher Muhammad knew someone

who knew a member of the Karzai family – well, by marriage – who had part of a house to rent out.

By dusk we we had four bedrooms, a sitting room and two bathrooms for $100 a night. The rooms were carpeted, and the landlord promised to provide some furniture and curtains. The family lived on the ground floor, but we used the back stairs to avoid giving offence to their womenfolk. It suited us fine – we had a south-facing balcony, and there were steps up to the roof with a view across the city.

Which was where I took Felix. I told him I wanted to show him the layout of the town. What I really needed to do was talk to him alone, and before Abdur Rahman turned up.

Felix was sucking on a cigarette. He never smoked at home, or in training. Only on operations. He explained the bad habit by saying it was an appetite suppressor, that it helped keep him calm.

He had a funny way of snapping matches in half when he'd used them. An army thing, he said. He also opened his cigarette packets from the bottom so his dirty fingers wouldn't foul the end that goes in the mouth.

'Felix—'

'I don't how you can do it. Christ on the cross, the bastard killed our people. He damn nearly killed the two of us.'

'I know.'

'So what the fuck are we doing? You surely don't trust the cunt. Tell me.'

'Look south.'

'South?'

I turned him by the shoulder.

'See the hill there, right on the horizon?'

'I see it.'

'The pale patch below it.'

'So?'

'Those are sandhills. It's the start of the desert, and goes all the way to the Pakistan border. Over to the left – the south-east – is the airport and the US base. You can't see it because the hill is in the way. Now follow the horizon westwards. Hold it due south. What do you see?'

'Two choppers.'

'Blackhawks, on patrol.'

'I bow to your superior knowledge in such matters.'

'They're patrolling the edge of the desert because they believe Taliban are slipping into the area from that direction.'

'Where's this leading, Thomas?'

'What do you see between the edge of the desert and where we're standing?'

'Villages, fields. A treeline at 800 metres.'

'And next door to us?'

'A destroyed house.'

'Destroyed during the Soviet occupation.'

'What's this got to do with anything?'

'Bear with me.'

'For fuck's sake . . .'

He was puffing on the cigarette and stamping his feet to keep himself warm.

'This house has been rebuilt since then, but at that time, when you were based at Shindand and I paid a brief visit to Kandahar, this was a stronghold of the People's Democratic Party of Afghanistan. They had mortars up here on the roof where we're standing. Over there – ' I pointed to our right, due west, where jagged blue hills sprouted from the plain ' – the Soviets had set up fire bases to provide artillery support for their PDPA allies in the city.'

'Okay. I believe you.'

'That treeline you mentioned – it marked mujahedin country. Today it marks Taliban territory. It's not black or white turbans, but a state of mind. Back then the young, educated people of Kandahar and other cities looked to the socialist bloc for reform, for development. Today, the young people of the cities look to the West for help.'

'So?'

'So what's changed? The Americans are at the airport. Twenty years ago when I was here I went up to the perimeter and watched Soviet helicopter gunships landing and taking off.'

'Nothing's changed. So what?'

'Back then the Soviets said they were fighting *basmachi*, bandits backed by Pakistani intelligence and the CIA. Today the Americans say they are fighting terrorism. In many cases they were the very same people. Freedom fighters or *basmachi* then, terrorists or freedom fighters now. What's the difference?'

'As you said, not much.'

'Right. And you know why? Because what you were fighting back then, and what the West is fighting now, is the same.'

'Which is?'

'Poverty, ignorance, illiteracy. A state of mind.'

'Bombing illiterates and the poor won't solve the problem. As we learned to our cost in Herat.'

'No, it won't. It didn't then and it doesn't now. You're right. Twenty years ago the young leftists were divided between the Dari-speaking urban intelligentsia who belonged to the Parcham faction of the ruling party and the Pashto-speaking provincials of the more radical Khalq faction. It was their quarrel that prompted the Soviet intervention. Today the young urbanites are again divided – between the Dari-speakers and the southern Pashtuns.'

'Thanks for the lesson, but what's this got to do with Mullah Abdur Rahman?'

'Abdur Rahman understands all that,' I said. 'He's come to understand it.'

'Bully for the mullah. When did this Damascene conversion take place?'

Hardly the appropriate phrase for a Muslim.

'I don't know, but he's onside.'

'I'm touched. I'm sure Curly, Philippe and Andy will rest easier for knowing that – to say nothing of our Hazaras.'

'He didn't know who we were. We didn't know who we were pursuing.'

'We thought it was the Taliban ex-governor of Herat.'

'Abdur Rahman thought we were American special forces.'

'We were both wrong – so what difference would that have made? What difference does it make now?'

I could hazard a pretty good guess when and how Abdur Rahman had changed sides – if he'd changed sides, and it was a big 'if' – but it wouldn't help matters to tell Felix. It would only make things worse.

'Abdur Rahman's our local help,' I said. 'Without him this job won't work out. He has the access, and I know the way. We need him and his people, Felix. We need him a damn sight more than he needs us.'

'That right?' Felix stamped on the cigarette. He was still very angry. 'I don't have to like the son of a bitch, though, do I?'

'No,' I said. 'You don't have to like him.'

Yannis returned with Sher Muhammad from their trip to the bazaar after dark. Yannis lugged a generator up the stairs, followed by Sher Muhammad with a jerrycan of petrol. Yannis went out to the car again and brought back a large gas canister with three alternative fittings – a heater, a light and a stove-like apparatus for cooking.

He was our communicator. He needed power. He would have to spend lonely hours and days waiting for word from us before encrypting our messages and passing them on to our mysterious masters. He needed to get himself and his equipment 'sorted', as he put it.

He was taken aback by the appearance of Mathilde, and when she told him the news about Joseph he was visibly upset.

'What are we going to do?'

'We're going ahead, of course,' Mathilde said.

'We're bloody blown,' Yannis said.

'Not necessarily.'

'And what about Joe? We just leave him, is that it?'

'What do you propose, Yannis? Any suggestion would be welcome, but we can hardly search Karachi – a city with twice the population of London.'

He looked around helplessly.

'I don't know,' he said. He was a short, broad-shouldered man, his sturdy legs, broken nose and shaved head emphasizing the impression of a pugilist. Only now he looked bewildered, and quite lost.

I tried to distract him. 'The gear's arrived, Yannis.'

He looked at me, but the words hadn't sunk in.

'Bloody hell,' he muttered. 'Poor old Joe. Poor devil. There must have been a leak. Someone's talked.'

He was jumping to conclusions.

'There may be a simple explanation,' I said. 'There may have been a problem with his passport or his visa. They're always changing the rules. He might have been mugged. It could have been a simple robbery.'

'Joe would have called.'

I said I thought it unlikely. '*En clair* – using his satphone? I don't think so. He wouldn't have thought it important enough. He was a stickler for the rules on comms security. He knows we would carry on, that none of us is indispensable. He had an emergency number – we all do – but I doubt he would have used it unless he thought it was an emergency.'

Yannis did not look convinced.

*

We were thinking about eating by the time Abdur Rahman appeared. I'd given up hope, convinced that Felix's outburst had offended him. I thought he wouldn't turn up for a day or two, just to prove a point and set us back in our hunt for the fugitive.

I was wrong. He burst in, Khaled in tow, looking excited. He was armed, and he wore a simple black *chalwar kameez*, matching waistcoat and a dark-grey turban. He resembled a pirate captain rather than a fashion icon. All he needed was an eyepatch. And yes, he looked every inch a Taliban commander. Which is what he was, of course.

Introductions followed, and the inevitable round of greetings. These were repeated once we had all sat, keeping eye contact as the questions and answers were repeated all over again. Khaled shook everyone's hand, moving from each person to the next before sitting down cross-legged.

We had a sofa, the low table and Felix and Yannis dragged in two more armchairs from the other rooms. We crowded together around the table, enjoying the warmth from the gas heater.

Abdur Rahman put down his Kalashnikov, leaning it against the wall within reach. Khaled followed his example.

'Here,' Abdur Rahman said, taking out from his waistcoat what appeared to be a DVD. He handed it to Mathilde with a broad smile. He ignored Felix.

Yannis set up the little DVD player.

Ahmed, the young Tajik who worked in the house as cook and cleaner, brought a pot of green tea for our guests, and we waited until he had left again before we started.

'I have all the names,' Abdur Rahman said in English. 'There are twenty-seven all told. You will know some of them. Unfortunately Khaled and I know them all – rather too well.'

Mathilde was the only one of us who seemed to have any idea what he was talking about.

'What you are about to see was recorded in Quetta,' Abdur Rahman said. 'It was taken last week – in secret, of course – and the lighting is not as good as one might have wished for. The camcorder was hidden in a bag. The buyers you will see are not the main players, but their representatives, their agents. We know who they are, too.'

It was a simple room with double doors at one end, curtained windows and a richly patterned carpet. Around the sides were flat cushions, blue, like thin mattresses. There were also round cushions, like bolsters. They were navy.

The host sat at the far end, opposite the doors. He wore white. His beard was hennaed and he wore a turban, and fingered prayer beads. He appeared to be in his sixties or seventies. He was smiling, half-rising to greet his visitors, all men of middle age or older like himself, grasping their hands and forearms in both hands.

The visitors then took their places around the room, sitting on the blue cushions and leaning on the bolsters.

'The buyers,' said Abdur Rahman.

A boy poured tea. Trays of dried fruit and nuts, including sugared almonds, were set out on the floor. Spitoons were strategically placed by each man.

The first girl was tall for her age and slim. I thought she looked about twelve, but Abdur Rahman told us she was fourteen.

The bidding started. It stopped at one point while an elderly woman in black undressed the girl, taking off her knee-length *chalwar kameez*, the baggy pants, until she stood naked.

The old woman forced the girl to pivot, turning right around, and even handled her budding breasts, showing them to the buyers as they sipped tea. One man rubbed himself quite openly. The bidding recommenced, faster now, as the girl was helped to dress.

'She's been bought for $3,000,' Abdur Rahman said.

'Who by?' I said.

'A Karachi brothel,' said Abdur Rahman. 'She's a virgin – and quite untouched.'

Next was a green-eyed nineteen-year-old. She too was stripped, revealing a wonderful figure, and bidding was fast and furious, but stopped at $2,400.

Abdur Rahman explained. Yes, she was a virgin, too. But she had been 'touched' – sodomized – and fetched less as a result.

'Many of them end up in the Gulf in harems,' Abdur Rahman said. 'Many others are sent to brothels in Pakistan, even India. The lucky few end up as housemaids, but even then it's a form of slavery. Sexual abuse is common.'

We watched two more 'bride auctions' before Mathilde said she had seen enough. I think we all had. The last was a fifteen-year-old with long black hair who was in tears, clearly frightened. She was both untouched and a virgin, and the bidding went up over $3,000. She was light-skinned, and her eyes were blue. That explained the price, according to Abdur Rahman.

'You don't want to see the boys?'

'I don't think so,' I said. 'Thanks all the same.'

'The boys – the small ones – end up as camel jockeys in the Gulf. Others are simply cheap labour – slave labour. In the refugee camps you can buy a boy from his family for a month's supply of wheat. That's what a life is worth now.'

'Cheery stuff,' Yannis said.

'The buyers are paying to marry the girls,' Abdur Rahman said. 'That's what they would say if questioned. Of course, they don't marry them. They're buying them on behalf of somebody else, and marriage is not on the cards. This is the south Asia sex industry, and it relies on Afghan slave children smuggled across the border to provide the raw material. The main market is the Gulf. The smugglers' route is the same for everything – drugs, guns or kids. It leads from Kandahar through the area known as Argestan – Thomas knows it well from his trips during the Soviet occupation – across the frontier and on to Quetta.'

Mathilde caught my eye and looked away.

I had used the pipeline during the Soviet era, but she knew perfectly well I'd been back that way again a lot more recently than that.

To retrieve our plunder from under HMG's azaleas.

Felix lit another cigarette.

'What's any of this got to do with us?' he said.

FIVE

Abdur Rahman didn't answer Felix's question. Instead, he asked Khaled to go to the one good restaurant in the city and fetch dinner, and to complete his mission before the start of the 21.30 curfew.

Khaled appeared to be daydreaming. 'What's that?' His eyes came back into focus. 'Oh, all right.' He got up. He was about five-eleven tall, and slender. His face was broad. His eyes were very large. I imagined they must be his mother's. The lashes were long and thick and quite feminine. His beard was trimmed close, but he had a strong, obstinate chin. His complexion was pale. He could be a Brahmin Indian, I thought, an Iranian, a Syrian or perhaps a Saudi prince.

I still couldn't remember where or when I had seen him before.

Khaled said in Pashto, 'What shall I get them?'

Abdur Rahman told him: 'Barbecued chicken. Better make it two. Lamb kebab, *karai*, salad, nan, yoghurt. The usual. And something to drink. A big bottle of Coke.'

'And the money?'

'Pay for it yourself, but make sure you get a receipt. In fact, we will drop you off and you can make your own way back with the food in a rickshaw.'

Khaled wrapped his *potu* around himself, and picked up his rifle. He went outside onto the landing and put on his shoes.

My grasp of Pashto was picking up.

Abdur Rahman turned to me. 'English, I want you to meet a friend of mine. He has asked us to dinner.'

It was more order than invitation.

Felix looked up. 'What about us?'

Abdur Rahman showed his teeth. It was a smile of sorts, but there was no humour in it.

He said, 'Don't worry, my Russian friend. You won't go to bed hungry. We are fetching your dinner. Too many foreigners moving about at night raises questions. There are only two places where you can find decent food; one is well lit and the diners can be identified from across the street. The other is small and cramped and I do not think we should be seen out together there. Not all of us at the same time.'

Abdur Rahman picked up his Kalashnikov. He didn't clear it, but merely checked that it was on safe. At the door he turned round again.

'Khaled is your fixer. He has some English. Enough, anyway. He will be the link between us.'

He made it seem final. It wasn't a question. He didn't look at Mathilde when he said it. It was clear Abdur Rahman was going to want to do things his way, on his terms. I knew how it would be. He was very much like myself. He liked to dominate, and if he couldn't get away with that, he would manipulate other people. Unless someone made it clear to him what his responsibilties were and where precisely they ended, he would take us over completely, and impose his will on us.

The notion that Mathilde might be consulted would never have crossed his mind. I wondered if she knew that.

There was very little traffic.

At city intersections the security forces had built bonfires both for warmth and to provide light to inspect drivers' identification cards.

We were not stopped. Perhaps they recognized Abdur Rahman. Or maybe they knew the car.

Our headlights stabbed the swirling dust, and Abdur Rahman wrestled the Pajero from one side of the street to the other to avoid the worst of the bumps and potholes. We dropped Khaled off, then Abdur Rahman pushed the Toyota through the bazaar until he turned off into a tight alleyway, high mud walls on both sides. There was room for barely a single vehicle, certainly not two.

He cut the lights and for a moment we sat in complete blackness until our eyes grew accustomed to the dark.

'Come on, English.'

Spectral figures had appeared, their shawls wrapped tightly around them from head to foot. A boy carrying a paraffin lamp led us down what appeared to be a tunnel. I had to lower my head to avoid bumping it. There was a fetid stench of human and animal waste and rotting refuse. It wasn't particularly offensive – just a stink it would take a little time to get used to.

We turned right, into a tiny doorway.

Abdur Rahman was behind me. 'Mind your step.'

The boy took me firmly by the arm.

We were climbing. The steps were small, the passage so narrow I was touching the walls on both sides.

The youth released me as we emerged into what appeared to be a courtyard.

'Look, English.'

A dark carpet of glistening stars seemed close enough to touch. The city centre lay all around us.

'Please. This way.'

I bent down and undid my laces, something I had to do several times a day. Our escort waited. I told myself that if I ever returned to Afghanistan I would use Velcro, not laces, on my boots. Perhaps I should design a pair of boots especially for Afghanistan – and for Muslims who take them off to pray five times a day.

Someone was holding aside the curtain that hung across a lighted doorway.

'Welcome, Thomas. Welcome.'

This was Abdur Rahman's home in Kandahar, I realized. I don't know why. I sensed it. It was buried inside the old city walls. Kandahar had originally been a few homes and a market inside a fortress and protected by its massive walls, the entrances barred by huge wooden gates at night to keep out bandits and packs of wolves.

'Make yourself at home, Thomas.'

Cushions were piled up around me. Abdur Rahman sat opposite, smiling, clearly pleased. A comfortable-looking bed stood in a corner, next to it a chest of drawers. There were no pictures or images on the walls, but the atmosphere was homely, comfortable, surprisingly neat.

The boy who had carried the lamp returned, bearing a tray crowded with long glasses of freshly squeezed fruit juice – pomegranate, orange and apple. One by one, Abdur Rahman's guests arrived, prompting hand-shaking, hugs and rounds of greetings, repeated again and again. Each man settled himself against the cushions until I counted eleven visitors, excluding myself.

While two youths unrolled a huge tablecloth on the floor, a lean, tough-looking man in his forties told amusing stories about life in prison in Quetta, and his friendships with foreigners held there on drug-smuggling charges.

Trays of food followed, a vast array of dishes to be spread among us and shared, the diners using their right hands, tearing up the bread and using it to shovel up the food.

I was introduced to everyone simply as 'Mr Thomas' or 'The English' and received friendly nods and smiles. Their questions were few and inoffensive. Where did I live? How many children did I have? Was the weather in London as bad as everyone said it was? What did I think of Mr Blair? Someone noticed me fidgeting, and told me there was no problem if I had difficulty sitting cross-legged all the time and wanted to stretch my legs out. They understood it was hard for foreigners

It wasn't until the meal had been cleared away and the tea was poured and cigarettes lit that we started to talk seriously.

'He has seen the video,' Abdur Rahman said.

'Ah.' A dozen pairs of eyes turned to look at me.

'And what did you think?'

The question came from the man on my left, a silver-haired gentleman in his sixties, with a rumpled, kindly face.

I hesitated.

He said, 'The children were beautiful, no?'

I wasn't sure whether I should agree with him or not, for fear of offending the honour of Afghan womanhood or of appearing to be a sicko who regarded children as sex objects.

'That people should be bought and sold—' I began.

'Is a crime,' he said, finishing my sentence for me.

'Absolutely.'

'Nowhere is man kind to woman. Not even in England. But here . . .' He shrugged, leaving the rest of the sentence unsaid.

Abdur Rahman came to my rescue.

'Suleiman is a businessman with many contacts across Afghanistan and over the border in Pakistan and Iran,' he said. 'He is very knowledgeable in the matter of trade.'

'Trade or smuggling?'

Suleiman smiled, and opened his hands as if to say, Well, it's all a matter of semantics.

'He helped us record the auction,' Abdur Rahman said.

Suleiman spoke quietly. 'Trade is our lifeblood in Kandahar, but in the matter of smuggling, it wasn't always like this,

Mr Thomas. Under Zahir Shah and his father, tribal leaders, district *shuras* and so on received royal patronage.'

'Meaning payments?'

'Exactly. Monthly stipends. It wasn't much, of course, but it satisfied everyone. The money flowing from the state coffers kept the machinery of governmment well oiled. The king's authority, the state's authority, operated through the traditional tribal system, and through the institution of the *shura*, or council of elders. You understand, I think?'

I said I did.

'It provided stability, even if it reinforced traditions and failed to allow for change or what you call human rights. It allowed a businessman like me to conduct my commercial affairs safely – and honourably. My family was safe.'

He repeated what he'd said in Pashto for the benefit of the other guests. Several heads nodded in agreement.

'When Daoud launched his coup against the king, the system broke down. People had to look elsewhere. You have seen the poppy fields. You know about the opium, the huge profits to be made by the big smugglers?'

'Of course.'

'You have seen the Japanese four-wheel-drive vehicles on our streets – smuggled in from the Gulf via Bandar Abbas?'

'Sure.'

'You know about the weapons – everything is available at a price, even Stingers. You know about the cars and the drugs. Now you have seen the video, you know there's a slave market as well.'

'Yes.'

'Everyone in this room was either a Taliban member or supported the Taliban. Why? We wanted to try to stop the kind of thieving, banditry and violence we experienced after the Russians withdrew in '89 and the mujahedin parties took over and started fighting one another. Our host, Abdur Rahman, was a famous Taliban commander. It was a simple thing for us. We wanted stability. We wanted order. We wanted an end to this criminality. Of course, Mullah Omar went too far—'

'And now?'

Suleiman was not to be diverted from a speech he had clearly thought about and prepared.

'The Taliban took a wrong turn. We know that. The commanders – including Abdur Rahman – wanted to get rid of bin Laden and his al-Qaeda network. They urged restraint on Mullah Omar. They called for moderation. It didn't work. He wouldn't listen. After the September 11 attacks, some commanders wanted to replace Mullah Omar with someone more pragmatic, more flexible. Pakistan tried to engineer an internal coup, but it backfired, and Omar emerged more closely aligned with bin Laden.'

'So—'

'Tell him, Abdur Rahman,' Suleiman said. 'Tell him the rest of it.'

'We fear the same disorder,' Abdur Rahman said. 'The same lawlessness. It's coming back. Our roads are unsafe. Motorists are being killed by robbers. The drug barons are still doing business. Some are even protected by the Americans. Our women – well, you have seen what goes on. The new government has been promised billions of dollars by the international community, but the south-western provinces have got nothing. Our country areas are starved of resources. People go hungry. They take up the Kalashnikov and solve the problem the only way they know. After all, every male between fifteen and sixty has fought at one time or another, and few have any other trade but war . . .'

'What's this got to do with me?'

'Everything, English. Imagine you are a poor farmer in Helmand province. A man comes to your door. He tells you he will pay you cash now – right now – for your opium even before the seeds have been planted. He will come back to collect the opium himself, he says. You don't have to lift a finger. And he offers you cash in advance for your cotton, your barley, even your fruit. He fixes the prices in advance. Yes, the prices are rather low, but he's giving you cash in hand. You desperately need the money. Do you refuse him? Your wife and children are hungry, they are crying all the time for food.'

'No, I don't refuse.

'Very well.'

'I still don't see . . .'

'Imagine you are a refugee. You have seven malnourished children, including three girls. A man describing himself as a marriage agent comes to your tent. He offers you $150 in cash on the spot for the twelve-year-old. What do you do? He gives you all the sweet talk about offering her a better life in the household of a devout Muslim. He even has photographs of the young man who will wed the girl when she comes of age. He talks about her being properly fed, the nice clothes she will have, even her schooling. You want to believe him. It's a wonderful dream. A fairy story. You are uneducated and poor, and females have never been considered to be important in your culture except as servants or childbearers. He counts out the notes in front of you. Do you refuse?'

'I suppose not.'

Suleiman sighed. 'You see? Twenty-seven people are involved in managing and profiting from this smuggling route. Twenty-seven major players. They'll handle anything. If it makes money, if there's a market for it and the profit margin is worth the risk, they'll do it. With heroin they increase their money a thousandfold, maybe more.'

'These twenty-seven – they're where, exactly?'

Abdur Rahman said: 'They stretch from Kandahar through

the Hada hills in Argestan down to Spin Boldak, across the frontier to Chaman, and then to Quetta, and from there to Karachi. There's a branchline from Chaman to Iran, too.'

'They have official protection,' Suleiman added. 'The same protectors they had twenty years ago when the Soviets were here.'

'How official?'

This prompted a round of hurried discussion in Pashto among those present. I couldn't follow it. It was too quick. There was disagreement of some kind, probably over what I should be told, and how much.

'All right,' Abdur Rahman said. 'The point is this. Some al-Qaeda people bought their way out through central Asia. Particularly from the Kunduz front. Others escaped to Iran.'

'I read something about it.'

'Some went down the smuggling route we've just described to you. Wounded al-Qaeda to begin with, in January. This year – 2002. Then senior figures. February. The same route, English, and they had the same protection.'

'You're talking about Pakistan's Inter Services Intelligence.'

'Of course,' Abdur Rahman said.

'You're saying the smugglers, with the active or tacit support of ISI, helped smuggle al-Qaeda and Taliban cadres out of Afghanistan, via Chaman.'

'Naturally.'

'Despite Pakistan's honeymoon with Washington.'

'Oh, yes. Pakistan's military feels it has Washington's blessing and can do whatever it likes. Just as before. Pakistan's military dictators have always needed America to thrive.'

'It's still going on – this ISI stuff?'

'Of course.'

'I've been there,' I said. 'In the Soviet period, I travelled from Quetta to Gulestan, then over the border and through Argestan to Kandahar and back the same way. We managed without food for a week while we hid in the Hada hills. I remember a spring there, an oasis, really quite lush, in the Lowrah valley . . .'

I didn't mention my trip in 1996.

'That's the place,' Abdur Rahman said. 'Suleiman and his friends know it, also.'

I knew what was coming, or thought I did, but it would be better to play dumb and not rush matters.

I turned to Suleiman. 'Why should you people care? You were all Taliban yourselves, or at least Taliban supporters. You should be pleased some of your comrades are escaping the Americans. Anyhow, why tell me – a British national?'

He leaned over and put a hand on my forearm and gave it a gentle squeeze. 'Because Abdur Rahman says you can be trusted. You are his friend. He says you and your friends can help us – provided, of course, that we help you.'

Trust. Friendship. Honour. Grandiose words, I thought. I looked at the faces of the men around me. These things mattered to Afghans more than most, I knew. They weren't just empty phrases. But I had no illusions. I was a foreigner, a Westerner, a member of a nation allied to Washington and its absurd war against the so-called axis of evil. I was a non-Muslim, too, and I had hunted down and killed such men as these – not for faith or ideology, but for money.

American dollars.

And yes, of course, I was in Abdur Rahman's debt. So was Felix, though he wouldn't admit it.

'How do you think you can help us?' I said.

The power had gone again; load-shedding, or problems with the supply from the big hydroelectric project built by the Americans a generation earlier in Helmand province. The city was wrapped in darkness. There were no stars now, the night sky blanketed by the dust rolling in with the cold south wind.

'Does the name Gul Yunus mean anything to you?'

Abdur Rahman was back behind the wheel. He was keeping to the backstreets, or trying to. Still, he had the password. It was changed every night, he told me, but his contacts at the governor's house always told him what it would be.

'Gul Yunus is head of the Khad – your secret police – in Kandahar.'

'Yes, English, he is. Gul Yunus has been an agent of Pakistan's ISI for many years. A sister of his is married to Sher Ahmed, a businessman in the Gulf. Sher Ahmed's business is legitimate as far as it goes, but the capital he used to establish himself was built on heroin. Ahmed is a dollar millionaire, and his heroin empire stretches to Frankfurt and London.'

'I didn't know.'

'Both men – secret police chief Gul Yunus and Sher Ahmed – are Gabizai, a sub-sect of the Achekzai. The Gabizai live in Gulestan on the Pakistan side of the frontier and they also live on this side, and in this area. They have had ISI protection for years.'

'Why should they need it?'

'They've had a running feud with the Achekzai chief and his leftist, pro-democracy party, the Pashtun Nation, on the other side of the border. It served Pakistan's interest to stoke the feud to keep the Achekzai in particular and the Pashtuns generally in a state of turmoil.'

'Strategic depth.'

'Shit depth. That's what it is,' Abdur Rahman said. 'They took a page out of the British imperialists' handbook, and elaborated on it.'

'So this Yunus is Pakistan's man in Kandahar.'

'If only it was just one. There are many. Hundreds, probably. Gul Yunus has an uncle, Haji Safar, who works in the secret police. I know him. He's another ISI man. He's the brother of Isa Muhammad, khan or leader of the Gabizais. You get the picture, English?'

'They keep it in the family.'

'That's Afghanistan for you.'

'It's like the Sicilian Mafia.'

'Worse, English.'

'Why do you keep calling me that?'

'It makes me feel more Afghan.'

'I'm glad I serve a useful purpose.'

'You will, Morgan, I promise you.'

'Why? Because I know the way?'

'That – and other things.'

'Go on. This Haji Safar . . .'

'It was Haji Safar who got three al-Qaeda fighters out in the first week of January. They were wounded; a Saudi, a Palestinian and an Algerian. They were driven to Chaman in a private ambulance. They were met by a major in the ISI and taken to a private clinic in Quetta. Later they were transferred to the city's Sandiman Hospital—'

'I know it. It's in the foothills on the city outskirts. A big yellow complex. New. There's an isolation centre for Congo haemorrhagic fever just a little further up the road.'

'After three weeks they were flown to Islamabad.'

'Then?'

'We don't know.'

'Go on.'

'In Chaman the head of the JUI – Jamaat Ulema Islami, the populist Islamic party in Pakistan – is Maulana Karim Khan. For thirty years Karim Khan was the family priest to Sher Ahmed's father, Lalai. Lalai and his brother, Daoud, entered Pakistan from Afghanistan in 1964 and were established in Gulestan with ISI help. So you see? The family and political ties?'

'I think so.'

'Karim Khan has been told to place al-Qaeda and prominent Taliban with JUI members' families in Chaman until they can be moved on. He's paid for it, of course. He skims a commission off the top for himself and pays the JUI members who provide hospitality for those fellows who are brought over.'

We were outside the house in Sharinau. No lights showed. I assumed everyone had turned in. Abdur Rahman killed the lights and the engine and we sat in the darkness and listened to the wind thundering across the plain.

'Gul Yunus has one brother living under a false name as a refugee in Germany, but he's not short of money. Another has refugee status in Britain and receives government money, but I'm told he's not exactly hard up. He drives an E-class Mercedes.'

I opened my door and the cold air swept in.

'English.'

'Yes?'

'This is the way he will come.'

For a brief moment I didn't make the connection.

'You understand?'

'How do you know?'

'You will not speak of this.'

'Abdur—' I was going to explain there were only four of us. We had a job to do, and we had to share the information we needed to get it done.

'Not even to your government. Not until it's over.'

'Look.'

'Promise me, man. Your word on it. You will tell no one until our work is done. You will not communicate this in any way, not to anyone. Promise, English.'

'I promise.'

'Not the woman. On your honour.'

How could a Brixton boy educated at Goldsmiths' possibly accept the word of a bounty hunter, and what could he possibly have against Mathilde? Perhaps he was more Afghan than I had thought.

'You have my word. Scout's honour.'

'You're no scout.'

'Neither are you, pal.'
'But I have your word?'
'You do, yes.'
Abdur Rahman seemed strangely reassured.
'Good night, English. Sleep well.'
Outside it was bitter, well below zero.
'Thanks for dinner.'
'You're most welcome.'

SIX

'You knew Zotov – when?'

'Back in '92,' I said.

'So you didn't know him here – in Afghanistan?'

'Felix was based at Shindand airport, in the north-east near Herat, and later Bagram. We're talking early eighties. The Sovs were gradually getting better at using airborne assaults to catch their opponents on the hop. Night operations were his thing.'

'Spetsnaz.' Mathilde stated it as fact, not a question.

'Two tours in Afghanistan.'

'And you?'

'I was here in the south, seeking Sovmat.'

'For us?'

'No.'

'Who then?'

'I was on loan,' I said.

'On loan?'

Mathilde was in the back. She was sitting very close. I could smell her perfume, her skin. She must have known the effect she was having. I could also smell Sher Muhammad's feet. He was driving, and I was glad of his presence. His feet served as an antidote – well, almost.

'Who was it?' Mathilde said.

'We didn't know until much later.'

'So?'

'It was the Pentagon.'

'You got leave of absence.'

'We were asked if we would like to volunteer for something that might be good experience. I stuck my hand up – I was still too young to know that in the army you don't volunteer if you've got any sense.'

It turned out to be the clandestine pursuit of Soviet war materiel.

We were heading south through the dustiest, busiest part of town. The main street, Judda, was packed with people, with donkey carts, rickshaws, with Toyotas flying the national flag and packed with gunmen – and with the US TV networks' cars and their bodyguards, and the big shiny Jeeps favoured by US special forces. Occasionally the Americans could be seen in the back of pickups – bearded, wearing baseball caps, pistols strapped to their legs with black Velcro, knee pads and the inevitable M-16s, along with 'I love NY' badges on their desert fatigues. They hung out at the Kandahar Restaurant and today several were crowded into a carpet shop.

Mathilde said, 'How did it work?'

'We flew to Pakistan, checked into local hotels, registering ourselves as aircrew. For Iceland Cargo or Icecargo, a chartered airline with headquarters in Helsinki. That was the cover story.'

'And?'

'I got the minigun off a Mil-24 gunship. It was a first, and it was in good shape.'

'Brilliant.'

'It was. The boss was chuffed.'

'I bet. You got paid, though, didn't you?'

'Bloody right. Three grand. It seemed like a lot of money in those days.'

'So you remember Kandahar.'

'Some. I walked along the fields towards the city in daylight, watching the Sovs and their convoys on the highway – the route we're taking now, only in the opposite direction.'

'Didn't they see you?'

Her hand touched my neck, just for a moment.

'I was just a peasant among many. I even had the requisite crab lice and fleas.'

'You were dressed for the part.'

'Sure. My clothes were filthy.'

'You went through this place called Argestan.'

So that's what this was about.

Mathilde said: 'Is that how you got your haul out after the embassy job?'

I didn't say anything.

'It wasn't through Landi Kotal, Thomas. It wasn't through Teri Mangal, either. Paracinar was out of the question. You couldn't use those routes, not then, not in '96.'

'No?'

'No. You needed friends. Friends you could trust. Like Felix. Like Abdur Rahman.'

Did I trust them?

For several minutes neither of us said anything.

'Tell me more,' Mathilde said. 'Tell me why this place fascinates you so much.'

'I was in Nuristan once—'

'Nuristan . . .'

'Kunar province. The mountains are huge up there. Like massive Pacific rollers. Never ending. You think you've climbed one ridge at 14,000 feet but behind it there's another at 18,000. And another at 20,000. And another. We couldn't use the valleys or the roads because they were in Soviet and PDPA hands. I was on my last legs. In fact, I wasn't on my legs at all. I was crawling, pulling myself up with my hands. It was exhaustion. The air was so thin. We'd been walking – climbing – for a couple of weeks on nothing but green tea and bread. An old man with a white beard strode past. He must have been at least seventy. He gave me a contemptuous look. It was a look that said: You wanker – you're a pathetic, self-

80

pitying prick, a soft Westerner, no better than those *kāfir* Russians.

'It was just a glance. I got up at once. I stayed up. He offered to take my Bergen. I refused. He actually tried to pull it off my shoulders, but I pushed him away. He set off at the same light-infantry pace, regardless of gradient. He didn't speak. He didn't look back. I stuck to him. I'd rather have died than fallen behind. I really think death would have been preferable to the shame I would have felt. That night when we finally halted a feast was prepared – it was our first hot meal in a long time. The entire village was assembled. I had the place of honour at the host's right hand. Far at the back, way down the pecking order, I saw the old man again. I saw how poor he was. His clothes were threadbare. I piled up food on my plate and carried it over to him.

'I couldn't think of another way of showing him respect.

'That night he found a charpoy from somewhere – one of those wood and string beds. He put it up on the flat roof of the tallest building in the village, then he wrapped himself up in his *potu* and lay down at the foot of the bed, clutching his rifle.

'He had appointed himself my bodyguard. For the next week we were inseparable. We never spoke. He moved at the same fast pace. I kept up. I forgot my blisters. I forgot to be tired. I carried my own kit. In a tight spot I know with absolute certainty he would have given his life to defend me. I still think of him and many others like him, even now.'

Mathilde said, 'And what of Kandahar?'

'This highway was in much better shape than it is now. So was Kandahar city. The Americans have done more damage and killed more people in five months than the Sovs did in the first of their ten years of occupation.'

'You don't know that, Thomas.'

Mathilde disapproved. It made me smile. She was so disgustingly loyal, a real zealot. I enjoyed winding her up. It

81

was unfair, of course. The Soviets had killed a million Afghans, mostly civilians. They themselves had lost upwards of 40,000 soldiers, but they'd only ever admitted to 14,000.

They'd gone in for massacres, for carpet-bombing. The Americans might have killed off a few wedding parties, and bombed schools and hospitals, but they hadn't gone that far.

Not yet anyway.

'No, you're right,' I said. 'I don't know. But it's what I see and hear, and that's a lot more reliable than any figures from the UN or anyone else. Médecins sans Frontières puts the death toll in those first months at 8,000—'

Mathilde was keen to get back on course. 'What else?'

I was riding my hobby horse. I wasn't about to dismount.

'Of course the Russians and their Afghan clients fired Scuds, scores of them, into the hills. Today the Americans are using weapons of mass destruction – thermobaric bombs and fuel air weapons – and they're killing all sorts. Very few are genuine Taliban or al-Qaeda. Washington has the nerve to lecture us on Iraq's alleged weapons of mass destruction . . .'

'You've become very cynical, Thomas.'

Again, her fingers brushed the nape of my neck, giving me gooseflesh. It was doing something else to me, too, elsewhere. Notwithstanding Sher Muhammad's unwashed feet.

Mathilde was completely out of order, but that had never stopped her in the past.

'I've had lots of practice,' I said.

'Tell me more about Kandahar back then.'

What she really wanted from me was a detailed description of the way in and the way out – even better, a detailed map.

Full marks for effort, Mathilde.

'I went around the airport perimeter, spent a few nights in the villages in the area, photographed the gunships and fixed-wing aircraft taking off and landing. Bandit country then, bandit country now.'

'That was for the US Department of Defense too – the pictures?'

She must know. Why did she ask?

'No. Wasn't part of the deal. I thought I'd bring our people a present. A freebie.'

'Tell me more about Felix and your Afghan days.'

I didn't tell Mathilde anything important. I was sure most of it was in the files her people kept back at Vauxhall Cross. I'd hunted for Sovmat in Kunar, Nangahar and Paktiya, Logar, Ghazni and Kandahar. I'd interrogated a captured Soviet official, a candidate member of the Central Committee well into his sixties, just before his keepers shot him. I watched the execution, and I didn't object. Why should I have? It hadn't occurred to me to do so. In those days I thought the only good Sov was a dead one, and the more senior the better, and I thought civilians were as good a target as the military, if not more so. Fuck 'em. The fact that the Afghan guerrillas wouldn't go after Soviet women and children was a source of major irritation. I used to suggest ways to attack restaurants and Soviet housing complexes, to gun down Soviet mothers and their kids in drive-by attacks, to hit them where it really hurt, but the Afghans always refused. They were shocked at the suggestion. It was dishonourable. It was un-Islamic. I didn't tell Mathilde that, either. I didn't tell her that we British and Americans had behaved exactly like the so-called terrorists we were now supposed to be fighting.

Hell, what was the difference between dropping a 10,000 lb bomb on a school from 15,000 feet and firing an RPG through the window of a Russian crèche?

Nothing.

The generation that was to provide recruits for the Taliban and al-Qaeda had been eager to learn, and we had taught them well. Too well.

And when the Russians pulled out, we turned our backs on the Afghans and forgot our promises.

I didn't tell her about the lack of food, the exhausting night marches, the blisters, the fatigue, the terror of being pursued by those Mil-24 gunships, the fear of night ambush, of unmarked minefields, of betrayal, of being maimed, of dying slowly, in pain and alone.

Kandahar had been easier because it was relatively flat. There were buses, trucks, motorcycles and donkeys. In the city itself I'd ridden a motorycle around the city centre, lit up by streams of red and green tracer, incoming and outgoing. I never thought of it as dangerous. Just massive fun. But the ease of travel was offset by Felix's buddies in Soviet intelligence. They always knew of my presence within twenty-four hours of my reaching a particular location. They were hunting me as I hunted them. I had to keep moving, sleeping in different places, never following a straight line or coherent direction for fear of people like Zotov coming in by chopper and lying in wait.

The Taliban and al-Qaeda had not forgotten those lessons.

Sher Muhammad lit a cigarette, and I opened my window.

By now we had left the city far behind. Kandahar's southern approaches were guarded by rusty T-52s, T-55s and T-62s, painted in the most exotic camouflage, as if graffiti artists had gone wild with cans of spray paint. The Soviet-built tanks would have been supplied to the PDPA at least twenty years ago, would have passed into the hands of the mujahedin, then over to the Taliban and finally to the forces of Hamid Karzai's interim governmment.

It would be a miracle if they could move at all.

The airport was an hour from the city, a turn to the right into the desert scrub.

'Thomas.'

The perimeter fence of iron posts and barbed wire had not changed.

There were the wrecks of old Soviet aircraft to the right, then a line of seven black-painted Chinooks in a row, special forces aircraft, I thought.

'You were saying . . .'

'What?'

'Felix. How you met. In 1992.'

'He was selling Soviet-era campaign medals and decorations on Moscow's Arbat.'

'He was broke?'

'We both were. Felix was a captain in military intelligence, based at the headquarters outside Moscow which we called the Aquarium. His monthly pay packet wouldn't have bought him a Big Mac at Moscow's McDonald's. He had to moonlight.'

'You didn't tell me this.'

Mathilde meant when she and I were sleeping together – during our disastrous 'fling'. That's what her friends had called it. An office fling, except I didn't work in her office. I was just her 'joe' – a head agent – and people like me never got invited to head office or anywhere near it. Prior to Mathilde's bedroom sessions, meetings with my handlers had been usually held in a Portuguese caff in Stockwell's South Lambeth Road or a pub just across the river in Pimlico. I had put it down to the snotty IOs keeping their expense accounts for classier company. After all, I was just some West Pilton yob with an incomprehensibly thick accent. Mathilde was supposed to report her sexual contacts, specifically ones that developed into lasting affairs, but I was pretty sure she hadn't reported on us for the very good reason that it would have ended a promising career in Operations.

'I had no reason to tell you,' I said. 'There's a hell of a lot you never told me.'

Mathilde didn't want to get into that. 'How did you work it – the uniforms, I mean?'

'I had orders for certain outfits. KGB, rocket troops, the

staff of the 20th Guards Army in what used to be East Gernany, you name it. People had specific requests. Collectors. Mainly in Germany and the States. They were very specific.'

'Such as?'

'One client wanted a paratroop general's dress tunic. It had to have certain campaign medals.'

'Felix helped?'

'Sure. I had the buyers. Felix located the potential sellers. I would give him the dosh and go and stand outside on the steps of the Frunze Military Academy with an empty sports bag. Within twenty minutes he would emerge with whatever it was I wanted.'

'You shared the commission?'

'Yes. I split my cut with him.'

'A fifty-fifty split?'

'Straight down the middle. Then we'd blow it on a decent meal and get rat-faced.'

I was going to ask Mathilde why she was so keen to know all this old stuff, but Sher Muhammad had pulled up outside the gates of Kandahar airport and I opened my door and jumped out. Mathilde followed.

Mathilde told Sher Muhammad to wait.

The gates were high, the lower half covered with fine mesh. On the far side there were coils of razor wire and log barriers, and about twenty-five metres back stood an American with a balaclava on his head, cradling an M-16 with grenade launcher attached. He advanced slowly. He was being very careful. Mathilde held up her ID. I wondered what it said. Surely not an aid agency.

'British embassy, Kabul,' she said in her Queen's English voice.

'Sure, ma'am,' the American said. He took the plastic card from her and stepped carefully backwards, still keeping us in view. He spoke into his radio handset.

Mathilde turned to me. 'So you recruited Felix for your embassy job.'

'That's right.'

'Why a Russian?'

'Why not a Russian? He had the training and experience. He knew the country. He needed the money. Three very good reasons. I also liked him. We got on. That's a fourth good reason.'

'You got pissed together, you mean. You went on the tiles. You went whoring together. Those awful clubs packed with tarts and flatheads.'

'If you say so.'

'You didn't think he was under control back then?'

'He could have been.'

'It didn't bother you?'

'The place was falling apart. The rouble was in a terminal nosedive. The KGB and what was left of Felix's old outfit were a mess. At war with themselves. Can't say I was sorry. I was delighted to see what a shambles it was. Served them bloody well right, or so I thought back then. The last thing they were bothered about was a few foreign tourists or the likes of me buying Soviet memorabilia.'

'Felix was a central Asia specialist.'

'He knew northern Afghanistan. He spoke Farsi. He knew the Tajiks, the Uzbeks and Hazaras. My experience was limited to the Pashtuns. He was fed up to the back teeth with the oligarchs and what they were doing to his country. He wanted out, a change of scenery.'

Moscow had shocked me rigid. It had made me realize the Cold War had been a sham, largely a Western invention, and I'd fallen for it like a lot of other people. The Warsaw Pact couldn't have fought their way out of a wet paper bag, let alone overrun Western Europe.

Before the Cold War it had been empire and a string of

colonial wars of subjugation. Bringing civilization to the natives.

Now this. The war against so-called terrorism.

George Orwell didn't know the half of it.

The American was on his way back. He handed over Mathilde's card and started to open the gate. He had to take off a glove to do so. I noticed a comrade of his had appeared, and was keeping his mate covered. They were both well wrapped against the cold.

'This is going to take some time,' Mathilde said. 'They'll have to get someone to escort us up to the base perimeter. Then they'll search us. We have to take off our shoes and they'll frisk us. Finally, we'll be escorted over to the terminal.'

She was shivering after the warmth of the Pajero.

'They don't let Pakistani or Afghan journalists beyond this point,' she added. 'They think they might be terrorists. It's all part of what they call racial profiling.'

'In that case I feel really privileged to be a member of the white race.'

'Thomas, be serious.'

'I am,' I said. 'I just hope it's all worth it.'

There was a strongpoint of logs and sandbags at the entrance to the Americans' base, and triple rolls of razor wire. I made out fighting holes dug in among the pines on our left. They had overhead cover and were well camouflaged and linked by crawl tenches. Directly ahead two soldiers of the 101st Airborne manned an M-60 squad machine gun on top of a wall of sandbags, and it was pointed at us.

We waited to be searched. One trooper had set up a folding table in front of the bunker, another was going through my jacket and Mathilde's shoulder bag.

'How was dinner?'

'Good,' I said.

'Abdur Rahman told you what you wanted to know?'

'I'm not sure,' I said. 'Wanted? I don't think so. Needed to know – maybe. I can't remember all of it, and I'm not sure I really understand it.'

I was deliberately playing it down.

Mathilde touched my arm, then quickly withdrew her hand as if the gesture had been unconscious, unintentional.

'So what did he say?'

'He told me all about smuggling. He explained how the main players were linked by blood or marriage, and he made me promise not to tell anyone, not even you.'

Mathilde shrugged. She was clasping her arms to her chest. She was feeling the cold. 'He does that with everyone,' she said, searching for a tissue in a pocket and blowing her nose. 'It makes him feel more important and he has the idea that it will give his product more weight.'

They were ready for us.

'Okay, ma'am,' said the trooper. 'Okay, sir. One at a time please.'

The Americans were very polite. Mathilde went first, kicking off her shoes and standing straight, arms held out. One trooper faced her. The second squatted down on his heels behind her and steadily worked his way from her ankles up to her collar. He was feeling her clothing like someone wringing out the washing, squeezing it in an effort to detect a blade or some other concealed weapon. In the meantime the M-60 was trained on me, its muzzle a black eye pointed at my heart at twenty paces.

Then it was my turn.

The Americans looked like giant turtles waddling about on their back legs. It was partly the helmets they wore, partly the bulky flak jackets, the baggy pants and all the military paraphernalia they strapped on to themselves, from knives and ammunition pouches to flashlights and gas masks. It was a wonder they could move at all. All that gear made me think of a child's comfort blanket. Emotional reassurance in foreign and hostile surroundings.

A second lieutenant wordlessly walked us over to the airport terminal, a battered concrete building without windows where we were invited – by a gesture – to climb into the back of a Humvee parked outside.

The runway itself was quiet, most of the aviation landing and taking off at night. We skirted the apron, passing an outdoor gym, an area that seemed to be occupied by more special forces troops, a storage area full of crates and large objects hidden under camouflage netting, past the detention centre where the Americans kept Taliban and al-Qaeda suspects bound for Camp X-Ray at Guantanamo, and over to the far side and what appeared to be a temporary hangar.

The Humvee rolled to a halt.

The young officer didn't smile. His face was a blank. Finally he spoke. 'Have a nice day, now.'

The lieutenant nodded to the driver and the Humvee moved off, leaving the two of us in the open.

'Come on,' Mathilde said. 'He's waiting for us.'

It was Quilty. He had the place to himself. He was standing at a trestle table. Maps covered most of it. Down the far end was a large thermoflask and several styrofoam cups, some of them already used. Around the table were half a dozen metal-framed folding chairs with green canvas seats and backs.

I had the impression that another party had left hurriedly before we'd arrived, and had slipped out the back way.

'Good of you to come. So glad you could make it.'

Quilty shook Mathilde's hand warmly, then mine. He even smiled and sounded as if he meant what he said.

'Coffee? No tea, I'm afraid. Milk? Sugar?' He didn't wait

for an answer but shot his cuffs and waved an arm in the direction of the chairs. 'Please. Take a seat. I'll be mother.'

He wore a grey suit, white shirt and silver silk tie. Mathilde wrapped both hands around her cup and sipped the hot liquid, grateful for its warmth. I took mine from Quilty and sat down on one of the chairs. It was as uncomfortable as it looked.

'Any news of Gerber?' I said.

''Fraid not,' Quilty said. 'Not a thing.'

'That's not good.'

'No,' Quilty agreed. 'It isn't. But we've no reason to think that we've been compromised in any way. We're going ahead, and I hope you both feel you can go along with that decision.'

I said nothing.

Quilty took a third chair. He put his coffee down on the table, careful to avoid marking the maps.

Quilty adjusted his glasses, pinched the crease in his trouser leg at the knee and self-consciously cleared his throat.

'Our information suggests the target is currently in the Ghazni area, and moving south-west. We believe he will move parallel to the Kafar Jan Ghar range of mountains . . .' Quilty's right hand swept across south-west Afghanistan.

'The route takes the sheikh between Kandahar and Qalat. We expect him to lie up in Argestan before he's taken into the pipeline for the final move south. Morgan, you visited Argestan some years ago.'

I nodded.

I said, 'How long do I have?'

'Our best estimate is between ten and fourteen days.'

Quilty pointed with a manicured finger.

It moved south over the pink desert.

'In the final stage, the target is likely to move initially into Gulestan, then to Quetta. I would suggest the last leg would be a Pakistani or Saudi military flight to a sovereign Saudi airbase.'

Quilty got to his feet.

'Clearly, as far as Riyadh and Islamabad are concerned, the target cannot be taken alive. He knows far too much. He's worked with the ISI and Saudi intelligence for too many years. Were he to give evidence in court, he would be a considerable embarrassment. On the other hand, he cannot be permitted to be killed by the Americans. Or ourselves, for that matter. He would become a martyr and far more dangerous dead than alive, both at home and in these parts. We believe the Pakistanis and Saudis are working together very hard to avoid these possible scenarios.'

'What then?' I said.

'House arrest,' Quilty said. 'That's the optimum solution. Permanent obscurity, without access to telecommunications. Probably a remote village in the kingdom, possibly the Hejaz, somewhere no Westerner can possibly venture, and where the Sheikh can be kept securely, in reasonable comfort and under permanent surveillance. And kept on ice for possible further use if that were to become desirable.'

They were both looking at me.

'Makes sense,' I said. 'He's removed from the scene of the action, effectively neutralized, Washington claims victory over al-Qaeda – yet again – and no one gets hurt. Pakistan avoids public humiliation at a war crimes trial. Saudi protects its own, but buries the embarrassment. There's no martyr to inspire future generations. Everybody gets what he wants.'

'Except us,' Mathilde said.

'If he reaches Saudi,' Quilty said, 'you do understand that there'll be nothing we can do.'

I finished off my coffee. 'Maybe that is for the best.'

Quilty and Mathilde exchanged glances.

'That's not what this is about, Thomas,' Mathilde said.

'I thought not,' I said.

'It's about setting an example,' she added.

The self-righteousness got to me. I stood up and reached

for the thermoflask. 'Retribution without recourse to the law is very primitive,' I said. 'It's called vigilantism. As a former bounty hunter I think I'm particularly well qualified on the subject.'

'Rubbish,' said Mathilde. She was angry.

Quilty walked round the table and looked down at me. 'Aren't you interested in your share of the reward, Thomas?'

'More than you could possibly know,' I said, pouring myself the last of the coffee. 'It's really the only reason I'm here – and the threat of being banged up in Belmarsh, of course.'

Two fingers to their bullshit.

Just give us the cash and drop the cant about standing shoulder to shoulder with our allies in defence of freedom.

Freedom for what? For whom?

'I'm glad you stopped shaving,' Mathilde said.

A hand appeared over my shoulder and cupped my chin.

'It's soft,' she said. 'I like it.'

I didn't object. Mathilde was in playful mood. I liked what she was doing, too, but I didn't want to let on.

'It makes you look less of a killer. More of a thinker.'

'That's a mistake, then,' I said.

'It makes you look more sophisticated.'

'I'm sure it's appreciated in Kandahar.'

'Bastard. You can't even take a compliment.'

The hand was withdrawn, but the sulk didn't last. In a moment or two Mathilde's cool fingers returned to caress the nape of my neck. Sher Muhammad didn't seem to have noticed, and if he had, he wasn't showing it. I thought he was probably too busy concentrating on the road back to the city. There was something about the man's fragility and particularly his eyes – the pupils seemed to fill them, and there were blackberry smudges below – that suggested a heavy and habitual hashish user.

Mathilde said, 'You don't like Quilty.'

I said nothing.

'He's really not that bad.'

'I feel better already.'

'He's good at what he does.'

'What does he do?'

'Don't be mean.'

The fingers were withdrawn.

'Tell me something,' I said.

'What?'

'When did Abdur Rahman first come across?'

'Some time back. I don't have all the details.'

'Yes, you do.'

'I don't remember everything, Thomas.'

'He was in Kabul. A senior Taliban commander with an intelligence role. Responsible for surveillance of foreigners in the capital under the aegis of the Khad. Who better to check out foreigners than a foreigner? Right?'

'You'd know,' she said. 'Why ask me?'

It was more than suspicion.

'Mathilde, you know very well.'

Silence.

Those cool fingers were back on my neck, probing inside my collar, beating a gentle tattoo on my skin. She was playing with me, testing me. Letting me know that under certain conditions, in certain circumstances, I might enjoy certain privileges again in my relationship with my case officer. As long as I behaved, and kept my objectionable views to myself. She liked control. It was her mission in life, and her private passion. Maybe we did have something in common after all.

'Ask him about it,' she said.

'He's still with the Khad, isn't he? New bottles, old wine . . .'

No answer.

Abdur Rahman had been a big shot in the secret police

under the Taliban when we'd lifted the embassy silver. I was sure he was still one of them. The Khad didn't really change, no matter how often they changed the colour of their turbans.

Mathilde was all take, no give.

We were back in Sharinau. Sher Muhammad pulled off the road onto the gravel verge and the blue flag fluttering above the UNICEF headquarters opposite our place showed that the wind had shifted. It was coming out of the west. It was still cold, but the air was extraordinarily clear this time. Distances appeared to have shrunk and every detail of the hills stood out.

I was thinking that I understood all too well how Felix felt about Abdur Rahman.

SEVEN

Surrounded by the contents of his Bergen, Felix was cleaning his rifle. Khaled was sitting next to him on the sitting room sofa. He was entranced by the care and attention lavished on the weapon. Every Afghan male loves a well-made firearm, and there's nothing better than the Kalashnikov, not even the M-16. Abdur Rahman sprawled opposite in an armchair, eyes shut, hands folded across his chest. Indifferent, or seemingly so.

The room was like a fridge, and the gas heater roaring away next to them didn't seem to make much difference.

'It's not that different from the AK-47,' Felix was saying. 'It even looks similar. Stamped metal parts. Easy to clean and maintain. Loads of tolerance. Never jams. But the big difference, the really important difference, is the bullet. Along with the silencer, of course.'

He held up a cartridge between thumb and forefinger.

'It's nine millimetres and we call it the SP-6.'

Khaled nodded. I was sure he didn't understand a word.

What he really wanted to do was handle the Rampart himself, heft it in his own hands, feel the weight and balance.

'Think of it as a moon shot,' Felix said. 'When you go to the moon, what do you design first – the rocket or the probe itself?' Khaled had no idea what Felix was talking about, but that didn't stop the Russian. I thought Felix a terrible bore on the subject of small arms, but he had found a captive audience, albeit an uncomprehending one.

'See, you design your lunar module, then the rocket to get it there. Same with a rifle or pistol. First you ask yourself what the target is, what its characteristics are, then you design the bullet to kill the target, and last of all the weapon to deliver the bullet.'

He had the Rampart stripped, the parts laid out neatly on the coffee table. He'd done it systematically, so he could shut his eyes and reassemble the rifle by feel. The ribbed magazine was also empty, the spring removed for cleaning. Felix had two brushes, one of them of bronze wire, a pull-through for cleaning the barrel, a small tin of oil and several soft cloths.

'We know this much. The target will be a man. He will be moving at night, or maybe at dusk or first light. Maybe on foot, or on horseback. Perhaps riding pillion on a motorcycle. We know he's someone important, and it's likely he'll be wearing body armour. He's got close protection, too, in the form of bodyguards – and the shooter probably won't get within one hundred metres.

'More like three hundred, I'd say, given the terrain.'

Abdur Rahman opened one eye and winked at me.

Felix was rattling on, caressing each part with an oily cloth. 'What's really special about the ammunition is that it will defeat all known body armour . . .'

Felix grinned at Khaled, who caught the evangelical enthusiasm and smiled back, pleased to be taken so seriously by the weird foreigner, but most of all wanting to handle the rifle.

Felix started to reassemble the Rampart.

He didn't have to look at what he was doing.

'She's a beauty. So simple. The second big difference here is the silencer. It's not like the ones in the West. You lose so much accuracy and range. Not with this. This is special, my friend. The effective range with a fully silenced round from the Rampart is four hundred metres. Believe me. Four hundred. Incredible, no? It doesn't sound anything like a gunshot, either. Right next to the firer all you'll hear is a quiet cough, or a soft clap. Like this.' Felix put the weapon down again and clapped his hands very softly.

'The VAL assault rifle – that's its formal designation – weighs in at 2.5 kilos with empty magazine included . . .'

Felix reached down into the special briefcase that was used for shipping the Rampart.

'One more thing,' he said. 'This is the nightsight, the NSPU-3. It's brilliant. You can't fucking miss.'

I felt sorry for Khaled. He was getting the full, unexpurgated sales pitch on behalf of the Russian arms industry.

'He's not got a clue what Zotov is saying,' Abdur Rahman said.

'I don't think Felix gives a damn.'

We were out on the balcony. The air was very cold, but the sun was still hot. It was mid-afternoon. I sat on an upright wooden chair at the end, out of the wind but with the sun on my face. Abdur Rahman was standing at the railing, one foot up on the lowest rung.

On a distant rooftop, children were flying their kites, dabs of red and yellow weaving across a deep-blue sky.

'Where's Mathilde?'

'With Yannis.' Abdur Rahman jerked his head towards the front room Mathilde had chosen for herself. He raised both hands and made a tapping motion with his fingers like a pianist. He meant she was using her laptop. Yannis was presumably encrypting her material prior to transmission.

'Are you ready, English?'

'I've got the kit.'

'What did you get?'

'The usual.'

I brought it out to him.

'Kandahar people like light colours,' he said when he saw the black tunic and trousers.

'But they don't fight at night and the Taliban always liked black. You wear black yourself.'

The second outfit was grey-green.

'Good camouflage,' was all he said, probing at a poorly stitched seam.

'I didn't want anything too upmarket,' I said.

'Turban?'

'Here.' It, too, was dark. Grey with a lighter stripe, a cotton–silk mixture.

I showed him the *potu*, a waistcoat, sandals, and the round cap that I would wear under the turban.

'You'll have to wear them in,' he said. 'Particularly the sandals. Otherwise they'll cut your feet.'

The whole lot had come to a little over a hundred US.

'Show me your hands.'

He turned the palms up, felt them with his thumbs.

'Too soft,' he said. 'Too clean. A paper-pusher's hands. You've been out of circulation too long, English. Your hostile environments course obviously wasn't hostile enough.'

He insisted on inspecting my feet.

'You have the feet of a child. Pink and soft. It comes from wearing combat boots and thick socks. You Westerners are so spoiled. We'll have to sort this out. And fast.'

You Westerners.

'What am I supposed to do? Use sandpaper?'

'At least you're not blond or blue-eyed, and you don't have to pretend to be an Afghan. That's something.'

'Some Afghans are fair with blue eyes.'

Abdur Rahman grunted. He was thinking hard how to turn a soft-living ex-soldier into a tough peasant whose appearance would not prompt a second glance.

'You look the part, English. But remember – you'll be living with these people. That means no privacy. They will watch you. They will watch you all the time.'

How could I forget?

'First impressions won't be enough. They're going to notice everything. Everything.'

'We will test your memory, English.'

As the *adhan* sounded, we walked from the house to the local mosque, just around the corner from the football stadium built by the UN and used by the Taliban as its local killing ground – for public executions, amputations and floggings.

First, we performed the *wudu*, the washing. Abdur Rahman and I squatted side by side at the taps. I washed my hands three times. I rinsed out my mouth three times, using bottled water. I washed out my nostrils three times, imitating Abdur Rahman and snorting loudly. I rinsed my arms up to the elbows. Three times. I splashed water on the top of my head, behind my ears and neck. Finally the feet, again three times.

I put my turban back on my head and we went in to pray, beginning the first *rak'ah*, or cycle of prostration.

Abdur Rahman was beside me.

He whispered: 'Woe to those who pray but are heedless in their prayer; who make a show of piety and forbid almsgiving.'

Woe indeed. Thanks for the warning.

Standing upright, I raised my open hands to the level of my shoulders, fingers almost touching my ears.

It was coming back. It was as if I'd never been away.

'Allah is great.'

I put my hands on my chest, right hand over my left.

'You alone we worship, and to You alone we turn for help.'

I bent forward from the hips, back straight, fingers spread out across my knees.

I heard Abdur Rahman's gravelly voice beside me.

'Glory be to my Great Lord and praise be to Him.'

We stood straight simultaneously.

'God listens to those who thank Him, O Lord, thanks be to You,' I muttered.

Down on our knees.

Forehead, nose and both hands on the floor.

In unison: 'Glory be to my Lord, the Most High; God is greater than all else.'

Kneel. Palms on our knees. I cast a furtive look over at Abdur Rahman. He ignored me. I counted up to four. Slowly.

'O my Master, forgive me.'

I bent forward once more.

Forehead, nose and hands on the floor.

We sat back slowly. We turned our heads; looking right, then left, paying our respects to the rest of the congregation.

'Peace be with you and the mercy of Allah.'

I was an imposter.

An atheist posing as a follower of the one true faith.

I felt strangely emotional.

I thought all the while of my Muslim friends no longer with us. They deserved my respect.

Abdur Rahman and I rose with the others and walked slowly out into the long afternoon shadows, put on our shoes and sandals and sauntered back home, the dying sun burning gold on the hills where the Soviets had once placed their guns.

No one paid me the slightest attention, not even the beggars, sharp-eyed when it came to singling out the foreigner.

I was behind the wheel of the Pajero, Abdur Rahman in the passenger seat, his AK-74 between his knees.

'You are Bilal, son of Iskander.'

I tried the sound of it on my tongue. 'Bilal.'

'Bilal was an Abyssinian slave,' Abdur Rahman said. 'A convert, and one of the earliest companions of Muhammad, peace be upon Him. Bilal called the faithful to prayer, using the words of the Shahadah. Bilal is a name of distinction, English, and epecially suited to a convert such as yourself. Islam is a way of life, and if you demonstrate an awkwardness in your manner, imperfections of any kind in practising the faith, people will put it down to the fact that you are a relative novice, a newcomer in the House of God.'

'I hope you're right.'

'If you're caught out, your true identity revealed, they will kill you. No question. You know that.'

'Yes.'

'They will make an example of you. I know I would. It would not be quick. It would not be painless, either.'

'I see that.'

'They might offer you an alternative.'

'I think I know what you're going to say.'

'A genuine conversion this time.'

Abdur Rahman looked at me.

'Which would it be, English?'

'The coward's way out.'

'Which is?'

'Conversion.'

'I did say genuine. The coward, on reflection, might find the bullet the easier option.'

'As you said yourself, it would be neither quick nor painless – and I'll do almost anything to avoid unnecessary pain.'

'I hope for your sake they never know that.'

'Damn right.'

'We're going to do what we can to make sure you are never forced to make the choice, English.'

'In Islam, conversion by coercion has no validity,' I said.

'Tell that to the Taliban and al-Qaeda.'

We were approaching the western edge of the city.

'Right here.'

'It's the graveyard.'

'I want to show you something,' Abdur Rahman said.

Beyond a cluster of mud compounds lay a canal, built by the Americans some forty years before. It ran roughly from north to south. It was dry. There were just a few stagnant pools here and there. The road we took ran along the top of the levee, and we moved south along it, raising a column of dust behind us. Over to the right, below the embankment, was a stony plain.

It was quite flat and desolate.

It was the city's main burial ground.

There were hundreds of boat-shaped mounds of stones, gathered in flotillas, entire fleets, all in formation, all in neat rows, heads to Mecca. Tall grave markers, a forest of bamboo poles, bent and nodded in the wind, their ragged flags of green and black and red and yellow streaming out like ragged telegraph signals strung from the yards and masts and halyards of these navies of the dead.

'Head for the crowd,' Abdur Rahman said, 'then park over there with the other cars. You see – where that fellow selling onions is standing.'

I did as I was told. There must have been two thousand people in all milling about, mostly women, and most of them dressed in the voluminous blue burkas.

'The *shahuda*,' Abdur Rahman said.

The martyrs of war.

As I put on the handbrake and removed the keys from the ignition, I caught sight of myself in the side mirror. I was almost unrecognizable. My clothes were black, and the dark turban, coupled with a week's stubble, presented the face and bearing of a stranger, someone I didn't know, a grim and savage and altogether swarthy figure. So much so I put a hand up to my face to check that this was indeed me I was looking at. This was no Englishman or Scot, and certainly no Christian. I was light years away from West Pilton and its gasworks and

the tenth floor of the council block where I grew up. And I
thank my lucky stars for it, I told myself. This stranger glared
back at me, a knowing expression, a look that carried the
severity of Ayatollah Khomeini. Abyssinia was far closer to
me now than the Firth of Forth, and the glimpse of myself,
seen in a dusty mirror, no matter how alien, was reassuring.

I can do this.

I took the lead, walking down the slope of gravel, watched
by the onion seller, whose calls to buy we both ignored.

The ocean of blue burkas parted.

'Taliban fighters in front,' Abdur Rahman said quietly.
'The boys who put up a last stand against the Americans at
Kandahar airport. About seventy or so are buried there.'

'Friends of yours?'

'Some.'

The biggest crowd, however, was focused on seven graves
off to the right – the six al-Qaeda fighters who had died in the
storming of the city hospital ward where they had held out
for more than a month before being overwhelmed in January.
The seventh was an anonymous Afghan who just happened to
be buried alongside them.

The Arabs – they included Saudis, a Yemeni and a Sudan-
ese – had fought to the last breath, quite literally, despite
multiple wounds.

'These people hope for a miracle,' said Abdur Rahman.
'They believe that the spirits of those who die in battle in
defence of their faith have a special power to heal.'

Malformed and disabled children lay right up against the
graves. Women rubbed stones taken from the mounds on their
children's limbs, across their foreheads, and clutched handfuls
of them to their own breasts. Some children were deaf and
dumb. Others had been paralysed by typhoid since birth.
People scattered flower petals and rice over the mounds.

'It's complete nonsense, of course. This isn't Islam,' Abdur
Rahman said. 'It has nothing to do with it. It has everything to

do with Pashtun custom. It's superstition. It's pre-Islamic. It's ignorance, coupled with desperation.'

We made our way back, out of the crowd, past fathers holding their children, mothers crying out aloud, as if the louder they prayed the likelier it was that their prayers would be answered. Brown hands reached out from the crowd to the graves, patting the muddy earth, smoothing it, caressing it.

Back in the car, Abdur Rahman watched the crowd through the windscreen.

'This is Taliban. This is Afghanistan. Look. This is what it means. This is poverty. This is ignorance. This is tradition.' He was shaking his head. He was angry and upset, and close to tears. 'People will always hope, English. They go on hoping when there is no hope, not for them or their children. They go on hoping when it is better they should stop hoping and face the truth. But the truth is too terrible for them. And for most of us. You know, English, most children in Afghanistan die before they reach the age of five. Their mothers will mourn, and say it's decreed by God. Did you know that, English?'

I didn't say anything.

'I hate this,' he said. 'I hate it. I hate this hope. It is the hope of utter despair. I hate it. Look on your enemies, English. Go on. Look. Your enemies are the poor, the dispossessed, the suffering. Look, English. For these people the future is no better than the past. It cannot be better. It is sure to be worse. I hate what we are, man, and I hate what we have become.'

At each mention of the word 'hate', Abdur Rahman struck the dashboard with his massive fist, and the car shook.

He sat back against the headrest, his eyes shut.

'This is not how it was meant to be,' he said.

I drove home in the dark.

'You have children, Bilal.'

It was more statement than question.

'I do, yes.'

'Speak to them tonight if you can. You may not be able to do so again for a while.'

He was watching me. 'You are one of us, Bilal. Listen to me. You are all that is left of your cell. A survivor. The network itself has gone. Finished. It was shattered by arrests across the UK. Almost everyone was picked up in a big round-up of suspects towards the end of September. Hear me?'

'Yes.'

'You don't know if anyone else is on the loose. Newcastle, Manchester, Leicester and London. No specific dates. No habeas corpus under the new British terror laws. You don't know the suspects, of course. You had no direct contact. It was a joint CID and Special Branch operation nationwide, but you have no details. You believe that. You stick to it. At least thirty people were picked up, you think, but no precise figures are available. Got that? No charges have been made against any of the detainees so far as you know. Nothing in the papers, either. You don't know the names. Of course you don't. You're not supposed to.'

'Okay.'

'You made a run for it. When Razaq – remember, it's his workname, Razaq – didn't make the final fallback in Battersea Park (you were to meet in the car park near the athletic track) you packed a bag and withdrew cash from your accounts. When no one responded to your emergency sign – a blue dishcloth hanging in your kitchen window – you ran. You gave it forty-eight hours, but it should have been only twelve. You took a stupid risk waiting that long, and you were very lucky. Very, very lucky. More than you deserved. Remember?'

'I remember.'

'Good. You took the Eurostar from Waterloo. You dithered about and deliberately missed the first train in case you were followed. You weren't stopped. No one asked you anything.

You spent a day in Paris. From there, a TGV to Marseille. You paid cash. Okay?'

'I think so.'

'You sweated it out for two days and two nights. You didn't sleep. You didn't check into a hotel. You walked a lot. You dozed fitfully in cafés in the port area. You didn't know what to do. You didn't know whether it was safer to duck and hide or cut and run. You decided to run. You never liked sitting still. And you were scared. Admit it. Strange country, strange city. Cops everywhere you looked. So you ran. Beirut was the next stop. You flew Cyprus Airways, via Larnaca. You bought a tourist visa on arrival in Beirut. You don't remember how much it was. You bought it at a counter at the airport. It was in local currency and you had to change money before you bought the visa. Got all that, Bilal?'

'What is this – a travel writer's nightmare?'

'Be serious.'

'Sorry.'

'You stayed at a fleapit in Bourj Hammoud. You don't remember the name. It might have been called the Ambassador. You remember the noise and the smell and the lumpy bed. That's all. But it was Bourj Hammoud. Lots of Armenians. Loads of shops selling cheap shoes and suitcases. You went to the bus station the very next day. Ugly, concrete place. Stalls selling snacks. Coaches going north, south, to Amman, to Damascus. It was October 7, the start of the American air offensive. You felt a sense of urgency. You were going to head for Damascus by bus, but you changed your mind. You had a bad feeling at the bus depot. Too many people hanging around doing nothing except taking an interest in everyone else. You took a service to Hamra and went instead to the local office of Pakistan International Airlines. It's in Ain al Mreisse, and you walked from Hamra. You bought a ticket to Karachi via Dubai. It was the cheapest available.'

'If they check?'

'They'll discover it's the truth. All of it. You left a clear trail for anyone willing to look hard enough. You left plenty of footprints.'

'Why the hell would I do that?'

'You were panicking. Running scared.'

'If you say so.'

'I do. You flew to Islamabad that night. It was just before midnight. You don't remember the exact time. Your body clock was already mixed up. The Dubai–Islamabad leg lasted seven and a half hours. Your British passport got you a seventy-two-hour visa at Karachi immigration. You slept on a row of empty chairs in transit and caught the flight the next day to Quetta. At 12.45. You paid cash. It was around forty dollars, but you can't be absolutely sure. You were exhausted.'

'Fine.'

'You knew the network by the name of Night Journey.'

'Mir'aj.'

'Mir'aj. That's right. Now repeat it, Bilal. All of it. Right from the start, please.'

'What did Mir'aj do?'

'We'll come to that. First, repeat all I've said. Don't leave anything out.'

Mathilde was whispering 'How do you feel?'

'Okay.'

'How did it go?'

'Fine. As far as I could tell.'

'Abdur's happy?'

'We're going to run through it all again in the morning.'

'So you're ready.'

'I've a couple of questions.'

A lot more than a couple.

Mathilde had tapped softly on my door long after the rest

had turned in. I was already in my sleeping bag, the warmest and most comfortable place to be on a cold night. After dinner in Kandahar there was nothing else to do but go to bed. There were no bars, no nightclubs, no television, no cards, no dancing girls. She had come in slowly, closing the door behind her, and found her way to the only chair in the room, dumping my gear onto the floor.

'Did I wake you?'

'No.'

'So what do you want to know?'

'How do I make contact?'

'How much did you know when you were taken in to Tirin Kot?'

'I didn't know my arse from my elbow. I kept blacking out.'

'So there you are.'

'What's your point, Mathilde?'

'They won't expect you to know. It's all arranged.'

'I'm not sure I like the sound of that. When people tell me not to worry, everything's fixed, it's usually time to abandon ship.'

She said, 'It's freezing in here.'

Mathilde was moving out of the chair. She was next to me, kneeling and leaning down over me. I could smell her hair.

Mathilde said, 'Why don't you use the bed?'

'I like the floor.'

'It's hard.'

'It's good practice.'

'Practice for what, Thomas?'

'Not what you're thinking.'

'Trouble with you, Thomas, is that you're only truly comfortable when you're uncomfortable.'

'It's my Calvinist upbringing.'

'Is there room for me in that sleeping bag?'

Mathilde did not wait for a response. She slipped in

swiftly, fully dressed. She had wanted to be asked, but when no invitation was forthcoming, she gatecrashed.

'That's so much better.'

She wriggled close to me, hip to thigh. Perhaps she had never been turned down, or if she had, had never acknowledged it. Perhaps she knew that a man like myself could never turn a woman like her down. She overwhelmed her victims. She was like a praying mantis. She mated with whomsoever she liked, then ate them up. Devoured them.

Trouble was, I liked her more than I was willing to admit, even to myself.

'What's the plan, Mathilde?'

'You're recovering from your wounds and temporarily out of action. You're on Washington's list of the top fifty most wanted Taliban and al-Qaeda.'

'I am?'

'You're notorious, Thomas. British national known as Bilal, aka Tucker, Gordon Alexander. Born Edinburgh. Along with a very fetching mugshot with beard and turban. Your picture, genuine this time, but you'd be amazed how similar you are. It's very impressive, I must say – I looked it up on the Web today, as a matter of fact. The FBI site is the best.'

And the real Gordon Tucker? Who was he, and what had happened to him?

One hand had found its way to my chest. It was moving gently upwards. With thumb and forefinger she squeezed a nipple. Hard.

I tried not to flinch.

'I'm flattered.'

'You're a big wheel in the axis of evil, Thomas.'

The hand stopped again, found the second nipple.

Harder this time.

Ouch.

'There's an Interpol warrant out for you. A British warrant, too. Seems you're very much wanted. Quite a fan club.'

The other hand joined the first, slid round, rested on my shoulder.

So that was what she had been up to all day: making sure there was only one way out of here. All other exits well and truly barred.

'Aren't I lucky – and it's thanks to you, Mathilde.'

She put her head against my chest, and her hands continued their journey independently, feeling their way around me.

'Did you ever think—'

'What?'

'Did you ever think, Thomas, when we were, you know, together . . .'

'Sleeping together.'

'Yes. Did you ever wonder what it would be like if we had tried to make a go of it?'

I didn't answer.

'Did you ever consider it?'

I kept quiet.

'I did, Thomas. For the record. I thought about it. I thought about you leaving your wife and moving in with me. I really did. I would have lost my job, but I told myself that wouldn't have been the end of the world.'

What could I possibly say?

She touched the scars on my back, tracing the broken flesh.

'Closer, Thomas.'

Then she was taking off her pullover. Next she pushed her combats and socks down to the bottom of the sleeping bag.

'Help me.'

She was taking off the rest.

Mathilde didn't ask. There was never any question of that.

Those long, smooth and muscled legs held mine, her thigh pressed itself against my groin.

I was never much good at undoing bras.

'You men are so useless. God knows you've had enough practice.'

Her skin was silky and well toned from the regular visits she made to the sports club near her two-bed flat in Clapham. I'd almost forgotten her swimmer's shoulders, her tiny waist.

'Touch me,' she commanded.

I remembered what she liked, and where.

'Like this?'

'Yes.'

I'd never really forgotten.

'You like that?'

'You know I do.'

Was this the sexual equivalent of the condemned man's last meal? Was this Mathilde's idea of charity, of preparing the troops for battle, a girding of the loins? Was it planned? Was this the prize Mathilde awarded to all her joes before she sent them off under the wire? Or was she just helping herself to something she felt like on the spur of the moment, the prospect of action stirring her sluggish civil servant's blood?

That was unkind.

It was her leaving present, for sure.

Mathilde said, 'What if I'd suggested it?'

'Suggested what?'

'Moving in to my place.

I didn't answer.

'The truth is, Thomas, I frighten you. I think every woman does. You're scared of any entanglement. You're more scared of facing up to feelings you can't control than you are of going off to places like this and getting yourself shot at. It's so much simpler out here.'

I wasn't going to argue. Her bags were packed. She was probably headed back to London along with Quilty where they could both watch things unfold from a safe distance.

It was better not to know.

Back-seat drivers the pair of them.

'Don't stop,' she said.

I kissed her hard to stifle the sound she was making.

She broke free, one hand grasping my hair, forcing my head back.

'Whatever you do, Thomas, don't stop, you hear?'

I couldn't.

Not now. Not even if I wanted to.

EIGHT

The Argendab River used to be the main source of water for the city of Kandahar. It would still have been the main source had there had been any water, but there wasn't. It had rained here and there in the south-west, intermittent showers for a few days in January, some of them heavy and lasting several hours, but not enough, not nearly enough, to break the stranglehold of four years of drought and undo its terrible damage.

I could picture what it must have been like before the rains stopped. In places the river would have been several hundred metres wide. I tried to imagine the sound of it, the colour of it under the sun, the sheer glory of its expanse. The gardens and orchards ran right down to the banks as if reaching for the water, seeking to quench their thirst in the summer months. People said the river had been full of fat fish, the reed beds ringing with the sound of innumerable birds and their nesting young.

Now it was a bed of stones, a beach white as sun-bleached bones, those orchards and gardens long dead, the trees lifeless sticks protruding uselessly from the cracked earth, railing at the empty sky.

We left early, Abdur Rahman and I, with Khaled at the wheel. We headed north through the city and took the road to Herat, passing the blue Mirwais mosque, the fortress at the northern exit.

Khaled swung the Pajero off the highway to the left, down an unmarked dirt track just before the bridge, bouncing down to the river and passing through a daily livestock market, weaving among camels, long-haired goats, herds of sheep and ponderous, long-horned cattle – and their owners haggling in the early sunlight.

We travelled several more miles, perhaps for twenty minutes in all, following the tracks of other vehicles. The valley broadened out to the west. The river meandered gently, shallow and slow – it would have done had there been water – except where it came up against the almost vertical and jagged teeth that were the hills guarding the city's flanks. Here the watercourse narrowed and deepened in the morning shadows, the reed beds still grew thickly and boulders guarded the bank.

Good cover among the rocks.

It wasn't hard to see what had happened.

'This is where Bilal died,' Abdur Rahman said.

He didn't mean the Abyssinian, but my alter ego. My stolen identity. The man whose real name was Tucker, a Scot like myself. I had to see with his eyes, Bilal's, feel as he felt, think as he thought.

Looking up at the cliff, I saw natural crevices, overhangs and caves which been excavated by human hand, enlarged and deepened. It was there, following the contour for hundreds of metres, that debris marked the destruction of ammunition caches. Wood mostly, shattered remains of ammunition crates, scattered about the scree, blown from the caves and thrown below the gaping rocks.

'Taliban and al-Qaeda storage depot,' Abdur Rahman said. 'Ammunition, mostly. Also spare parts.'

Khaled stopped the car.

'Watch your feet,' Abdur Rahman said.

I got out, very carefully.

My companions made no attempt to follow.

The sky was clear, the sun bright but without warmth as yet. The wind cut through my cotton clothing and I wound my *potu* tight round my torso and shoulders.

Abdur Rahman's warning referred to the US cluster bombs and the harvest of anti-personnel and anti-tank bomblets. Yellow, the same colour as the containers of food they had dropped in their 'hearts and minds' campaign.

I didn't have to ask what had happened.

It was all around us.

A BMP-1 armoured fighting vehicle had been tossed into the air, performing a somersault and landing upside down. It was blackened from the explosion and ensuing fire.

A T-62 tank lay disembowelled and beheaded in a hollow. The turret had been torn off and flung aside like the lid of a jam jar, its gun barrel bent and buried in the river bank. The chassis had been ripped open, as if by a giant butcher's knife, revealing pistons and engine casings, cracked and scorched. Right next to it was a vast crater, perhaps eighteen metres across and ten deep, a greasy puddle at the bottom.

I walked very slowly, watching the ground in front of my feet. A mistake would cost me a leg or a lot more.

The pebbles were worn and rounded, shades of pastel grey, blue, slate grey and white.

The Americans had caught them in the open. There had been nowhere to run and hide. The Taliban thought they could insert the armour among the trees, in the reed beds, using the terrain to conceal the tanks and armoured fighting vehicles.

They were wrong.

The attackers had infrared goggles, heat-seeking weapons, image intensifiers, laser designators. They could blanket the area with high explosive from a safe altitude, then come in low and slow and loiter, picking off individual targets at their leisure, inviolate.

Here was the evidence. There were ball bearings, bits of blackened uniform and boots, clusters of electrical cable, scraps of leather tank crew helmets, cartridge cases, an entire tank engine thrown about like a toy, unidentifiable lumps of carbonized material that could have been, well, yes, human.

I could almost hear the explosions, the inferno, and feel the blast waves.

I squatted down and scratched away at the stone and sand. There was no doubt about it. It was bone, a broken shaft, a split femur.

'Bilal died here,' Abdur Rahman said. He'd come up behind me, stepping in my footprints for safety's sake.

I was still clearing the debris with my hands, brushing lightly, like an archeologist. Only this stuff was weeks old, not centuries.

'He brought some of his people here to replenish his ammunition,' Abdur Rahman said. 'It was bad luck. Could have happened to anyone. He wasn't to know. There was nothing left of him to bury. No sign of him ever having been here.'

No evidence. No witness alive to tell the tale.

I said, 'You knew him.'

Abdur Rahman said nothing.

'A friend of yours?'

'He was like you, English. A white boy. Tucker looked every bit the way you do now. Why do you think they chose you? Miss Mathilde had hundreds to choose from, but she chose you. Didn't you ever ask yourself why? You're just like him, man, that's why. You could have been twins, for sure. Only he was Muslim. A good man. His men loved him.'

Could anyone wish for a finer epitaph?

I stood up and opened my hand, showing him what I'd found.

'Maybe these were his,' I said.

They were human teeth; three molars.

'You are Bilal,' Abdur Rahman said. 'Tell yourself you are Bilal. Think like him, eat like him. Walk like him. Be him. Think of yourself as him.'

It was good advice – apart from the fact that I knew so little about him.

'In that case,' I said, 'you will have to stop calling me English. I'm no Sassenach, but I'm beginning to think of myself as one. So start calling me Bilal. Okay?'

Abdur Rahman just smiled, showing me his teeth.

I said, 'Tell me about him.'

'He was middle class. A little younger than you. Not like us. Different. His people were educated. His father was a teacher. So was his mother. They were smart folks. He told me his home was full of books. Hundreds of them.'

'Do they know he's dead?'

Abdur Rahman shook his head.

'You mean they're sitting at home back in the UK waiting for news of him? Waiting for a call from their son, rushing to pick up the mail every morning when the letters drop through the letter box?'

I could picture it all too vividly.

'Christ's sakes, when did they last hear from him?'

'I don't know.'

'Bloody hell, don't they deserve to know?'

'Of course.'

'You're a cold bastard.'

'Talk about the pot calling the kettle . . . What's the alternative, Bilal? Should I pay them a visit? Think it would help to tell them in person, do you?'

He was right, of course.

'Does he have brothers? Sisters?'

'A sister. Married. Two kids. Lives in Aberdeen.'

I wondered if brother and sister had ever been close and if so, if they were still. How did she feel, what was she doing to try to trace her lost brother?

We were driving back to the city now, climbing up to the highway, heading south through the dust and noise of a city waking to a new day.

I thought of those people, thousands of miles away, leading very different lives who, through no fault of their own, were connected to this land and its never-ending conflict. I would have liked to have called the Tuckers, got the bad news over with. But it would never be over.

Not for them.

'Why did he convert?'

Abdur Rahman took time before answering.

'He wasn't a Muslim when he first came here,' he said, speaking carefully. 'He was drawn into it gradually. It wasn't like a sudden revelation. There were no angels, no visions. He visited the country twice. He worked as a student volunteer in Logar province, then here in Kandahar. For UNICEF. With Bilal it happened slowly. He met Afghans at university. They encouraged him to come out here. It took time, see. The religion – it was a slow awakening, know what I mean?'

It was plausible, but I felt there was a lot more to it behind Abdur Rahman's impassive mask. Such as guilt, remorse. A sense of responsibility for his death.

'You were one of those friends of his?'

Abdur Rahman didn't answer.

'You really are a cunt,' I said.

He tensed. He was still smiling, but the eyes weren't. He didn't know if I was preparing to tear his head off and piss down his neck or make a joke of it.

A real Afghan wouldn't have taken it.

'He was looking for a cause,' I said. 'He was young, idealistic, angry about an unfair world. You gave him what he was looking for. You recruited him. No one else. It was you. Afghanistan and its poverty held an appeal for him. It was a fine cause, quite hopeless, and to the young quite irresistible. Mir'aj was your outfit and he signed up. He was one of your night riders. He found an affinity with these people. It was heady stuff. He could make a real difference, or so he thought. His family was horrified, but that only underlined his sense of

119

being on the right track. The anti-Western, anti-American edge all helped, too. Then, to make the final leap, the last step, you gave him his new faith. You opened the door marked "no going back". It was the total commitment that did it, pal. That had been your goal all along. To find converts, and to sweeten it with the promise of a clandestine life, working against sociopaths like Rumsfeld and Sharon and that grinning twat, Tony bloody Blair.'

Half a century back and it would have been CND, the Communist Party of Great Britain, the IRA or Scottish Liberation Army or some bent don offering impressionable gays at Oxbridge the allure of a secret life on behalf of the Soviet proletariat.

'I didn't give him anything,' Abdur Rahman said. 'He went looking for it. He found it, man. Just like I did.'

'You really are a shit. How do you feel now he's dead?'

Abdur Rahman turned around in his seat and faced me.

'How did you feel when your friends died in Oruzgan, English?'

'Don't call me that,' I said. 'I'm Bilal now.'

'All right. Bilal. How did you feel?'

I wasn't finished, and I wasn't going to be thrown by that question, either.

I said, 'He worked for you, didn't he? He went the whole hog. He joined the Taliban. He joined one of your cells. You sent him off for training in his summer hols. You gave him some experience. One taste of the action and he was all yours. Don't shit me. You turned him from a do-gooder into a fighter. You taught him, armed him, took him out and showed him how to kill.'

'He was good, man.'

'I'm sure he bloody was. Humans make excellent killers. It's one thing we can do all do well at. It's so easy.'

Why was I so angry? The British Army was no different. It took kids out of school and off the street and turned them into efficient killers, and society applauded them for it, paid them a wage and gave them medals. Gave them respect.

What did I care?

Bilal. Born Gordon Alexander Tucker April 10, 1968. Aries. You were a scholarship boy, Gordon. You went to grammar school. A bright lad. A clear mind. Steady. Good at everything to do with books. No sportsman, mind, but you tried your best. A Hibernian supporter, God help us. You sailed through your SCEs. Nine Standard Grades, four Higher Grades. You had everything going for you – or so it seemed. Dropped out of your psychology course in the second year, aged twenty-one. It was sudden. Family problems. Split up with your first real girfriend. She thought you were a mite dull. Too reticent, and you couldn't afford your own wheels and that threw a spanner in the love life. Romance on the number 18 bus didn't appeal to her. If you'd had wheels you could have had all the totty you wanted, pal, and more. You and your mum were close, though. You never got on with Dad, did you? Not from the very start. He was a bully. Gordon, my son, I've been there. I know. It's the story of my life, but then find me a lad who does get along with his father. Whoever he is, he's a lucky little sod. At least your old man wasn't a drunk who beat you senseless when you were fourteen and took the strap to you until you were big enough to lay him out in the yard, taking the poker and breaking his jaw and a couple of ribs to make sure he stayed down. It was payback for all that he'd done to my mum, the useless pathetic cow that she was. Might have been better if you had done the same, Gordon. Got it out of your system. But on your side of the tracks things were done different. I know. You swallowed the anger, shoved your fists in your pockets and resisted the temptation to tear the bastard a new arsehole. But you suffered. We just solved our problems in our own individual ways, you and I.

121

Then you met Abdur Rahman.

I could imagine him at university.

Quite the suave persuader, the fisher for men's souls.

Abdur Rahman took it all off your shoulders. All that pain and confusion and embarrassment. Showed you how life could be lived. Helped you lighten the load through prayer. Helped give you back your self-esteem by helping others. He played up to your liberal's sense of guilt. Great thing about Islam, its great charm, the magnetic pull for most Westerners, is the attraction offered by the demand of total acceptance, of unreserved submission.

Giving in and giving up is such ecstasy, Gordon.

It's almost physical.

It's so simple, too.

Easy.

Mir'aj was your new family, your new love.

For the first time you could remember, you were truly happy. Until you came to the Argendab river one day in January.

'What do you think?'

I didn't answer.

Mathilde let herself in and sat on the edge of the chair. I was resting on my bed, fully dressed except for my boots and gazing at the display she'd prepared on my wall.

She said, 'It really is a remarkable likeness.'

'What did you do?' I asked. 'Go through lists of active and former contract workers and their pictures, looking for someone who was a match?'

'Something like that.'

I ticked off the characteristics on my fingers. 'Had to be male, between thirty and forty, widowed, single or divorced, active service experience, of saturnine appearance, between five-nine and five-ten, stocky ... preferably with some familiarity with south Asia, someone handy with a gun and with an overdraft. I suppose you just programmed your computer and it ran through records and found what you wanted.'

'You forgot bad-tempered, bloody-minded and grumpy.'

'I did say saturnine, love.'

'It's the head,' Mathilde said. 'The shape of the head and the eyes and accent, the tone of voice. The scowl helps, I must admit. We knew DNA, fingerprinting, all that stuff, wasn't going to matter. It had to be low tech.'

We?

'Where did you get all this?'

I meant the happy snaps.

'Foreign Office, mostly. They borrowed them from the family, we copied them.'

There were thirteen photographs in all. They'd been copied and enlarged, and Mathilde had mounted them on sheets of white card. They showed Bilal aka Gordon, aged around five, sitting in a rowing boat, holding the oars. Probably playing pirates. He was looking at the camera, frowning. In the next shot, he was two years older, wearing a coat, clutching a fishing rod in his right hand and in his left he held several mackerel, strung through the gills on a piece of twine. It was raining, but he was smiling in triumph, not frowning.

'The child – father of the man,' said Mathilde.

Bilal, aka Gordon in his first school uniform, blazer and grey flannels, standing on the doorstep of his parents' terraced house. Gordon aka Bilal starting grammar school, aged thirteen. Same place, but in the backyard – a patio they would call it today. Proudly carrying his school bag. Next Bilal aka Gordon with his friends, three of them, the frown in place, striking a tough pose, but with the pimples of adolescence.

The undergraduate, this time, marching in a street demo in leather jacket and jeans, hair over his ears and collar, a cigarette between his lips. Three grainy shots on high-speed film from different angles in black and white, police shots, I

123

thought. Trying to act the street tough, but innocence – no, more than that, a bookish earnestness – in those eyes, the face still soft, unmarked by life. Princes Street. Raining hard on Palestinian flags and red Socialist Worker placards. Lots of very wet and pissed-off cops, some of them on horseback.

Mathilde turned to look at me. 'Is it you, Thomas?'

The penultimate series was blurry, out of focus, blown up into three big prints. They showed a group of bearded men outside a mosque. It was winter, and they wore padded jackets and anoraks. Taken from a surveillance van, probably, parked across the a street.

'That's—'

I pointed at the second picture in the series.

Mathilde said, 'Abdur Rahman.'

'There's Bilal.'

Bilal. No more Gordon Tucker. It wasn't the full beard or the white skullcap, but the eyes. I went up close to the picture. He was in the rear, behind Abdur Rahman, looking over his shoulder. The neophyte. They'd just emerged after prayers. Perhaps it was my imagination. Maybe I was reading too much into it. It was the expression of a man who knows. He had accepted Abdur's gift of absolutism, of certainty. Individual responsibility had flown. In its place, Abdur Rahman's certainties.

It was written. It was decreed. It was God's will.

It was scary.

'He was thirty-one in that picture,' Mathilde said. 'It's the Finsbury Park mosque. The place opened by Prince Charles, cost a million and the Saudi royal family pitched in. Then it came under the control of Abu Hamza – the one-eyed, one-armed imam and Afghan vet. Remember? These come from police files. I don't think his family would like them very much, do you?'

'I can see why.'

'You could be twins,' Mathilde said. 'You really could.'

She stood next to me, close enough to feel her warmth, to smell her skin and hair, that scent of hers – Remember Me – but we didn't touch. The bedroom door was open behind us.

The last was Bilal in Afghanistan.

'It was his first visit,' Mathilde said.

He was crouched down, resting on his haunches, in mountain terrain. He was doing something to his backpack, adjusting the straps, maybe. He wore a green *chalwar kameez*, a dark-brown waistcoat, his *potu* slung casually over one shoulder and a green and gold turban on his head. His head was turned over his shoulder, and he was looking at whoever was taking the picture. He was bearded. He looked fit and healthy. Confident and self-assured. He seemed to be saying, 'Hey, no pictures!'

'It really could be you,' Mathilde said. 'When I first saw this I thought we'd made a mistake and it really was you. Then I realized we had found what and who we were looking for.'

She squeezed my fingers with her left hand.

Mathilde closed the bedroom door and came back and sat down next to me on the end of the bed.

'Remember Suleiman?'

Of course I did. He was the 'businessman' at Abdur Rahman's dinner. The silver-haired gentleman who had helped organize the clandestine video of that obscene auction of little girls and boys in Quetta.

'He took you in,' Mathilde said. 'You were taken to him. You were in bad shape. You were delirious, you'd lost a lot of blood and you were badly dehydrated. He did the right thing by you. He looked after you. He put it about you'd been killed. You stayed quietly at his farm in Maiwand district for

125

weeks. You didn't show yourself. You didn't dare send out news that you were okay. Meanwhile he paid for the surgery. He protected you. He took very good care of you.'

'So what's changed? Why leave?'

'They're on to you, and you don't want to land Suleiman in the shit. He's done so much. You're grateful, and feel responsible. You don't want him or his family caught in the firing line on your behalf. He's a former Taliban supporter, a Pashtun, and you feel indebted to him.'

'Fair enough. Who's on my tail?'

'The Khad. A former Taliban commander now working for the interim government. He's taken charge of your case. His people are already sniffing around Suleiman's farm and his house here in town. Suleiman knows. He's feeling the pressure. You left before it gets any worse. You did the decent thing.'

'Name?'

She said, 'You know him.'

'I though you might say that.'

'Abdur Rahman.'

'It figures.'

'You don't seem the slightest bit surprised.'

'He's part of my cover, and it's just your style.'

Devious, I meant.

Mathilde said, 'It's his cover, too. He's been ordered to look for you. The British authorities have been pestering the governor about you. He will look for you. Actively.'

Poacher turned gamekeeper.

Just how active, I wondered.

'And the Sheikh?'

'He's on the move. That's all I can tell you.'

Bull.

It was all she was prepared to tell me.

If Quilty was right, my window of opportunity stood at nine to thirteen days.

'It's the old need-to-know,' I said. 'Carrot in front, stick behind. But well and truly fucked, whichever way. When?'

'Tonight.'

I waited.

'You're going to turn up on the doorstep of your prospective father-in-law. He'll be pleased and a little disconcerted at your sudden reappearance. He's got a lot on his plate right now, but he won't turn you away. He can't. The real test will come when you are reunited with his daughter.'

'Whose daughter?'

'Nabibullah's eldest.'

'I've never met him, or her.'

'Bilal has. He's met Nabibullah at least twice. Maybe more often, but we rather hope not. We think Bilal met the daughter only once, and then it was formal. We hope we're right. For your sake.'

'So?'

'Aisha is the woman Bilal was engaged to marry.'

Mathilde turned her head and looked at me. She smiled. It seemed to amuse her.

'She's your betrothed, Thomas.'

NINE

I walked all the way.

I couldn't see the dust, but I could smell it.

It was close to midnight, and more than two hours after the start of the curfew.

I hugged the walls where I could. I tried not to fall into any ditches along the way. Much as I wanted to look, sound and smell like everyone else, I didn't want to end up covered from head to toe in shit. Nabibullah might baulk at that.

There was another blackout, extending across the city. I stayed off the main roads and away from the major intersections. There was no need to bump into the street patrols, or get hauled up at a roadblock.

The few vehicles on the move could be seen from a long way off, their headlights punching the murk. Standing still in the shadows, waiting for them to pass, I could smell my own company: a familiar, pungent reek of armpit and foot, scrotum and greasy beard. The tanning lotion had a slight orange tinge to it, but otherwise it was a fine impression of the unwashed and sunburnt. In the dark no one would notice, anyhow.

The dirt under my nails was real enough.

Afghanistan was a bit like a boozer. I got grimy just breathing in and out or, in the case of lifting a couple of pints, sitting or standing at the bar counter.

My clothes had been worn a week without change. I'd slept in them. I had washed only in cold water, and without soap.

Of course I was poor. I resembled a landless peasant, or hoped I did. Or maybe just a Talib on the run. But I was no beggar selling the *Big Issue* and living rough under Waterloo Bridge. There was no self-pity, none of that repetitive whining at commuters for small change to pay for my crack habit. On the contrary. I told myself I was a prince among men. In the dark I practised walking with Pashtun attitude: a swagger, a swing to hips and shoulders, a long stride, head up.

No man living was my better.

Everyone was my equal, or considerably less so.

My only possession of any consequence was a 5.45 mm AK-74 – and it was very clean, much cleaner than me – along with two full magazines, strapped together for swift reloading.

Mathilde said she would take personal care of my watch and the Barrett.

So kind, Mathilde.

No money, except two very grubby 20,000-Afghani notes. At nearly 500 to the Pakistani rupee, and with sixty-one rupees to the dollar, it wasn't much. Under a quid.

Asking for refuge would be like trying to get an English student grant from the Blair government. I would be means-tested, and I meant to demonstrate I had none.

A filthy grey woollen blanket was folded inside a square metre of plastic. The plastic had stones in diagonally opposite corners, twine held the stones in place. The plastic sheet was then rolled up with the blanket and my one change of clothing inside, like a sausage. I carried it across my back and chest. Back home we called it a Hudson Bay pack.

One corner of the *potu* I had flung hard across my left shoulder, then wrapped the rest of it around me like a high-lander's plaid.

I told myself that if I kept up a steady pace I wouldn't feel the cold.

I felt so much better now I was on my way. The waiting

over, the queasy sense of trepidation had vanished. It felt good. I worked best alone, and Quilty knew that.

The sandals would get a good wearing-in.

So would my feet.

It was going to take me half the night to get there.

The backstreets were like tunnels. High mud walls on either side, the narrow, dusty streets uneven underfoot and stretching ahead pale in the starlight. Orion was almost directly overhead, standing out with the Plough in the jewel-studded night sky.

This wasn't like a Western city. There was no glow, no orange light from street lights. No rumble of traffic, no directional signs and no street names.

Just the scuffle of my own feet, the yapping of feral dogs in the distance, the murmur behind a wall of men's voices, low and deep, the odd burst of music from an unseen window, the occasional shadow flitting by, the shape of a curfew-breaker on a bicycle or a pedestrian, as nervous of me as I was of them.

To the south, the drone of aircraft using the US airbase.

I piloted by the North Star, helped by the Plough and Cassiopeia, by the layout of the main streets, and by the hills to the west and east. I traced an irregular path, a tacking west and south, west again and south a little. As time went on the cars became fewer, the fires at the police checkpoints dimmed to heaps of coals, the security men themselves squatting down and dozing under their shawls.

The city was sleeping. The bazaars were shut, even in the main street. Honest men were in bed.

When I came out at the canal I was too far north. I had to retrace my steps, scuttle crabwise round a couple of blocks to come out again at the bridge Abdur Rahman and I had crossed earlier in the day on our way to the burial ground. It took an extra twenty minutes, but I wanted to avoid walking along the exposed canal bank and showing up against the skyline any more than I had to.

The wooden stall at the crossing was boarded up. The guards, watchers – whatever they were – had also packed up for the night.

I walked over to the other side.

I tapped on the big metal doors.

Nothing.

I used the flat of my hand, giving it three loud slaps.

Roused from its sleep, a neighbour's guard dog barked and fell silent again.

Minutes passed. The cold crept up my legs.

I hammered on the gate until it quivered, using my fist.

Several dogs responded. A man's voice, slurred with sleep, asked who it was.

'Bilal,' I said.

The sound of sandalled feet came and went. He was in no hurry. There was a murmured conversation, too far away to make out. The sandals shuffled back after what seemed to be an immensity of time, and I thought I heard the clink of a rifle sling.

'What do you want?'

The guard was standing right opposite, separated from me by the metal doors. Not a hostile voice. Not welcoming, either. Just cautious.

'Refuge,' I said.

I could sense the hesitation.

'I am Bilal,' I said. 'Nabibullah's friend. I need help.'

'Wait.'

The sentry called to his companion.

The bolt was inched back with a good deal of noise of metal grinding on metal. The door opened a few inches.

131

'I am Bilal.'

'What do you want?'

The question-and-answer session was circular and would continue for some time, until someone or something broke the cycle and a decision was reached. It would not be taken by either of these men. It would require the attention of a member of the family.

'I'm seeking refuge.'

They could not refuse me *nanawati* out of hand, friend of Nabibullah or no. They lacked the authority. *Pashtunwali*, the code of honour, was taken very seriously, and *nanawati*, the obligation to provide refuge for those who ask for it, was obligatory. It was a matter of reputation.

Only it could be a ruse.

Either way, the two gunmen would not want to take the rap.

More talk. Who was I? What did I want? One guard slouched off into the darkness. Obviously he'd picked the short straw and had to wake someone up. The second stood still, holding the door, staring, but I guessed he could no more make me out than I could him. He was trying to establish if I was armed.

My legs were frozen, and I felt the cold penetrate the *potu* around my shoulders.

This was the way it was. There was nothing more I could do.

The mud walls were about twelve feet high. The gate perhaps eight, topped with spikes. The walls were vast at the base, and tapered up. They were cheap to build, would last decades with care and maintenance. They were far better suited to defence against modern firearms than brick.

A light appeared through the gap in the gates. It illuminated a long, low building not unlike a bungalow. A terrace ran its full length.

It was the traditional guest house.

132

It stood well back, a vast and empty mud yard before it.

The light was a paraffin lamp, and it rocked gently as whoever was carrying it advanced.

He stopped short and gestured to the guard.

The gate swung open.

'Come in,' he said in English.

'I am Bilal—'

'I know,' he said.

I put out my right hand. We exchanged greetings. I shook hands with the guards, too.

'You're welcome,' said the man with the lamp, in Pashto this time.

He was young with an intelligent face, dressed in white and wearing a white silk turban.

We went through the ritual of greeting.

'I am Mansour,' said the young man. 'Nabibullah is my uncle. Please. You will rest. Our home is your home. This way. Please.'

There would be another gate in the wall somewhere, to the rear, leading to the family home or homes. There would be a narrow passage, a gateway, easily blocked in case of attack, and there might be gardens and servants' quarters, all in their own rectangular sections.

To the left, up against the mud wall, was a car port. It was a thatched structure of rough poles. There were three large utility vehicles parked there.

Mansour saw me looking.

'See the white one?'

'Yes.'

'It was one of Mullah Omar's cars,' he said.

It was huge, the 2000 model, with tinted windows. I read the name Galaxy on the rear.

'Come, Bilal. This way.'

Mansour waited for me, insisted on my going ahead up the steps. He didn't know me from Adam, in all likelihood.

He was just a polite Pashtun, observing the usual courtesies. I saw him glance at my AK-74 and look away.

Behind us, the gate had been shut and bolted.

'You're most welcome,' Mansour repeated. 'You are our guest. Please, make yourself at home.'

It was an enormous room with a high ceiling. Several low windows ran down the western wall, looking out on to the terrace. The windows were double-glazed in effect, with double wooden frames and fly screens between the panes. They were shuttered, and heavy curtains were drawn across them.

At the far end was a doorway that led to a storeroom where the bedding was kept, and to a bathroom.

A massive television set stood at the end. The place was carpeted with two gigantic Afghan rugs of Persian design and equal size, and bolsters and cushions lay against the walls. There were power sockets at regular intervals. The structure itself was concrete. I thought it very ugly, yet the specifications were similar to any traditional mud house. Why bother with concrete? Mud was cool in the summer, warm in winter. It was also much cheaper, and it looked good, too.

The walls were unplastered. The concrete was a nasty grey. Maybe they'd run out of cash, or Mr Nabibullah just hadn't had time to get round to it, what with America's war against terrorism and the fall of the Taliban.

Tea was brought by a sleepy-eyed teenage servant with a sullen expression. A plate of dried fruit and another of home-made biscuits followed.

Mansour was apologetic. It wasn't a proper meal. I would have to wait until breakfast. Would that be all right? He carried out mattresses and blankets and laid them out for me. I was not permitted to help. It was his duty, he said, and his pleasure. I should rest. No doubt longing for sleep, he nevertheless squatted down with me at the end of the room farthest from the television and bathroom, and drank two cups of green tea he probably didn't want. One cup was polite. Two was courteous. Three would have been more than enough, four excessive.

He watched me, taking what information he could from my appearance and my strange Pashto. He smiled. He asked no questions.

'I'm tired,' I told him. 'I hope you won't mind if I sleep.' I was giving him the excuse he needed to return to his own bed. We both knew it.

He left the paraffin lamp and the tea.

The bathroom was a very modern affair by Afghan standards, just like the ones in our house in Sharinau, only this was bigger. It had a white-tiled floor and the tiles went halfway up the walls. There was a proper lavatory, a washbasin, a shower with hot and cold taps and another tap that opened directly onto the tiles for the *wudu*. There were two pairs of plastic flip-flops at the door, and two large plastic jugs for pre-prayer washing. The floor sloped towards a central grate. I ran both the basin taps, but there was no hot water from either.

I went back into the main room. I doused the lamp and waited for my eyes to get used to the darkness. I opened the door a crack. I waited. I heard nothing, and saw no movement. Then I stepped out onto the porch. I didn't bother with my sandals. I would make less noise barefoot.

I stood still for about two minutes, which was as long as I could stand the cold. The sky to the east was begining to turn grey. I could make out the pale mass of Mullah Omar's Galaxy.

Of the guards there was no sign.

*

I woke early to the sound of the call to prayer from a nearby mosque, the voice greatly amplified by loudspeakers. I couldn't have had more than a couple of hours' sleep, but it felt like it had been enough. I lay on my back, thinking about the day ahead. I wondered what role Felix and Yannis were supposed to play, and what had really happened to Gerber. There was method to Mathilde's particular brand of madness, but God alone knew what it was. Sooner or later my hosts would come round to take a look at me, and I wanted to be on my feet and not flat on my back when they did.

I rolled out of my blankets and stood.

It was light outside. I thought it must be around seven, because the sun wasn't high enough to make itself felt.

I went into the bathroom, stripped off and turned on the water. There had to be a cistern somewhere, but I didn't know where. I put up with the cold water, but I was very quick.

Back in the main room I folded my bedding and put it against the wall along with the AK-74. I put on my turban.

Live your cover, the instructors always said.

Facing east, I spread out my *potu*.

I had to get it right. All it took was practice.

Nabibullah was a big man in his sixties. He must have been six-two at least. He was broad and carried a big gut. He wore his turban tipped back on his bald head. He moved slowly, and he had the habit while talking of running his right hand over his beard, which was quite long but not thick. He wore rimless glasses. He looked more like a prosperous banker or director of a large corporation than a big drug dealer with a private army numbering thousands at his command.

He was retired for health reasons, or so he said.

He had turned down offers of public office, blaming it on what he called a sickness in the head. He tapped his temple when he said this. It wasn't clear whether he meant he suffered from bouts of schizophrenia or simply migraines.

We had breakfast together at around nine. Mansour, the nephew, joined us. The kid poured the tea, kept our glasses full, replenished my plate while Nabibullah and I talked.

I contrived to sit with my back to the wall, facing the door and windows. My rifle lay behind me, the stock against my backside so I'd know precisely where it was at all times. I'd thrown my *potu* over it. I had no idea what to expect and I wasn't taking any chances.

We drank; it was the kind of tea that's boiled up with the milk and sugar and flavoured with something or other. At any rate, it was delicious and I must have drunk four glasses before I told myself I was being greedy. We ate nan, goat's cheese, olives, and a cake with a sticky brown crust and yellow on the inside.

'We thought you were dead,' Nabibullah said.

'So did I.'

'You're better? Fully recovered?'

'Much better, thank God.'

'God be thanked. You were in hospital?'

'I had surgery. I was looked after. It took a long time before I could move.'

'Your arm?'

He was looking at my hand, where the stitches had been across the ball of the thumb and right round the other side. The flesh was puckered, and greyish-pink.

I said, 'I was hit in the back.'

I showed them. Whether or not they wanted to see. I didn't care if my big turnip-shaped scars put them off their food. They had to see. Mansour helped me, and I'm sure he must have got a good whiff of Afghan peasant to go with it.

We spoke in Pashto, but when it became too much and too quick, I turned to English and Mansour translated. He didn't do a bad job. His English was probably better than mine. All it lacked was practice, just like my prayers. I told them about what happened to me at the Argendab river base. I told them in detail and bored them silly because I'm sure they knew most of it, but I wanted them to have it because it was real and about the only thing that was.

'What do you think of this?' Nabibullah said, gesturing with an arm to indicate the guest house. 'It's new. I designed it myself. It was my first effort at designing a building.'

'Brilliant,' I said. 'Really fantastic.'

Mansour translated.

Nabibullah beamed.

I went on to explain that I had to leave the place I was staying because enquiries were being made about my host. I didn't say where and I didn't say who. I had left despite my host's protests. I did so because I didn't want him to come to any harm. He had little protection. He was simply a business-man, and I didn't want him or his family to be hurt in any way on my account. They had cared for me for many weeks, had provided me with the best medical attention. I was grateful.

Nabibullah stroked his beard and listened.

'Who's asking these questions?'

'People are sniffing around. Strangers. Asking things strangers ask when they're up to no good.'

'What people?'

'Khad. Least, that's what people said.'

The ice was perilously thin at this point.

Nabibullah did some more beard-stroking.

'Why did you come here?'

I feigned embarrassment, a reluctance.

He waited, watching my face.

'Who else could I trust?' I said.

This was a man who had helped arm the Taliban and fund its conquest of the country. At precisely the right moment he had switched horses, putting his private army into the field alongside the opposition forces led by the governor in the final push on Kandahar the previous December.

He was smart. He would buy opium when the price was rock bottom and sell when it was high.

So smart that he had let Mullah Omar slip away in the night. He had left the back door open for the Taliban leader to escape into the hills as the deadline for Kandahar's surrender expired.

He denied it, of course. In his version, he'd simply been tricked by the one-eyed cleric.

As for backing the Taliban, he explained it away by saying he was just paying his taxes.

'I made sure I wasn't followed,' I said. 'That's why I came at night. I hid for two days in Maiwand district before coming into the city.'

He was still waiting for the answer he wanted to hear.

'I am still betrothed to your daughter, God willing,' I said. 'I think of this place as my home.'

He took off his turban and scratched his bald head. 'She has waited for you, Bilal. She refused to believe what people were saying. She absolutely refused. She always said you were alive. She is still waiting.'

He sipped his tea noisily, watching for my reaction over the rim of his glass.

We stood and embraced, trying not to kick over the breakfast things.

'Thanks be to God,' I said.

Nabibullah was smiling, too.

'*Nashkur Allah.*'

If he hadn't been wearing glasses, I'd have sworn that I saw tears in the old rogue's eyes.

'Welcome home,' he said.

*

The big test was still to come.

Trouble was, I knew so little about whatever had happened between the loving couple. Had they seen each other's faces? Had they held hands, whispered sweet nothings to each other, had his hands strayed under her burka? Had they had a little nookie behind the Afghan equivalent of the bicycle shed?

I doubted it very much.

I hoped Mathilde's intelligence was good or I could be in a lot of trouble.

After Nabibullah left the guest house there was something of a hiatus. Mansour had clearly been delegated to look after me. Or was it to spy on me? Once the breakfast things had been cleared away, he asked if I'd like a walk in the garden. I said I would. He said I could leave the AK-74 where it was. It would be safe. I said I was sure that was the case, but I wouldn't feel comfortable without it. I never went anywhere without it, I said, not even the bathroom. Sorry, and all. It was the habit of a mujahed. He shrugged, and seemed to accept my explanation.

I needed to learn as much as I could and as quickly as I could. In fact I learned several things. The last was a big surprise.

The first was the layout. My pre-dawn recce had got as far as the doorway through to a second compound. Now I saw that this had a lawn, a rose garden and an L-shaped, single-storey house, almost a replica of the guest house. Mansour's family lived there along with other relatives. On the far side was another gateway that led to a third quadrangle where Nabibullah lived along with his wife and children. It looked like a large village house. It was the most attractive of the three.

As we set out, Mansour apologized on behalf of his uncle. I would be moved into Mansour's place later. Because of the hour of my arrival I had been put up in the guest house. They hadn't been sure who I was. I said it didn't matter. No, I would be moved, he insisted. I was family. I interpreted this to mean that they needed the space. Something was up, guests were expected, and they wanted to keep me away from whoever it was.

Maybe I was being unfair.

After all, I was male and a bachelor. Or so they thought. Custom dictated that I had to be kept away from any womenfolk unless they were chaperoned.

Mansour said Aisha and her mother were visiting relatives, but would return that afternoon. There would be a dinner to mark my visit.

Just the family.

In the meantime I could rest. If there was anything I needed, anything at all . . .

'She will be there, at dinner?'

'Not at the meal, but you will see her.'

He was shy discussing such matters, but he wanted to appear reassuring. He wanted to please.

We walked right around again without either of us saying a word. I noted there were no guards in the corner towers, and none inside this particular compound.

'You speak very good English, Mansour.'

'My father and my uncle gave all the children a good education,' he said. 'I was training as a lab technician when the September 11 attacks happened. Our parents are very traditional in many ways, but in education they're very modern.'

He added with a sideways glance, 'Very un-Taliban.'

An odd thing to say to a former Taliban fighter. If that was what he believed I really was.

'Where did you go to school?'

'Peshawar Grammar School for Boys,' he said.

'What about the girls? Your sisters and cousins?'

'They went to school in Pakistan, too.'

He looked at me, expecting a reaction. There wasn't any.

'Aisha has a university degree. From Delhi. You know that,

141

I think. She speaks very good English. The Taliban stopped all girls' education except home study. But Aisha finished her education abroad. She spent a year in England with relatives. She did a master's degree. In London. It was a family secret.'

What was it that Bilal had that Aisha's father would have so willingly offered her in marriage to a foreigner? Bilal had been a devout Muslim, certainly. But what was it that the foreign Talib had to bring to this family? He wasn't wealthy. It wasn't as if the marriage would have forged a strategic alliance between clans of comparable influence. He was a fighter, like so many others.

Something didn't add up.

Mansour stopped. He touched my arm.

'You don't remember me,' he said in a low voice.

It was our third circuit of the roses.

I thought he meant Bilal's previous visits to the house.

'We both look so different,' he said. 'I hardly recognized you.'

I was still trying to grasp what he meant, and I had the sense that I was losing control of the situation. It seemed as if Bilal – the real Bilal, aka Gordon Tucker – had spent time talking to Mansour, and I couldn't compete.

But I was wrong.

He said in English, 'You do remember the donkey, don't you, English? In Oruzgan?'

TEN

The sun shone.

The walls sheltered us from the wind and the sun was high enough to drench the courtyard with its warmth. Mansour brought out cushions. I sat with my back to the house. That way I could see the two exits, one over to my extreme left that led to the guest house where I'd spent the night, the other to my right and leading to the Nabibullah family home.

The rifle lay next to me, wrapped in my *potu*.

More tea was brought.

'You'd better explain,' I said.

'I'm Barakzai,' Mansour said. 'My father was Barakzai.' He added, as an afterthought, and just in case I didn't fully understand, that the governor, Gul Agha, was also Barakzai.

'But Nabibullah is Noorzai,' I said.

I knew little about the Noorzai. I knew they were numerous. I knew they formed one of the biggest Pashtun tribes in the south. I knew they lived right across the south-west, all the way from Quetta, throughout the border region and up to and including Kandahar and beyond. You didn't mess with the Noorzai if you could possibly avoid it, and that was one reason why Nabibullah was living quietly at home and wasn't rotting away behind bars.

He was too powerful, too rich, and his followers too numerous and well armed.

I also knew there was a Noorzai in the interim government

who had helped the US special forces recover Stinger missiles at $100,000 apiece. There were other things the minister was widely rumoured to be good at buying and selling.

'My mother is Nabibullah's youngest sister,' Mansour said. 'My father died during the Soviet occupation.'

'They killed him?'

'The communists took him from his house. We never found his body. The PDPA took all the men from our village. Every male over the age of twelve. Forty-three in all. It was because of an attack on one of their convoys. Some people said they were shot. Others that they were drowned in the Argendab river. No one knows. There were reports they were forced to dig a pit and then made to stand in it and a bulldozer buried them alive. They did this so we could not bury our dead. To dishonour the dead . . .'

'So Nabibullah paid for your schooling – and that of the rest of your family?'

He nodded.

'He's not all bad then, your uncle.'

Mansour frowned. 'Good, bad – what do these words mean? He looks after his family like every Pashtun. He's just a little more up to date than most. He can afford to be. He has money. He's travelled. He has seen something of the outside world.'

'How did he make his pile – his wealth?'

Mansour gave me a knowing look.

'How do you think?'

'It doesn't bother you?'

'Of course. But he doesn't need the poppy fields. He's rich enough that he doesn't need to plant another single seed.'

'What about the Americans?'

'What about them?'

'Do they ever come here?'

'Sure. I've seen Americans here. The special forces. Just two or three at a time. They come at night.'

144

'Are they protecting him?,

Mansour thought for a moment. 'If he is protected, whoever's doing the protecting wouldn't get away with it unless
the Americans approved.'

'I see.'

It amounted to the same thing.

'My uncle was arrested by the Americans. They took him
to the Kandahar airbase. They questioned him. He said they
gave him his own room with a carpet and a bathroom. They
treated him with respect, he said. He was their guest for nearly
a week.'

'That's nice,' I said.

'He said they didn't ask him about drugs. They asked
about Mullah Omar and Osama bin Laden.'

'What did he say to them?'

Mansour shrugged. 'Who knows? He probably said what
everyone else says – that he'll do his best to help find them
and pass on any information concerning their whereabouts.'

'Do you believe that, Mansour?'

'Do you?'

'What were you doing with Abdur Rahman in Oruzgan?'

Mansour was refilling our glasses. He shrugged. He didn't
want to answer.

'Does Nabibullah know Abdur Rahman?'

'Of course.'

It was a small world, after all.

He was holding the teapot in mid-air, looking past me.

'Don't look,' he said. 'Don't turn your head.'

I put out my right hand and grasped the AK-74.

Doors opened and closed. Car engines revved and died.

Voices, both male and female, from the direction of the
guest house.

'They've arrived,' he said. He looked away from whatever
or whoever it was. He picked up a teaspoon and stirred his
glass vigorously.

'Who?'

'Aisha,' he said in a low voice.

There were three women.

Two were covered by blue burkas, the third wore a white headscarf, all of them hurrying along the gravel path to the house. I turned my head slightly and used my peripheral vision.

The woman with the headscarf pulled the white material across her face when she saw us. All I made out was a lock of dark hair and the tip of a nose before she turned her face away.

I would never say it to Mansour, but I still thought male–female relations – or the lack of them – were sick in this part of the world. Furtive. Repressed. Fucked up. Notwithstanding my own considerable failures in that area. It wasn't the religion. It was tradition, and as far as I was concerned, most tradition – at least this tradition – sucked.

'Who are the others?'

'Aisha's mother.'

'And?'

'Her friend.'

'Aisha's or her mother's?'

He was going to say but changed his mind.

'What's the matter?'

'Nothing.'

Mansour seemed to feel he'd already said too much.

'So what are you so worried about?'

Mansour looked over both shoulders. He looked at the residence behind us. He made sure no one was in earshot.

'Yes?'

He looked down like a child who's been caught doing something he shouldn't. 'We're not supposed to talk about it.'

'But you're going to tell me.'

He shook his head.

No.

'What's her name?'

Mansour had gone the colour of old Camembert.

'It's okay,' I said. 'No one's going to know.'

I wasn't going to let him off the hook. He was scared. I wasn't sure why. I didn't particularly care. I felt close, but I didn't know how close. Or what I was close to.

'I can't,' he said. 'Not here. We're not supposed—'

'What's her name?'

He leaned towards me, looking past me, our heads so close our turbans touched.

'Amarayn,' he whispered. 'It means two moons.'

He sat back, fiddling with a grass stalk.

Mansour was sick with worry.

'I know what it means,' I said. 'It's a pretty name.'

I changed the subject to cut him some slack.

'Tell me about Aisha.'

'Like what?'

'How old is she?'

About twenty-eight. Maybe thirty. I'm not sure.'

'Old for an unmarried woman.'

He looked at me, a little shocked. 'No, no,' he said. 'She's a widow – you didn't know?'

I shook my head.

'She was married. Her husband died.'

'How?'

'How what?'

'How did he die?'

'In the civil war.'

I said, 'He was a Talib?'

A nod. Mansour looked away from me. Evasive.

He was sweating, and it wasn't just the sun.

'What was his name?'

'Tiryolai.'

147

A very Afghan name.

'He was Barakzai?'

There was a moment's pause.

'Gabizai.'

I gave no sign it meant anything to me.

'And his father's name?'

Mansour fumbled in his clothing, producing a packet of cigarettes.

'Haji Safar.'

Things were coming together now.

I changed tack again.

'What's she like, this Aisha?'

The colour was returning to Mansour's face, but he was still uncomfortable.

'You can imagine,' he said. 'The man is rich and powerful. A drug baron, I think you say in English. He lives in great style. You haven't seen inside his house yet, but you will. It looks nothing from the outside, but you will see. He has three daughters. He spoils them. There's nothing they can't have. They're used to this life. Can you imagine finding husbands for them?'

'Why not?'

He put a cigarette in his mouth and took it out again.

'Any son-in-law would have to cope with a wife who expects a certain standard of living. She likes luxury. She has her opinions. She is educated, probably more so than the husband. She likes short skirts and high heels. She likes stuff to put on her face—'

'Lipstick,' I said. 'Make-up.'

He nodded.

'Right. She won't stay home. She always wants to go out. She won't put up with a husband who tries to beat her when she won't obey him. She is outspoken.' Mansour opened his hands. 'You see? And then there's the business . . .'

'I don't follow.'

148

Mansour put the cigarette back in his mouth. He said, 'If a man marries into the family, he has to go into the business. Understand? You can't say no. Not everyone wants that. It's everything or nothing with Nabibullah.'

'But you make money. A lot of people around here would jump at the opportunity to make some decent money, and they wouldn't give a damn how they made it, either.'

Like me, for instance.

'The father is choosy, you see. Nabibullah won't take anyone. He wants to make an alliance – ' Mansour meshed his fingers together ' – to build a stronger empire.'

'But Bilal—'

I meant the real Bilal. I also meant myself. I meant that I wasn't anyone important.

He found matches, lit the cigarette.

'She's a widow,' Mansour said.

I saw what he was driving at. 'Meaning she's been fucked by another man so she's worth a lot less is what you're saying. She's no virgin, and hence no catch. An expensively schooled old maid at thirty. Another mouth to feed.'

Why not call a spade a bloody shovel?

Mansour was embarrassed by four-letter words.

'That's what you mean,' I said. 'Isn't it?'

Mansour went to collect my bedding. He wanted me to stay on the grass while he did so. He didn't like it when I followed him. I saw why when I went back into the first compound. There were dozens of men waiting, some standing, most squatting. They were on the guest house terrace, in the yard itself. Smoking and chatting. All armed. A rapid count reached seventeen, but there could have been more on the far side. None paid me the slightest attention, but I backed out the way I had come anyway, and waited for Mansour.

They did not wear Western-style camouflage uniforms.

149

They weren't members of the security forces. They were tribesmen.

They all had Kalashnikovs. Several carried RPG launchers and quivers on their backs full of the grenades themselves. There were a couple of 61 mm mortars, too, and a DhsK 12.7 mm machine gun mounted in the back of a Datsun pickup.

'Who are they?'

Mansour didn't answer.

'Look—'

I was getting pissed off. I grabbed his arm and spun him round to face me. The mattress, blankets and cushions flew out of his hands and fell to the ground.

I shook his arm roughly. 'Who are they?' I said.

'Nabibullah's people.'

'What's going on?'

He started picking up the bedding, but I went over to him and yanked him upright.

'I asked you a question.'

He flinched, expecting a blow.

'I'll tell you.'

'Tell me now.'

'The American and British troops have attacked places near Ghazni. They have sent hundreds of their soldiers there. The Americans are dropping bombs. They say they are fighting Taliban and al-Qaeda, but how can they possibly tell? They can't. Afghans don't wear labels. There are no Taliban or al-Qaeda fighters there, anyway. They slipped away before the attack started. Just like it was before, in Khost and Paktiya and Nangahar.'

He started to move again, but I blocked the way.

'Why didn't you tell me?'

'I thought you knew.'

'And these people?'

'They have come from there.'

'They fought with the government forces?'

Mansour shook his head. 'No. The government forces in that area are Hazaras and Tajiks,' he said. 'We will never fight with them.'

'Who, then?'

He looked down at the ground.

'Explain it to me, Mansour.'

'The Americans and the British are with the Northern Alliance. It's their government in Kabul, not ours. Hamid Karzai is a Pashtun. From Kandahar. He's a good man, but he belongs to America. He does what they want. The foreigners are attacking us Pashtuns. We must fight back. We don't have Qaedaa choice. It's not Taliban or al-Qaeda any more.'

He was visibly upset.

'Why did the Americans attack Ghazni?'

He clutched the bedding to his chest. I helped him by collecting the cushions.

'We sell information to the Americans, and they believe what they buy. You know yourself, Bilal. The higher the price, the better they believe it. They kill the wrong people. They make enemies of their friends. They say they win big victories, but we know it's not true. You know it better than I. Same as Gardez and Khost and Oruzgan. It's to draw them off.'

We were moving over to the house.

'Draw them off? Draw them off from what?'

Mansour gave me a withering look.

How could I be so stupid?

I told myself Nabibullah was a businessman. He hedged his bets and played both sides. He had made a token surrender of arms and vehicles stolen by the Taliban. He had agreed to give up his opium production. He had made his peace with the fragile interim administration. He received Americans in his home. But he also sent his men off to fight these same Americans, or at least to lead them a merry dance away from the Sheikh. He kept his door open to the Khad, and to men like Abdur Rahman. He had family ties with with the smugglers of Chaman and beyond. He gave me protection in his home, though I was being hunted by Abdur Rahman, and was even – so it seemed – prepared to marry off one of his daughters to a British Muslim.

Abdur Rahman was no different, not really. He worked for the interim government and the British simultaneously. Yet he was a former Talib. He kept up with his Taliban comrades. He had ties with Nabibullah, with Suleiman and with me.

The same went for Mansour.

He worked as a personal assistant to Nabibullah.

He was the old crook's kith and kin.

He was my ally.

Maybe.

And Abdur Rahman's.

It was language and tribe, tribe and clan, clan and family. It was balancing obligations and hedging options. It was a matter of contacts, opportunity, and timing.

It was survival.

'Come.'

Mansour led.

We kicked off our sandals at the foot of the steps.

I'd never seen anything like it. That was because there was nothing else like it.

On closer inspection, the Nabibullah residence wasn't mud at all. It was concrete just like the two other buildings. Only the concrete had been moulded and rounded. It had been plastered to give it a rough, uneven texture. It had then been painted a colour somewhere between orange and pink so it resembled a traditional mud house.

There was a carpet of grass out front. It was lush, soft and very green.

'It comes from France.'

'What does?'

'The grass,' Mansour whispered. 'He imports it specially from France and it's watered every day.'

The interior was the real shock. The massive front door, of wood and studded with iron and approached up half a dozen steps, opened to a vast reception room. Inside it was all white marble underfoot, domed ceiling above, and a white fountain like a wedding cake dribbling in the centre.

It seemed to go on forever. There were nests of armchairs and sofas around coffee tables. There must have been a dozen different suites, from black leather to midnight velvet.

The reception was empty.

'Presents,' said Mansour as he led the way. He meant the overstuffed furniture. 'Presents from friends and admirers.'

Bribes, more like.

It was like Selfridges furnishings department.

A wrought iron staircase led someplace upstairs, or the roof, maybe.

Grand piano.

A huge and garish oil painting of Nabibullah himself, wearing traditional robes and clutching a sabre, hung above a big stone fireplace of smouldering logs.

Soft music. Jazz piano from hidden speakers.

Rugs from Herat, from Baluchistan and Bokhara.

The interior walls were sliding glass, looking out on a central courtyard of what looked to me like ferns and bamboo.

Stones, forming shapes and patterns.

A Japanese garden in miniature.

Christ.

This was more Beverley Hills than Kandahar.

Mansour led the way down a very white corridor lit by brass lamps that threw weird shapes on the walls and ceiling.

A fine Qalat runner underfoot.

'In here.'

Mansour stood aside, pressed himself against the wall, swung open the door.

As I stepped inside, the hubbub of voices – male and female – ceased abruptly. I was conscious of the door closing, shutting off any retreat.

Heads turned to look. Several pairs of eyes took in my turban, my face, my grubby clothes, my dusty feet. The AK-74 reversed and slung across my back.

I was being inspected. Thoroughly.

Nabibullah was on his feet.

He wore a striped gown or cape over a grey silk tunic and his bald head shone like a brown egg in the artificial light.

He looked very grand.

It was a small sitting room in traditional style, only the cushions and rugs were richly embroidered. They looked as if they'd been ordered direct from Liberty's in Regent Street.

Maybe they had.

'Bilal,' he said 'My son.'

I saw her at once.

There were three women. None wore a burka.

The oldest, a woman in her fifties, wore a simple white scarf around her shoulders. Her head was uncovered. She was very plump. Her expression was kindly, maternal, but the lines on her face said she'd led a life of hard work, worry and not a great deal of fun. She probably didn't know what the word meant.

Mrs Nabibullah.

As I entered the room the young woman on the mother's immediate left lifted the edge of her own white scarf and pulled it up over her hair, a swift and instinctive movement in the presence of a male stranger. Just like the one I'd seen outside.

A space had been made for me and I was directed to it. The men were talking to me, shaking my hand. I heard the Pashto greetings, the enquiries after my health, and I heard my own formal replies, but my mind was elsewhere.

The third woman was tall and preternaturally thin.

Her head was uncovered. She didn't bother with the scarf that lay about her neck. She put a hand up and with long fingers moved her hair away from her face.

She had enormous, wide-set eyes. They were like the eyes of a calf. Huge, very dark and underscored with kohl.

A long jaw.

A wide, slightly lopsided and stubborn mouth painted in scarlet lip gloss. A sensual, hungry look.

Her hair was black, long and parted in the centre.

Gold flashed at her throat and on her wrists and fingers.

Aisha.

My wife to be.

She wore a deep-blue tunic of soft, woven fabric and matching pantaloons. She leant on a plump, tasselled cushion, her legs tucked under her.

Her hands were long and wrists fragile like porcelain, the skin so pale I could see the veins beneath.

This woman might enjoy doing flower arrangements, but I was pretty sure she had never had to cook a meal or wash her own clothes or make her bed.

She had certainly never drawn water from a village well.

Aisha was not beautiful.

She was awesome.

I sat on Nabibullah's right, the place of honour.

Men and women in the same room, and not all of them immediate family.

It was unusual to say the least.

Nabibullah was introducing me to the only two other men present. A brother, Rasul. We shook hands, exchanged greetings. I caught the name Haji Safar, and had a fleeting impression of a white beard, pale eyes and brown fingers clicking away at amber prayer beads.

Just like a luxury-loving Gabizai to strike a pious pose.

I took a chance. I addressed the woman I felt sure was Aisha directly, and without introduction.

'How are you?'

She answered at once. Her voice was deep, husky.

'I'm well, Bilal, thank you. Very well. How are you? Have you recovered completely?'

Cool. Unperturbed. Even faintly amused.

'Yes,' I said. 'I'm fine.'

'Your wounds are healed?'

She looked at the livid weal on my left hand and away again.

'Oh, yes,' I said.

I realized we were both speaking English.

'You look different,' she said.

'I do?'

'You sound different, too.'

'Yes?'

'Your accent is stronger, Bilal. And you're a little older than I remember.' Her lips twitched into a half-smile. 'Better-looking, though,' she added.

She was flirting with me in the knowledge that the others present did not understand. Or if they did, she didn't care.

'You haven't changed a bit,' I lied.

'Are you sure?'

She was teasing again.

Her English was almost perfect – there was the faintest touch of the subcontinent in her tone. It was not unattractive.

If there had been an Afghan edition of *Hello!* magazine I knew she would be the cover story. No question. Draped across the fountain. Barefoot in the Japanese garden's bamboo, smiling winsomely under the bougainvillea on the French grass out front.

I said, 'You're just the way I remember you.'

'It's been such a long time. Are you certain? It wasn't somebody else, perhaps? Do you remember what I was wearing—'

I ignored the question and interrupted her. 'It's great to see you again.'

I was in over my head and sinking fast.

How could I possibly know what she'd been wearing?

It was one of the inevitable lacunae in Mathilde's briefings. I just had to improvise.

Aisha arched her eyebrows. 'It is? Really?'

Her tone was mocking. She was looking at me intently, not quite managing to place either my hairy face or my accent.

'Of course,' I said. 'Now I'm here I hope we can see a lot more of each other.'

Aisha was the very antithesis of a village girl, cowed and submissive, raw and unsophisticated. This was someone who had dined at the Caprice, danced at Tramps and shopped at Harvey Nichols at the top of Sloane Street, just a short and agreeable stroll from her Mayfair pied-à-terre.

It didn't have to be London. It could be Paris or Rome, New York or Madrid.

Thanks to Daddy.

Thanks to his trade in morphine sulphate.

A Jordanian prince in Versace and behind the wheel of a Ferrari would be far more to Aisha's taste than an Afghan with mutton fat in his whiskers, a Kalashnikov on his back, toe-jam in his sandals and less than a quid in his pocket.

At least I thought so.

Our conversation was interrupted by the television news from al-Jazeera, the independent Arabic-language station in Doha. Apparently it was an evening ritual at the Nabibullah household, courtesy of the massive satellite dish on the roof.

Rasul offered me a Marlboro Light and I shook my head.

The bulletin led with another suicide bombing in west Jerusalem.

Second was an earthquake in south-eastern Turkey. Hundreds feared dead. Pictures of mountains, snow, helicopters and aid workers in woolly hats.

Then Joe Gerber's face appeared.

It was a still photograph in full colour.

Joe was holding up a three-day-old copy of the Karachi newspaper, *Dawn*.

His wrists and feet were chained.

A pistol was pointed at his head.

His captors had issued a statement demanding the release of twenty-two Pakistanis and five British Muslims held by the Americans at Guantanamo and their Kandahar airbase.

On behalf of Mir'aj, a clandestine organization of militants the newsreader said was believed by Western intelligence to be linked to al-Qaeda. It was active in western Europe, although its networks had been depleted by arrests, especially in France and Britain.

Then it was my face staring back at me.

Bearded, turbanned.

The orange suntan in place.

Looking down to one side and fuzzy, out of focus.

The group's elusive British leader.

Bilal.

Christ, it was me.

Wanted by the FBI and half the world's law-enforcement agencies, and believed to be in south-west Afghanistan.

ELEVEN

I woke up.

The shooter kept his weapon on single fire. He squeezed off three rounds, paused, and loosed off three more.

The flat cracks of the AK-47 were evenly spaced.

He had chosen well. A dark night, stars and moon obscured by cloud or dust or both.

I had no precise idea when it started. Around 3 a.m. would have been my guess. When the metabolism was at its lowest ebb, the sentries at their most sluggish. For me it began with a wave of light that washed into my room, followed immediately by an immense thump. The explosion was very close, right outside. It cracked the glass in the windows and made the floor shake and debris rattle on the roof.

It sounded as if the shooter used the flash and bang of the impact – that of a rocket-propelled grenade – to alter his position.

He fired again, but from further off. Four rounds, one-second intervals. Very steady. This time over to the right, to the north-west.

I rolled out of my blankets, ducked under the window and headed for the door, rifle in hand, slamming a round into the breech and pushing the safety off.

The occupants of the Nabibullah residence were waking up.

A long panicky burst from an RPK, like cloth tearing only a lot louder, sent a stream of tracer out over the wall.

Futile.

A sentry trying to make amends for sleeping on his watch.

I found my sandals on the porch, pushed my feet into them.

Already hundreds of rounds had been expended by the groggy defenders to the attacker's economical twelve or thirteen, less than half a magazine in all. The shooter was still at it on the northern side. He knew what he was doing. He would fire and move, fire and move. Within a few minutes he was joined by a mate on the high ground to the west. They worked in concert. The second shooter could see down on the three buildings, or at least the upper part of the structures. He too was firing single rounds in groups of three and four.

They took turns.

It was unhurried, deliberate, passionless.

They weren't shooting to kill. They were content drawing the defenders' fire and keeping our heads down.

They were playing with Nabibullah's people.

It really was too good.

The question was who, and above all why.

Another loud thump.

I guessed there were three of them now, one with the grenade-launcher. A trio, working well together.

Firing RPGs at the mud walls was like poking a stick into an ants' nest. They made holes and impressive bangs, but not much else. Nabibullah's people were pouring outside, tripping over each other in the dark and racing off towards the northern and western walls and blasting away at nothing very much.

There were no visible targets.

Not even a muzzle flash that I could see.

They were shouting a lot, though.

Every Pashtun likes to be the boss. Everybody was giving orders, and absolutely no one appeared willing to obey any of them. In Afghanistan it's called democracy. In the West it's known as sheer bloody panic.

Whoever was out there was gradually enticing the defenders away from the main gates in the southernmost wall and the guest house towards the northern side.

I headed south because if there was going to be an assault, that was where it would be.

A man cannoned into me with his shoulder. I grabbed hold of him to regain my balance.

'Dickhead—'

'Bilal – I came looking for you. This way.'

Mansour held a Kalashnikov.

He pushed me through the gate ahead of him.

'They're waiting. Over there. The white car.'

He meant Mullah Omar's Galaxy.

'Key's in the ignition.'

Mansour ran round the other side, jumped into the passenger seat. There was already someone in the back because whoever it was leaned across the seats to open the driver's door for me.

All that trouble to get me into Nabibullah's good books again, and now I was exiting. Fast.

I reversed out. Spun the wheel over. Lined the four-wheel drive up with the double metal gates, and held it there, dead centre.

Snapped the headlights full on.

A sentry stood at the entrance – exit in our case – blinded by the light, transfixed like a deer on a country road.

Mansour had his window down and was waving his rifle at the man, yelling at him to get out of the way.

In my side mirror I saw we had a number of interested parties in pursuit. There was more shouting. Tracer was hosing prettily through the night sky above.

This was not a time for elaborate Pashtun farewells.

No time to ask my hosts to open up, either.

I put the big car in first and stamped on the accelerator.

There was a nasty crash, a rending of metal and the doors crumpled. The bolt snapped and the padlock flew off

We shot out into the night.

Mullah Omar's white Galaxy wasn't pretty any more. The paintwork had been spoiled all down the left side, and the front offside had a couple of nasty dents where we'd wrenched one door off its hinges and taken it with us. One headlight was bust.

Our pursuers loosed off a long burst from an automatic weapon, and the tinted rear windscreen collapsed, but as far as I could tell no one had been hit. They were shooting far too high for the most part, on full automatic and from the hip.

The car bounced down the slope, reared up towards the canal and rocketed over the bridge.

No one followed, and there were no more rounds in our direction.

I put a couple of mud buildings between us and them and eased up, slowing to around twenty-five miles an hour.

Heading towards us and the fireworks under way at Nabibullah's compound was a pickup driven at a furious pace, bouncing and rolling from one side of the rutted street to the other, a huge Afghan flag fluttering from the bonnet.

The Ford was packed with gunmen, their faces covered against the cold and dust.

'Police,' Mansour said.

They didn't spare us so much as a glance.

We passed a second vehicle from the city cop shop a couple of minutes later. The same thing happened. They didn't pay us the slightest attention.

Our lone headlight picked out the pall of dust behind the two pickups like a firestorm.

Mansour was giving directions through the centre of town. I began to be aware of our passengers at the back. One of

them was Aisha. The other was an unidentified – and unidentifiable – woman in a burka.

Whatever it was that lay behind this abrupt and violent
departure of ours, I was sure it had everything to do with our
passengers.

'Over there.' Mansour pointed to what looked like a garage,
the shutters drawn. There were several four-wheel-drive vehicles parked out front on the greasy, diesel-drenched pavement.
There was nobody about, and no lights showed.

'Park next to the Jeep,' he said.

I did as I was told. He took the Galaxy's keys and, turning
round, dropped them into Aisha's palm.

We all got out.

Aisha and the tent-like woman hugged each other.

I couldn't hear what was said, but it seemed to be an
emotional parting.

Aisha took my place in the driver's seat of the Galaxy.

'This was your show,' I said to her through the open
window. 'Those were your people. You arranged it, the whole
damn shooting match. Right?'

Aisha didn't deny it. She didn't confirm it, either.

I had been given a part in someone else's local melodrama,
but I didn't know my lines and had no idea how much this
performance fitted in with my own mission, if at all.

'And the lady?' I meant the woman in the burka who was
now clambering with some difficulty into the Jeep. Mansour
had the door open for her, but there was no point in offering
her his hand because he knew she wouldn't have taken it.

'Amarayn is my dearest friend,' Aisha said. 'You'll take
care of her. Promise me. I know I can rely on you.'

I slipped the mag out of my rifle, cleared it and put it on
safe. Then I replaced the magazine, and slung the weapon
over my shoulder.

I said, 'And your father? What are you going to tell him?'

She put her head back and shook the long hair out of her face, then ran the fingers of her right hand through it. It was a self-conscious and flirtatious gesture I could imagine her making on a beach in Mustique or Mauritius, not the middle of the night in Kandahar after she'd got her own people to shoot up her father's house.

'I can handle him,' she said.

'I'm sure you can. But why me?'

'Abdur Rahman. He said you could do it. He said you had the skills. He said they would trust you – over there.'

'Do – do what? What's this "it"?'

'Get Amarayn away from here. Take her back to her people. Safely.'

'And where's over there, exactly?'

Aisha started the car.

I said, 'You owe me an explanation. That stuff about marriage, about waiting for me to show up—'

'It's nothing personal. Really, Bilal. I never appreciated my father's choice of suitors. Marriage isn't on my mind right now. It just seemed a way to get you to help, and it kept the family off my back . . .'

Meaning that while we were engaged she was saved the trouble of meeting more unsuitable suitors dredged up by her heroin-trafficking father. No wonder she chose not to believe Bilal had died. It suited her not to.

Not that I had had any choice.

I watched the Galaxy roll out onto the street and turn back the way we had come. Aisha stuck an arm out of her window and waved. She was going home to Daddy. I wondered what Nabibullah would make of the episode. It was quite a party. Especially the broken front gates, the gaping holes in his walls and the thousands of rounds of ammunition fired off into the night sky by his Noorzai tribesmen.

To say nothing of his guest who fled into the night.

The only people likely to have been hurt were those who had fallen into the rose beds or shot themselves in the foot in their haste.

I wondered what cock and bull story Aisha would cook up and whether it would be believed.

Mansour beckoned furiously from the Jeep, the woman in the burka a shadow behind him on the rear seat.

Beyond the eastern hills the horizon was purple, broken by a single brush stroke of pallid pink.

It would be light very soon.

Mansour drove. I ordered him to head south.

Amarayn curled up and slept, her back to us, like a large parcel wrapped in blue satin.

Just before the southern entrance to the city, I told Mansour to pull off the highway, scooting east between a deserted factory and a ramshackle petrol station, taking us on a wide detour across the desert, a half-circle, rejoining the highway a couple of miles south of the city gates where the governor's men had a checkpoint and a clutch of Soviet-built tanks.

The Jeep's tank was full when we left Kandahar. Someone had thoughtfully seen to the oil and water, too, and checked the tyre pressures. There wasn't much traffic, just half a dozen trucks loaded with scrap metal coming down from central Asia, a trio of buses from Herat and a couple of tractors. We overtook them all without difficulty, our headlights stabbing the clouds of dust, Mansour's hand slapping the horn.

I asked him to slow down with the onset of daylight. I was looking to my left, watching the desert slide by.

'Hold on everyone,' I said. Once again we left the road, the car bucking and bouncing out onto the scrubland. I thought of the ten million mines the Russians had left behind when they pulled out in '89 and the 40,000 bomblets dropped by the Americans in the past six months or so.

Mansour looked worried.

'Don't worry,' I said. 'No mines. No bombs. Not here.'

There were other tracks. Not many, and not fresh, but the fact we were following them made Mansour feel a lot better.

We were headed for the saddle I recognized in a range of hills running north-east to south-west. The ridges looked arid, bereft of vegetation, impossibly steep. Impenetrable.

Which was why most people gave them a wide berth.

We started to climb, and I remembered how the hills were a lot higher and wider than they appeared to be from the road.

In minutes the road behind and below was a straight pencil line on a beige table top. Kandahar was hidden beneath a smear of dirty smog on the northern horizon. Above our heads a pair of eagles cruised the thermals, wings barely moving, searching for breakfast among the stone peaks on a white sky.

We left a plume of dust in our wake, a clear trail visible for miles. I wished for wind to disperse it, but the air was calm for once.

Amarayn had sat up. She had pushed the burka headpiece up and was looking back the way we had come. Reassured we were not being followed, she turned to the front again. That was when I saw her face for the first time.

'She asks you why.'

We were following a watercourse, a wadi cut deep in the sandstone by flash floods. It was the sort of watercourse that has been dry for years, the hard surface ground to deep sand, the Jeep wallowing in it and sliding about as if it were mud.

The ground rose steeply on either side, layers of rock rising to a strip of blue high above. Perfect ambush country.

We were in deep, cool shadow.

Almost invisible from aircraft, unless a helicopter came down very low and examined every crevice.

'Why what?'

Mansour was translating. I had taken the wheel again.

'She wants to know why you.'

'I could ask her the same thing,' I said.

Amarayn had prominent cheekbones, a pert nose. Her most striking feature was her green eyes, which were oval, almost oriental. They had that flat intensity I'd seen in wild animals, predators especially. Utterly focused, entirely without guile. It was difficult not to stare at them. Her hair, or what I could see of it, was auburn, short, curly, almost like a boy's. Her hands – clutching the back of the front seats – were small, the fingers shapely, but they were capable hands, practical and strong, equally at home doing the flowers or pumping water from a tube well.

'It must be bad luck,' I said.

She smiled at that, but she didn't look at me.

'She says you are making a joke. She doesn't think you're truthful.'

'Ask her why – why she's doing this.'

'She says she was a prisoner at the Nabibullah house.'

'Yes?'

'She says it's difficult to talk about.'

'Try.'

There was a prolonged exchange, too quick for me to catch much of it. It sounded like an argument. In any case, I was concentrating on the roller coaster ride in the gully, trying to keep us upright.

'She says she is married to someone very important.'

'I gathered that much. Go on.'

'He had to leave Kandahar. She lived alone. In an ordinary house. You know, a couple of rooms, a kitchen, privy outside. A mud house. Like a village house. It was rented by him.'

'Yes?'

'He would come to her once or twice a week. Then less often.'

'Go on.'

'He would lie on the bed and rest. He liked to be left alone to think. He didn't discuss his business with her. He didn't talk politics. Mostly he didn't spend the night.'

I glanced round at her. What was she saying? Maybe it was the translation. Surely she wasn't telling me the husband wasn't interested in her sexually. She was sitting behind and between us, those green eyes fixed unblinking on the track ahead. Maybe she was telling me that without realizing what she was saying. Too innocent even for embarrassment. Maybe I'd got it wrong and her place was just the Afghan equivalent of a fuck pad and he'd come and get his rocks off and go away again.

'Children?'

'She says no.'

'What happened then?'

'He said he would have to leave the city. He said he might be away a long time. He would send for her.'

'Did he?'

'Not then.'

'So—'

'The Americans bombed the house in January. It was destroyed. Aisha took Amarayn to our home. Looked after her. Kept her there secretly until her father found out.'

There was another intense exchange between Amarayn and Mansour. I had the feeling Mansour knew a lot more than Amarayn wanted him to let on.

'Aisha's father, Nabibullah, discovered who she was. Who the husband was. He forbade her to leave the house. She became a hostage. She was treated well. As a guest, but she was still a prisoner. She was watched all the time.'

'Why was that?'

'Aisha's father thought he could lure her husband into a trap, then make him captive and sell him to the Americans for a lot of money. That's what Aisha said. The Americans would pay a great deal of money.'

'So?'

'He didn't come. He never sent any message. Eventually, Nabibullah decided not to wait any longer. He decided to sell her to the Americans. She knew nothing important, but the Americans wouldn't know that until they'd already paid Nabibullah.'

'This happened when?'

'Ten days ago. They made a deal.'

'So rather than be arrested by the Americans—'

'Aisha arranged her escape. Yes. That's how she says it was. She was frightened they would tie her up and put a hood over her head and torture her and take her to that place they have in Cuba and she would never see Afghanistan again.'

'Who is the husband?'

'She doesn't want to say.'

'Does she know where he is?'

'She thinks so.'

'But he doesn't know she's trying to find him?'

Another exchange, but very brief.

'No.'

'No? No what?'

'No, he doesn't know she's trying to find him. That's what she says.'

Mansour looked as if he didn't believe it.

'So it's going to be a surprise if she succeeds.'

'Yes.'

'Does she think he'll be pleased?'

Mansour translated.

'She says she doesn't know. She's not sure.'

I said, 'She must miss him.'

Mansour shrugged.

'What does she say?'

'She didn't answer. I don't think she wants to talk about it.'

*

169

The sandstone had worn away laterally, forming natural layers like a sandwich. Some were wide overhangs, and we stopped under one of them. The Jeep couldn't be seen from above.

We all got out.

It was chilly in the shade, and we'd have had to climb up several metres to find the sun, but none of us felt like being a mountaineer.

'There's some food,' Mansour said.

It was wrapped in newspaper and still warm.

Barbecued chicken, chips and a salad of onion, parsley and cucumber. Nan for four people and a lukewarm two litres of Coke. Thoughtful of somebody.

We spread out the newspaper on the back seat. We stood outside and leaned in and helped ourselves, using our fingers. Amarayn on one side of the Jeep, Mansour and I on the other.

We didn't speak while eating.

Mansour found cigarettes and matches and lit up. He tossed the match away and took a step away from the Jeep.

'Where's your rifle?' I said.

He answered me by gesturing with his chin towards the vehicle's front seats.

'Go round the other side,' I told him quietly. 'Move slowly. Climb in, pick up your rifle and come round here again. Slowly.'

There was no point in telling him off. It was careless, but he was no trained soldier. He was barely fifteen, and so far he'd done pretty well.

'Why, what's going on?'

'Don't look round,' I said. 'Just act normal. Okay?'

'Okay.'

He was looking at me. He was frowning. Nervous.

'Just go and get your rifle, Mansour. Quietly. No fuss. Just like I said.' I stepped back for him to slip past me. 'When you've got your rifle come back over like nothing's happened.'

'Okay.'

'Take it easy. Act naturally.'

'All right.'

He got his rifle, cradled it in the crook of his arm and climbed back out again, the cigarette in the corner of his mouth.

I licked my fingers and wiped them on a bit of tissue I found in my pocket.

'Steady now,' I said. 'Come back over here. Take it easy.'

Amarayn had climbed quietly in the back of the Jeep. Either she sensed something wasn't right, or she understood more English than I thought she could.

Mansour asked, 'What's going on, Bilal?'

'We're being watched,' I said.

There were two of them. Both were armed. They came slowly out of cover, scrambling down into the gully.

They walked towards us down the dusty slope and stopped.

Twenty paces between us.

No one spoke.

They took in our weapons, our clothing, then they looked hard at the Jeep. They noted the woman in the back. I could tell they wanted to have a look inside. They wanted to check out what else we carried – arms, ammunition, food, communications gear, perhaps.

The first man was bearded and very swarthy with a lined face and sunken cheeks. He wore shades. He was stocky and dressed in a *chalwar kameez* and a grubby Nato-style combat smock. He carried a large knife in a sheath at his waist and an airborne version of the AKM with folding metal stock. The rifle was slung around his neck, and lay against his chest where he could get at it easily.

On his head was a *baqul*, the round lamb's wool hat favoured by northerners and members of the Northern Alliance.

His companion was clean-shaven and dressed as a tribesman, complete with turban, *potu* and sandals. He carried a pistol in a shoulder holster under his waistcoat. In his right hand, kept down at his side, was a cellphone or radio handset.

He was long-haired, black curls protruding from under the turban over his ears and collar.

I guessed both men were in their forties. The man in front was the elder. I took him to be a commander of some kind.

'Where you guys from?'

His English took me by surprise.

It had a North American twang to it.

'I was going to ask you the same thing,' I said.

The first man removed his shades. He smiled broadly, his teeth showing white in the midst of his beard.

Whatever the hell they were, they weren't Pashtuns. Or if they were, their manners were nothing short of insulting.

'Seems we have something of a stand-off,' the first man said.

I waited. I was in no hurry. Mansour was on my left, slightly behind me, close to the rear of the Jeep. He hadn't said a single word, but I thought I knew what was in his mind. He was marking the second man, and would use the Jeep as cover if push came to shove.

Which it might well.

'Anything we can do for you?' I said.

'Well, yes,' the first man said. 'As a matter of fact there is. You can tell me who you people are and what you're doing here, and when you've done that you can turn round and go back to wherever it was you came from.'

His tone was an arrogant sneer.

'I wasn't aware this was private property,' I said.

'It's a restricted area,' he said.

'The whole mountain?'

'As far as you're concerned.'

The smile had gone. The shades were back in place.

I said, 'And who the hell are you?'

'You got it the wrong way round,' the first man said. 'We'll tell you who we are once you've said who you are.'

Mansour cleared his throat.

'Chief . . .'

I glanced back over my shoulder very quickly.

There were more of them behind us, and I hadn't heard their approach.

And even more up on the ridge.

'Let's not try anything stupid,' the first man said.

'I wasn't planning to,' I said.

There was really nothing we could do.

But Mansour thought otherwise.

The bullet went in under his left arm as he tried to dodge round the Jeep. It went through his ribs and then his lungs and I don't know where it ended up because there was no exit wound.

God alone knows what he thought he was doing. Maybe he imagined he could get the Jeep started and run the blokes down – the ones right in front of us. Their mates in the rear wouldn't dare open fire for fear of hitting them. Maybe that's what was in his mind.

He never even reached the door.

It was heroic but stupid.

He was still breathing. For some of the time he was conscious. I stopped the bleeding, but I knew the real problems were internal and out here there was nothing we could do about that. I rolled up my *potu* and put it under his head, covered him with his own shawl and squatted down and held his hand and talked to him.

All I could do was make him as comfortable as possible and wait.

It wouldn't take long.

'We'll take him in the Jeep,' the man in shades said.

I ignored the remark. The drive would only cause him severe pain and kill him sooner rather than later.

Mansour opened his eyes and looked at me like I was a very long way off.

'Sorry,' Mansour whispered. 'Sorry, Bilal.'

That's all he ever said after he was shot. He closed his eyes like someone taking a nap. His face started to change. His skin seemed to stretch tight over his face, especially his cheekbones. It lost its lines and seemed strangely smooth and unblemished.

The cheeks became sunken.

His eye sockets got deeper, the skin around them darker.

I'd seen this before.

Mansour was dying.

TWELVE

We were prisoners.

At least I was. I couldn't tell whether my captors regarded Amarayn as their prisoner. They left her alone. Ignored her. They didn't even speak to her. She was a woman. She posed no danger. As far as they were concerned, she was of no account.

I hoped that was true, for both our sakes.

They took my rifle, cleared it, emptied the rounds from the magazine and gave both back to me to carry. They searched my pockets and found nothing else of interest or value. The man in shades shrugged and turned away. He looked disappointed. I don't know why – perhaps he thought I might be carrying some form of identity, or something of value. Something he could use.

They didn't bother with my grubby Afghanis.

They left the Jeep where it was after a thorough search. It had picked up enough dust so it already seemed part of the terrain. Two gunmen used their bayonets to cut some scrub and Shades ordered them to pack the vegetation around the outside wheels so anyone coming up the gully wouldn't immediately recognize it for what it was.

I picked up Mansour, using the fireman's lift. His weight was distributed across my shoulders and his head hung down, banging against my shoulder blade. I gripped his right wrist in my left hand, my right hand went around right thigh.

Mansour was my cross. My road to Calvary was about half a mile, uphill along the gully.

A dead man is a lot heavier than a live one.

I staggered, stumbled twice, dropped Mansour once and the sweat got in my eyes. The AK-74 didn't help.

Amarayn was right behind me.

I counted seven of them.

They had put me and my burden up front. If there was a mine or a bullet waiting, I'd be the one who'd collect in full.

I'd have done the same thing.

At the top the gully opened out into a level clearing.

I put the body down gently.

The back of my shirt was crusted with Mansour's blood.

Someone thrust a long-handled spade at me.

'Over there,' said the man in shades, pointing.

He meant away from the clearing. While I dug I had a good look round. We were in a dish-shaped hollow, high ground on all sides, providing natural protection from the surrounding desert plain. There were two entrances to tunnels that I could see, each dug into the sides of the hollow. The entrances had been shored up with wood.

We were close enough to Pakistan for them to have been prepared two decades before with the help of Pakistan's Inter Services Intelligence. They would have been used then for storing CIA and Saudi-funded munitions destined for the mujahedin.

Mostly Chinese and Egyptian.

The only direct potential danger to this bunch was from above, the empty blue sky.

It was surprising the Americans hadn't already paid a visit. Or perhaps the fact they hadn't should have told me something about who these people were.

I had stripped down to my baggy pants.

Nobody objected and that made me think. Afghans are funny about nakedness. Even male nakedness. Especially male nakedness in a lot of cases.

I hit rock at four feet.

'That'll do,' said Shades.

Two men pulled my arms behind my back and lashed my forearms together. One of them kicked me in the shoulder so I fell sideways, then they bound my feet at the ankle and at the knees, cutting off the blood supply.

'Can I have his boots, boss?'

'Leave him alone,' Shades said.

He got up from where he was sitting and came over and looked at my bindings.

'Comfortable?'

'Not really.'

'Too bad.'

'Who are you waiting for?'

'Who says I'm waiting for anyone?'

I said, 'You are waiting. And it's not for Ramadan.'

'So?'

'You know who I am, I think.'

'You're a Talib.'

'So tying me up like this – a prisoner – says something about who you people are.'

'Yeah? So what?'

Shades had knelt down and was peering at me.

I said, 'So you're clearly not Talib-friendly. Where would I go, anyway? I wouldn't get far. You know that. Why not let me have the freedom of your camp? If the people you're waiting for check you out and see me around, it might persuade them it's safe to approach.'

Shades thought about this. Then he smiled.

'Our tethered goat,' he said.

'It won't work if I'm tethered, though, will it?'

He stood up. He hesitated a moment.

To the man who'd kicked me, he said, 'Cut him loose.'

Mansour's shooting had been a grievous error, but that aside, the ambivalence of Shades towards Amarayn and myself should have been enough for me to have drawn the correct conclusion straight off. Shades was Inter Services Intelligence, or ISI. He commanded Pakistan's reception committee for bin Laden. Only I had expected the ISI to be waiting at the far end of the pipeline, at Spin Boldak, just on the Afghan side of the frontier, or possibly over the other side in Spin Boldak's twin smuggling town of Chaman.

Not here, not this far along the smugglers' route.

Surely some mistake.

Shades said something and I had to ask him to repeat it.

'The lady – your wife?'

We ate freshly slaughtered goat in a stew flavoured with oregano and garlic. It was delicious. Wonderful thing about meat that hasn't been chilled. It tastes so much better. I wiped my plate clean with the nan.

'What's it to you?' I said.

'Just asking,' Shades said. 'No offence. I mean,' he added, looking round slyly at his men, 'we wouldn't want to stop you fucking her if you are man and wife.'

There were guffaws and sniggers all round. Shades put his head back and had a good laugh at his own vulgarity. It gave me a nasty whiff of his breath and a good look at his teeth.

Two expensive gold caps.

Not the kind of dental work generally available in Argestan. Not the kind many residents of Kandahar could afford, either.

'I can tell you're the type who likes to watch,' I said when the sniggering stopped.

He didn't find that at all funny and for a moment I thought he'd change his mind and have me tied up again.

In my presence they spoke Pashto. Three were almost certainly Pashtuns, but not necessarily from the Afghan side of the border. They looked tame. Too much city. Too soft. Quetta or Peshawar born and bred. The other four were a puzzle. The cook might have been Tajik. I really wasn't sure. That left two. They seemed to be Baluch, landless peasants. Ruffians. Hired guns who knew no other trade.

Shades was a Punjabi. I would stake a goodly portion of my share of the reward money on it. Not Pashtun, not Sindhi and obviously not Baluch. Not Serahi, either. Doing a good job of hiding it, but he was a Punjabi nonetheless and a military man to boot. All he needed was a shave, a short back and sides, moustache, swagger stick and blancoed puttees and he'd be the very model of a modern Pakistani major general.

Well, a major, maybe.

Khyber Rifles, possibly, regiment of the late military dictator General Zia ul-Haq.

I wondered how long it would be before Shades called me 'old chap' in imitation of a Sandhurst-trained officer.

He could even be a Sandhurst graduate himself.

I said, 'Aren't you going to give her something to eat?'

Nobody stopped me when I got up and went over to the pot and heaped what was left of the stew onto my tin plate. I tore off half a nan and walked over to where Amarayn sat, well away from us, her back turned.

I stood in front of her. I handed her the plate and the bread. She took them without saying anything.

I walked back and sat down.

'Who are you?'

I didn't answer.

Shades fumbled for a fag and lit up.

I had a feeling he already knew.

'You're not Afghan,' he said in English.

179

'That right?'

'You're too damn cheeky.'

Cheeky. The story of my life.

Tea arrived, but I wasn't offered any.

I said, 'You're no fucking Afghan, either.'

'Why you say that?'

'Because you've got bloody awful table manners.'

Shades bristled.

'What you mean?'

'What kind of Afghan doesn't offer a guest tea before everyone else?'

'You're my prisoner, not a guest.'

He said it with a sneer.

'To an Afghan there's little difference. A prisoner is a guest who can't leave, that's all.'

Not quite true, but did he know that?

Shades turned and gestured to one of his men. The gunman brought me a glass and poured tea up to the brim. There was a bowl with boiled sweets. Lacking sugar, the custom was to put a sweet in one's mouth and then drink the green tea, which I did.

'And the woman,' I said.

Shades didn't argue, but I could tell from his expression that I wasn't very popular.

He'd lost face.

Anyway, he probably treated a dog better than he did a woman. The bastard. Not that I was any kind of example.

I got up to wash in preparation for prayers.

'You're British,' Major Shades said.

I didn't respond.

'You're a Talib.'

I didn't answer that, either.

*

The cold kept waking me.

I dozed off and on, but the *potu* wasn't enough to keep me warm or dry from the dew that wetted the sand. It gave me a chance to think, to consider my position. To review what had happened since I'd left Kandahar and how Mansour had died.

We'd cocked it up somewhere along the line, blundering into this bunch. I hadn't been briefed, and Mansour hadn't said anything. He'd paid for our mistake.

I told myself that if I'd paid more attention to our rear he'd still be alive.

I felt his loss. Mansour was my link with all that had gone before, with Aisha and Nabibullah, with Abdur Rahman also, and indirectly with Mathilde and the others.

With him around I had not felt entirely alone.

I did now.

Shades seemed to accept me as a Muslim, but for some reason did not seem to think I posed any threat, or perhaps he had some other purpose in mind. I'd suggested one, after all. Maybe he did know, and really did see me as an asset. The rest was show for his goons.

His men had built a fire – not the most sensible thing to do at night on a mountaintop in my view, but understandable with the temperature plunging below zero – and they lay down around the embers. Several smoked hashish before sleeping, and Major Shades didn't seem to mind. Amarayn and I got our heads down well beyond their circle. We were also far away from each other, almost on opposite sides of the fire. I knew she must be cold. The burka was thin. I didn't know exactly what she had on underneath, but it was probably loose-fitting cotton trousers and a blouse or tunic. No socks or tights, almost certainly.

Shades had two gunmen on watch on three-hour stretches. One squatted at the head of the gully, looking down it.

The second clambered up onto the rim of scrub and rock that formed our perimeter, watching the slopes and the plain below.

Neither paid me any attention.

After all, where could I run to?

Now and then the second gunman would move to keep himself warm, and check another sector of the roughly circular patch of ground we occupied.

Occasionally I would hear them murmuring together. They'd share a cigarette, glancing back at their boss to satisfy themselves that he was still asleep and wasn't watching them. Major Shades obliged them by snoring loudly and it was only when he stopped that they would both turn and stare at the place where he lay curled up under a blanket, fully dressed and with his boots still on, the laces loosened.

By the sweet stench I knew it wasn't tobacco the sentries were smoking in their shared cigarette.

Seven gunmen. Too many. These two wouldn't be a problem, and I could make it to the Jeep and jump-start it. But what then? Where would I go? I was meant to be here, quite why I wasn't entirely sure. Much as I didn't like it, I had to bide my time. I needed intelligence about my captors' intentions. I assumed it was what Mathilde would have wanted. All I could hope for was an opportunity to swing the odds more in my favour when show time came around.

Which it would. I just had no idea how soon.

They had established a routine of sorts, suggesting they had been in the area a while. They'd got a good position. They had prepared it for a long stay. There was a rubbish pit, not far from where Mansour was buried, and a primitive latrine had been dug on the far side among some boulders.

Each man had his own tasks. The more mundane jobs were switched around to share the load. There was a system in place. There was even a cook who used oregano and garlic.

Major Shades made sure the place was kept tidy, just as a professional soldier would be expected to do. His men carried their weapons with them at all times, even if some of them were dopeheads.

They were waiting.

I was wide awake, but it wasn't the cold.

This time it was a scuffling noise. I thought it might be rats, or something larger rooting around for something to eat, scraps left over from the evening meal. A jackal, maybe.

I couldn't be bothered to move. I lay on my side, eyes closed, listening to the noises, wondering vaguely why the sentries didn't scare whatever it was away, and trying to identify the source. I wished it would go away. I think I slept again. When I woke I realized there was a struggle in progress. Something was being dragged along the ground. It was heavy, whatever it was.

Reluctantly, I rolled over and opened my eyes.

The sentries were nowhere to be seen.

The fire had died. Five grey lumps showed the positions of the other men.

Although unwilling to lose what little warmth I had under my *potu*, I twisted round.

Jesus, it was cold.

I clenched my jaw to stop my teeth chattering.

My feet were numb. I couldn't feel my toes.

I thought maybe she'd changed her position. Moved elsewhere to sleep. Somewhere more sheltered, more private.

More comfortable.

I sat up. Still no sign of her.

The chill crept up my back, my neck.

A murmur of voices reached me from over on the far side, among the boulders. A laugh, quickly suppressed.

Amarayn had gone.

When I found her she was on her back. One man pinned her arms to the ground above her head by kneeling on them. He had his hands on her shoulders. He was leaning on them.

Amarayn moved her head from side to side, trying to raise herself. She couldn't speak or cry out because they'd gagged her with a rag, but she was fighting hard.

The second sentry sat astride her legs, facing his comrade. He was giggling. He grabbed hold of her burka and ripped it as far as her waist. He leaned over her and ran his hands up under the garment and clutched at her breasts.

He sat back again and attacked the waistband of her trousers.

Neither gunman saw me.

They were too excited to notice.

Both had their rifles slung across their backs.

'Hurry,' said the sentry holding her arms. 'Come on, quick.'

The second man pulled her trousers down to her thighs.

He started to undo his own clothes. It was never a simple business with Afghan clothing, even in a rape. He had to fumble under his tunic to find the knot in the cord that held the baggy pants up, undo it with the fingers of both hands, and then let the trousers drop.

While he was busily engaged with both hands I stood up straight. I took a step forward into the open.

I picked up the stone with my right hand. It fitted nicely. It had a good edge. I swung my arm back and let him have the full force of it.

Like a sledgehammer on a pendulum.

There was a dull crunch and he went over onto his side without a word. He didn't move or make a sound.

His mate stopped what he was doing. He tried to rise and at the same time free his rifle and bring it up to the firing position.

He was trying to do too many things at once.

His trousers fell down.

He just wasn't quick enough.

He took the stone in the teeth before he could cry out.

I threw myself at him.

I'm not sure how many times I hit him. I only know that when I got up off his chest he didn't have much face left.

My right hand was wet and slippery.

I dropped the stone and took his Kalashnikov, wiping my fingers on his shirt.

There were signs of life among the remaining five sleepers.

Someone was talking loudly, insistently, rousing the others.

I recognized the voice. It belonged to Major Shades.

The moon went in again and the world darkened.

Amarayn was going through the dead man's pockets.

I never wanted it to happen.

'Hold it,' I said.

Shades and one of his men were advancing towards the boulders, but they couldn't see where I was. They moved apart to make it more difficult to take them on, but their night vision wasn't fully there yet, and mine was. I could see Major Shades moving his head this way and that, searching for the source of the two words I had flung at them.

They hesitated for a moment, then kept coming.

'Drop your weapons.'

Shades complied immediately.

His companion was a touch slow.

I breathed in and held it.

Held the foresight steady.

My forefinger took up the slack.

He wasn't just slow. He was going for a shot.

Bloody stupid thing to do.

The moon came out again.

I double-tapped him. Saw him go down.

Major Shades flung himself to the ground, too, made a grab for the Kalashnikov and raised it.

That was a mistake, also. So unnecessary. Again, I fired twice. I had the satisfaction of seeing one of two rounds go in, just above the knee. The moon peeked coyly out of the cloud and gave off enough light to see the flick of his clothing as the bullet hit.

Shades dropped his weapon.

He squirmed about, holding his leg.

To his credit, he didn't make a lot of noise.

Not that he needed to.

Everyone else was awake now, even the dopeheads.

There were still three unaccounted for.

One burst out of his blankets in a panic and made a run for it, racing for the far side of the hollow.

He was probably the cook.

I wasn't about to waste my rounds.

Two other targets in view.

One knelt right where he'd been sleeping, brought his weapon up, waiting for a sound or movement, a muzzle flash, something to go on. He was the clean-shaved one with long hair, the bloke with the cellphone.

The last man dodged off to the left, out of sight, in a running crouch.

I didn't want him on my left flank or working his way round to my rear, so I changed my position, rolling right.

The kneeling gunman saw movement, loosed off a long burst.

Too long. Too high.

I moved again, working my way on my stomach round the edge of the hollow to the south-west where the gully was. I'd lost my turban and a sandal in the scramble among the rocks.

'Bilal.'

She hissed my name. She was right behind me, an arm extended, holding something. How she got there I didn't know. She must have followed close behind. Or maybe she'd reached there before me, intending to flee down the gully and get to the Jeep.

She thrust it at me.

'Take.'

It was cool and smooth, about three times the size of an egg and a lot heavier. A grenade, frag or phospherous I couldn't tell. It was too dark again to make it out.

I didn't know if it was a four- or a seven-second fuse.

She must have found it on the assailant whose face I'd effectively removed. I remembered her searching his combat jacket. Now I knew why.

I pulled the pin. Let the lever fly. Counted one and two and three, then spun the grenade in an arc towards where the fire was, a bit to the left.

Pressed myself down. Pushed Amarayn's head down, too.

It seemed like eternity.

A flower of white heat burst into blossom, lighting up the mountain. An upside-down firework fountain of white light, sizzling and burning prettily, it sent sprays of fire in all directions like the tendrils of a monstrous jellyfish.

'Talk,' I said.

'Where did you learn to do that?'

Shades meant the dressing.

'Never mind,' I said. 'Just talk.'

'About what?'

'Who were you blokes waiting for?'

'I don't know what you mean.'

'No?'

I didn't have time to piss about.

'Talk.'

I kicked the leg that had taken the bullet.

Hard.

Major Shades screamed.

'This is getting boring,' I said. 'Talk, or I'll tear the dressing off and you can bleed to death.'

'My God,' he said. 'My God. What kind of person are you?'

'God's got fuck all to do with it. Now talk.'

I raised the stock of my AK-74 and held it over the wound.

'You'll black out,' I said. 'It's only natural. But don't worry, I'll bring you round again in plenty of time to feel the pain. You're fit and healthy. Your heart won't pack up.'

'Please. What do you want to know?'

'I told you already what I want.'

'All right, mister. Just stop, okay?'

'Talk. Starting with name, rank and number.'

'I am Captain Jameel. Pakistan Army. Number—'

'Forget the number. You're ISI.'

He nodded.

'Yes?'

'Yes.'

'What are you doing here?'

'My orders are to wait.'

'Wait for what?'

'I don't know—'

I hit the knee with the rifle butt. Just where I said I would.

'Don't fucking lie to me.'

I gave him a minute or two and when he'd calmed down a little and stopped blubbering I lit one of his fags and put it in his mouth. Snot was running down from his nose into his moustache. I remembered the Afghans and their hospitality in Oruzgan. They were noble people. I wasn't.

'Come on,' I said. 'I'm getting really impatient.'

I turned the weapon around and rested the rifle barrel ever so gently on his knee.

He shivered and shook.

'The Sheikh,' he said. 'We were waiting for the Sheikh.'

'When?'

'I don't know.'

I lifted the barrel off his knee, moved it up, held it over the dressing. About four inches away. I told myself this creep wasn't going to get between me and my share of the money.

Nothing and nobody was going to do that.

'When?'

'We were told – I was told – any time in the next ten days.'

Ten days in Afghan time could mean three days or twenty. But neither Jameel nor the Sheikh was Afghan.

'Starting when?'

'Yesterday.'

'So this is day nine?'

'Yes.'

'Why was he coming here?'

'He was on his way out.'

'To where?'

'Across the border, then I really don't know. My orders were to receive him here. To escort him to the border and into Gulestan.'

'You were going to sell him to the Americans.'

'No. No way.'

'You're a freelance. A bounty hunter. You're not army. You're not Jameel, either. You're full of shit and I'm going to shoot you like a fucking dog. Right here. Now. After I've had a little fun hurting you.'

'No . . .'

I raised the barrel higher, the muzzle a couple of inches from his face.

He shook his head. 'I'm Captain Jameel—'

'How many with him?'

I waved the weapon over his leg.

'An advance party. Maybe three or four. Maybe the same number with him, and another group bringing up the rear. That's what I was told, but the numbers vary. For God's sake—'

'Why's that?'

'It's a question of balancing protection with the need to remain inconspicuous – and move quickly.'

I didn't believe him. It was far too few.

'Moving at night?'

'Oh, yes. Of course. Only at night.'

'How did you stay in touch with your people?'

'Satphone.'

'The handset your chum was carrying?'

'The one you shot just now. Him.'

'Who's your contact?'

'My CO.'

'Who is?

'Brigadier Muhammad Asifi Orakzai.'

'Christ, another Pashtun working for the Punjabi military. Where is he?'

'Quetta. But he'll be moving down to Chaman tomorrow. What are you going to do with me? You can't shoot me.'

'I can leave you. You won't be going anywhere. The wolves will get you.'

'Please.'

'Shut the fuck up.'

'Look—'

'Did you report my capture – and the woman?'

'Yes.'

'How would you signal the Sheikh's arrival?'

He didn't say anything. For a moment I thought he'd passed out. He seemed to be trying to decide what to say, so I touched the dressing with the AK-74's large muzzle brake. Captain Jameel started to shake all over again.

'I was to say the party had arrived.'

'Just that? Nothing else?'

'Nothing else.'

'How did you charge the satphone?'

'There's a generator. In the tunnel we use as a base. We only use it for that, and for emergencies.'

'All that shooting might have scared him off.'

'It's possible.'

'Are you in touch with the Sheikh?'

'No.'

He looked at me like I was crazy.

'Crap.'

'Mister—'

'You lying prick.'

I poked him with the muzzle.

Again. Much harder this time.

He screamed again. It sounded convincing. I didn't think he was putting it on.

'Why didn't you put a guard on me? Lock me in the Jeep or tie me up? And give the woman a safe place?'

'You are the Englishman. Everyone talks about the English Talib. The one they call Bilal. You are Bilal, aren't you?'

'I'm asking the questions, pal. What else do you know?'

'You're a Taliban commander. You have a reputation as a fighter. I thought I would make use of your presence. It would be helpful to have you here. You said so yourself.'

'You could have sold me too.'

He shook his head. 'No.'

He looked terrible. Punjabis are often dark-skinned, but right then Captain Jameel's face was ashen.

191

'Any morphine in that medical kit of yours, captain?'

He nodded.

'You want some?'

Jameel grunted.

I said, 'I need the who, the what, the when, the where, the how and the why. I need all of it.'

He said yes.

'You're just going to have to tell me the truth. Tell me the truth and I'll keep the pain away. Lie, keep stuff back – and I'll hurt you so bad you'll beg for a bullet. Don't think I won't know the difference between the truth and a lie, pal. And don't think I won't do it, either. I have a really low boredom threshold. I could do with some entertainment. Do we understand each other?'

He said we did. He said it in a persuasive way. He was crying when he said it, and just this once I believed him.

'Can you use this?'

Amarayn shook her head.

I put Jameel's weapon down next to her.

'You stay,' I said. 'You see something ... you call me. Okay?'

I gave her the thumbs up.

'All right?'

She looked at me. Nodded.

She squatted in the tunnel and I left her there.

I was taking a chance. She could have come after me and shot me in the back for all I knew.

Still, I shouldered the AK-74 and shaded the flashlight with my free hand, walking doubled up down the sloping tunnel. I moved slowly, alert to the possibility of tripwires laid by Captain Jameel and his crew.

It descended steeply for about twenty-five metres, then turned right. This next section was wider and higher. There were Chinese anti-tank mines, but without the fuses. Bulgarian and Egyptian Kalashnikovs. Polish and Czech RPG launchers, yet no grenades. Russian 12.7 mm machine guns, greased up in their boxes. All of it crated up and piled up to the roof on either side, leaving just enough room for me to squeeze through.

I thought they'd wisely stored the ammunition separately, in the other bunker.

The cave-turned-tunnel turned right again.

Abdur Rahman had been both smart and lucky. He'd worked for Quilty. He'd worked for the Taliban. He'd worked for Captain Jameel of the ISI. He'd played them off against one another. He'd even worked for me, helping to get the embassy silver out of Kabul and down south, using his protection as a senior Khad official to get my people and the goods down the road to Kandahar and through Argestan to the border at Spin Boldak, then employing his ISI credentials and links with the notorious Gabizai to get us through Gulestan to Quetta.

Behind a doorway screened off with a blanket lay a subterranean chamber.

In effect a bomb shelter.

There were five bunks, a table built of ammunition boxes.

Blankets neatly folded on the bunks.

Sheets and pillows, still in cellophane.

Nestlé drinking water from Karachi, boxes of plastic one-litre bottles with their distinctive blue labels.

A large aerial map of Afghanistan on one wall, courtesy of the US military, with a sticker showing it had been bought in a Covent Garden map shop.

A pack of video casettes.

Shiny, unused paraffin lamps. Candles in their wrappers. Five jerrycans of petrol. A generator painted bright red, presumably the one Jameel had mentioned. Waterproof matches. Rechargeable battery-powered flashlights (five). Cheap porcelain plates and glasses.

Tinned fruit. Tea. Biscuits.

A cardboard box of pills of different kinds. Antiobiotics and painkillers.

There was enough stuff for someone to live here in relative comfort for weeks rather than days.

What I was looking for would probably be on the other side, in the second tunnel.

There was a colour poster of Saudi Arabia.

Even a kiblah sticker so the sheikh could pray facing Mecca.

A nice touch that, I thought.

THIRTEEN

I dragged two bodies to one side, one at a time, grasping their ankles under each arm and walking backwards. I dropped them next to each other and covered them with their *potus*. I wanted to stop the flies from clustering on the mouths and eyes of the dead once the sun rose and warmed the place up.

Humans are never particularly pleasant dead or alive, but seeing them being gorged upon by bluebottles is obscene.

'We'll be doing a lot of walking, but it can't be helped.'

I started digging one grave for both men.

Amarayn watched.

I said, 'We'll move at night, lie up in the day.'

The work warmed me up.

It was going to be a tight fit.

She was clutching her torn burka to herself. She didn't react in any way to what I said. Her face wasn't covered. She looked at me with those troubled and troubling green eyes. A searching look. I could only imagine what she might be thinking. So. This foreigner was no different. He killed, and perhaps he too would take his crude pleasure wherever he found it. A predator. Perhaps that was all she knew of men, or expected of them.

I took a break from the spadework and found her some Afghan men's clothes that seemed clean. At least, they didn't stink and were without bloodstains or bullet holes. With a series of gestures I suggested she change into them.

'You can be my younger brother,' I told her. 'Or my son.'

195

She shook her head. No.

She preferred her own torn clothing.

When I'd finished digging I drank some water – breakfast – and rolled the bodies into the hole, one on top of the other.

They did not look comfortable, but they'd never know it.

I took a stick and drew a picture in the sand. I drew the outline of a tall man in a robe with a turban and a beard.

'Osama bin Laden,' I said.

Amarayn stared down at it.

'You're his wife?'

I could manage that much in Pashto.

She shook her head.

'No?' I said.

She shook her head. Emphatically. She reached over and took the stick from me. She drew another, smaller figure next to mine. No beard this time. Shorter. Slimmer. A man – or a boy.

She said, 'Son of Osama.'

Osama was reputed to have three or four wives, and several children – perhaps as many as two dozen. It was empire building at its most basic. Or, in the case of bin Laden, network building, cementing international relationships among the world's dispossessed, its outlaws. Building al-Qaeda.

'What's his name?' At first I thought she meant that the figure she'd drawn in the dirt was her son. Her child by Osama. But he was too old for her to be the mother. She was the last wife, after all, and probably the only Afghan. Then I grasped what she meant.

'The son of Osama,' I said slowly in Pashto, 'is your man, your husband.'

A nod. 'Yes.'

So that was it. The man who had come to her mud house and wanted to be left alone to rest and think wasn't Osama at all, but one of his sons.

'His name?'

'Naim.'

I pointed at the drawing of Naim. I gestured, making a beckoning motion with my hand.

'Naim's coming – here?'

A nod.

I took the stick and pointed at Osama bin Laden.

'Osama?' I made the same gesture.

She nodded. Less certainly.

'Yes?'

I pointed to both figures, then repeated the come-hither.

She looked unsure now. She shrugged. She pointed at me, using her thumb, because to point a finger directly at someone is considered downright rude, as it is in the Arab world.

She imitated someone holding a firearm.

Then she pointed at the two figures.

Made a shooting noise with her lips.

Drew her hand across her throat, then pointed at me.

She was asking if I was going to kill the two of them.

In which case she had no reason to tell me what she knew.

I smiled. Shook my head.

I wasn't going to kill the kid. I didn't have any reason to. There wasn't any money on his head as far as I knew.

He wasn't part of the contract.

Osama was a different matter entirely.

'No,' I lied. 'Of course not.'

I don't think she believed me.

'You're going to walk all the way there with the woman? Why not take the Jeep Cherokee? It would be four or five hours instead of two or three days.'

I didn't answer. There was only so much Jameel needed to know. I had carried him into the shelter and put him on one of the beds. I left water and food and what remained of the morphine next to him.

'You better go,' he said. 'They'll be along soon, the Americans, along with my people.'

'I know.'

He was looking better. He'd slept and had eaten. He looked stronger.

'But you have to complete your part of our deal,' he said.

'And if I don't?'

He looked at me. We both knew the answer. There was nothing he could do, other than bear a bigger grudge than he did already.

He didn't know it, but I still needed him.

I took out the satphone. This was what he meant. It was about three times the size and weight of a normal mobile cellphone, with a short aerial. I had let him make one call earlier that morning. I listened. He spoke in English so I would miss nothing. God knew what his brigadier thought, but I didn't care. Jameel reported that he was wounded, that half his men were dead in an attack during the night.

He got no further.

I'd snatched the phone out of his hand, switched it off.

He hadn't got round to saying anything more about Amarayn and myself.

Now I held it up. I switched it back on. It was fully charged. The phone had GPS software. While it was on, its location could be monitored down to a few yards. But he'd have to take it out into the open to establish a signal.

'I'm going to leave this with you.'

'Let me have it.'

It was the type the US special forces handed out to their Afghan allies.

'Please.'

I could see what he was thinking. He knew our plans from what he'd told me, and from my questions. He could tell his people and they'd be able to head us off. They had plenty of time. All was not lost. Captain Jameel still dreamed of a field marshal's baton in his knapsack, or the Pakistani equivalent.

I did want his employers to pick up the GPS signal. But that was all, and I thought I had found a way to achieve both objectives.

Jameel tried to pull himself up into a sitting position, but stopped because it hurt too much.

Or maybe that's what he wanted me to think.

I'd changed his dressing, and that had hurt, too.

The tissue was a healthy pink. It was growing back. It didn't smell. There was little necrosis. He was in good shape, all things considered. He was going to live if I let him, and with a little effort he'd be able to hobble out of here into the open once we'd left.

'Did you kill them all?' he said.

'No such luck. Two ran off. Escaped. One of them was your cook. One of the would-be rapists got away, but he's in bad shape. He left a trail of blood. He can't have got far. He was crawling on his hands and knees. Probably concussion. I killed two with a phosphorus grenade. Not a pretty sight. Grilled to a turn, you might say. I took out one of the men who was trying to rape the girl. I'm afraid I lost my temper and bludgeoned him to death. I shot another who was with you, and who went for his weapon after I warned him . . .'

'He didn't understand.'

'Bollocks.'

'They were my men.'

'You should have taken better care of them and shouldn't have listened to me. You should've kept me tied up. Put me in here with a couple of guards. I'd still be your prisoner now. As for your men, less hashish and more discipline might have saved their lives.'

'And the woman?'

'What about her?'

'You're taking her with you?'

'Why not?'

'She'll be a burden. What use is she?'

'Better than leaving her here to run the risk of being raped all over again.'

'Why bother?'

'You mean why didn't I just let those two arseholes get their jollies, have their way with her? Maybe I should have woken you up so you could take your turn. Is that what you would have wanted?'

Truth was I felt bad about what had happened. I blamed myself. I hadn't thought. If I'd said she was my wife – or sister – then Amarayn and I would have slept near each other. It would have been some protection – and a lot better than being left on her own to tempt the goons.

Odds were it would never have happened.

'What was she to you?'

I felt almost sorry for Captain Jameel. He hadn't a clue. He was little better than a thug, but he had failed in his mission, and failure had reduced him to a pathetic figure.

He was still hoping, and trying to hide it.

He said, 'We both made mistakes.'

'I'm making one now.'

'How's that?'

'I'm leaving you here alive, Jameel, and to be honest I really don't know why I'm doing it. The world would be better off without you, and that includes the officers' mess of the Khyber Rifles or whatever unit it is you belong to.'

'Bastard.'

'I'm all heart, Jameel.'

I could sleepwalk it I knew it so well.

From above, the Hada hills looked like a cloven hoofprint in the sand. The hoof pointed north-east. The back end of it was clipped by the Kandahar highway like a bent straw fallen across the spoor – it was marked on maps as the A75 – that ran all the way to the Pakistan frontier town of Chaman.

I could see it with my eyes shut.

I'd been here twenty years before, and again in 1996.

It seemed like last week.

The indentations left in the sand by the hoof were the gullies and valleys, marked by tracks running from the south-west to the north-east. They were used by farmers and were to be avoided for obvious reasons. The ridges left by the hoofprint formed the high ground in the huddle of hills Amarayn and I were now forced to traverse on foot. There was no vegetation extensive enough to provide cover, only the rocks and the shadows they cast on the beige landscape.

A secondary road – secondary in the theoretical sense, because even the highway wouldn't be classified as any kind of road anywhere but Afghanistan – skirted our position to the south and east, running along the slopes and then up to the village of Argestan that gave its name to the area. The village lay on the floor of the valley, and commanded a crossroads.

From the crossroads one minor road led north through Khoram Khel village and on to Qalat in Zabol province. Another broke out to the west, eventually joining the Kandahar highway at Mandi Sar, just to the south of the city. The third ran east to Maruf, then north-east, roughly parallel to, but south of, the main Kandahar–Kabul highway.

It took two hours to reach the north-western edge of the hoofprint. Here the Hada hills descended steeply to the plain some 500 metres below. We had used the ground as best we could, taking care not to show ourselves on the skyline. We didn't speak. It took all our concentration to negotiate the boulders and rocks, climbing up and scrambling down. The sun was warm on our faces, the west wind chilled our backs.

Now we rested, staring at the land stretching out ahead

and below. A simple goatherd's track went across our front, east to west. In the distance I could make out Argestan village, and far beyond it, on the very edge of my vision, the misty blue slopes of the hills rising from the plain that formed my objective.

It was a desolate place, and down on the plain there was no cover.

I decided we would eat, then sleep.

We would wait for nightfall, then cross the low ground.

Our first visitors appeared just before 10 a.m.

Amarayn crawled under the rocks in her tunic and pants, rolling up her burka in a bundle and taking it with her.

They came from the north-west. Two Blackhawks, probably from the 101st Airborne or the 10th Special Forces Group at Kandahar airbase.

We heard them long before we saw them. The first stood off, the second passed under it and circled the Hada hills, riding a long lazy circle on its side, leaning right over, the rotor blades slapping the air like a motorized egg beater.

As he swept by us at the north-east end of the hills I could see the machine-gunner in the open door, strapped in and wearing body armour, ballistic helmet on his head, legs sticking out, braced against the gravitational pull, the wind beating at his clothing, gloved hands on his twin M60s.

Looking for targets.

Dropping its nose, the Blackhawk came in low and stopped, raising dust and dirt. Then its partner danced in over the top. They played this game for several minutes, airborne go-karts trying to draw fire, sliding over and under each other, playing point then back-up, switching roles constantly, a war-like aerial ballet seeking signs of life, signs of panic, signs of resistance.

Tempting whoever was on the ground to break cover.

No way, gentlemen.

They droned away again, one forward, one back, drifting back to the airbase south-east of Kandahar.

I could imagine the aircrew, setting out full of gung-ho enthusiasm in their clean desert fatigues. Virgins in the business of war, gum in their cheeks, still smelling of aftershave, eager to test their manhood in action.

Then the disappointment settling in, the crackling voice over their headsets ordering the boys to turn for home, guns unblooded, turning back to flapjacks and maple syrup and American coffee and the prospect of another day spent hanging about, hoping for something to happen to break the routine of letter-writing, card games, press-ups and jerking off.

Killing people like us on the ground would be as remote, as detached, as stepping on ants.

They didn't see us. I was pretty sure of it.

It wasn't us they were interested in, but the encampment where we'd spent our eventful night.

A recce.

'American?' Amarayn wanted to know.

'Yes. American.'

She showed no expression. Just the green eyes searching my face, reading me in places words didn't work.

They'd be back. Or someone would be. I was sure of it.

She pointed at me with her thumb again.

Then she patted the air with the flat of her hand, palm down, between hip and knee. As if measuring the height of something.

She meant children.

'You?'

She meant did I have kids.

'No,' I lied.

'Woman?'

'No.'

Incredulous. 'No woman?'

That was why I had lied.

To tell an Afghan he or she is divorced was arguably the worst possible insult. It didn't get any nastier than that. And to be divorced was to be disgraced, to be unworthy, a social outcast. It was far worse than being an opium addict. At least addiction was something deserving a little sympathy.

It wouldn't do any good to try to explain that it was different in the West, that it was in fact better our way.

Amarayn looked at me, head on one side, her mouth open slightly, lips parted, white teeth nibbling at a thumbnail. She regarded me thoughtfully.

'Why?'

I shrugged. I patted my AK-74.

My job, in other words. My calling.

I could tell from her expression she didn't understand. In Afghanistan every male from the age twelve could use a firearm, use it well, and aspire to owning his own. It was no bar to marriage and a family.

What was so off-putting about being a gunman that marriage was out of the question?

As excuses go, it was pretty lame.

In time of peace, Afghan communities would expect never to know of cases of divorce, separation, sexual assault, rape or molestation of minors. Especially in rural areas. These things were unheard of. Whatever miseries, cruelties, vices or abuses occurred between men and women, they happened behind closed doors, behind the high walls of a family compound, within the very private world of the marital state – but never, never in public.

Affairs discovered were settled in blood, or blood money.

Extramarital affairs didn't get the option.

What had almost happened to Amarayn back there in the

Hada hills was a symptom of the exceptional times, of the general lawlessness, of a twenty-three-year-long lapse in social order, of men released from ties of family and community.

I looked at her. I couldn't help myself.

Give a man enough time out here and the merest twitch of a burka, just the way the hips made the cloth move, the hint of a kohl-lined eye, the wave of a feminine hand, would be enough to stir the blood.

For me it was the delicacy of Amarayn's hands and feet, the curve of her neck, the soft and pale throat, the wide and full mouth, the long eyelashes, those large eyes.

I was suddenly aware that we lay close enough below the overhanging rocks to feel the warmth from each other's bodies.

And she a married woman.

We were already adulterers in thought if not deed by the standards of her people.

Amarayn saw me looking at her. She looked – straight back, quite unabashed.

There was boldness in her look, and a curiosity that matched my own.

The moment passed, and she started to move.

'Not yet.'

I held her forearm, then peered out cautiously, lifting my head very slowly.

No sudden movements.

I let go, but she didn't pull away.

'All right.' I nodded to her. 'It's okay.'

When the sun reached its zenith our second party of visitors arrived. There were dozens of them. They came over the crest of the hill on foot.

Soon they were all around us.

We heard their feet daintily tip-tapping and skittering on

205

the rocks, their teeth ripping at the meagre vegetation, their stomachs rumbling, and finally their rank smell.

The goats nearest our position saw us, but didn't so much as pause in their pursuit of food. We were entirely ignored by the long-haired creatures. The goatherd's whistle came from below. He was calling to them, talking to his charges, grunting and whistling, urging them off the hill.

As their keeper turned away, his feet kicking up gravel and dust, I raised my head very slowly. He was a boy, barefoot, no more than fourteen, with only a stout stick for his protection.

No dog.

Thank Christ.

Afghan dogs were aggressive, powerful creatures, as big as mountain lions, with massive jaws. Their sense of smell would have given us away.

I didn't want to think what I would have had to do.

The goatherd was nothing but a child.

Amarayn was looking at me, reading the death in my mind.

She knew. At least, that's how it felt.

Sometime in the afternoon a tractor and trailer appeared, leaving a trail of dust behind it. It moved from our left, the north-west, across our front to the right, and appeared to be heading for the village of Argestan. Three men were on the tractor. They were going at a fair crack, although at this distance – perhaps a mile – it was difficult to judge speed with any accuracy. From start to finish they were visible for about twenty minutes.

I prayed while Amarayn kept watch, her back turned.

When I'd finished, I raised my chin at her.

'You, Amarayn? Pray?'

She didn't answer, just turned away.

I thought she might want to use my *potu* as a prayer mat. I picked it up swung it around my shoulders.

She was listening, head on one side.

'What is it?'

'Shhh.'

'I don't hear anything.'

She waved a hand at me.

Shut up.

I could hear the wind, though, and the high-pitched call of eagles or falcons or whatever they were, circling unseen above the rocks behind us.

It was a good three minutes before my ears picked up the sound. It was an aircraft. A helicopter. At first I thought there were two.

Amarayan had wriggled on her stomach backwards into her hiding place, but I stayed where I was. I just kept still.

The big-bellied beast of a Chinook clattered overhead, rotors at both ends.

It went down slowly, nose first, as if testing the plain for a place to rest. It halted near the track where the tractor had passed by not long before. The back hatch opened and troops emerged. Within a few minutes a tent had been raised, and a Humvee rolled out the back of the helicopter.

The Chinook rose up in a ball of yellow dust and lumbered away.

The camp was about 800 metres in front of us, to the north-east.

'What are they doing?' Amarayn asked in Pashto.

A second tent went up. A long aerial protruded from it.

Camouflage netting was being put up over both tents.

The Humvee described a wide circle around the position.

Groups of men dug foxholes and filled sandbags, three of the outposts parallel to the track. One more to the north-east, another to the south-west, nearest us, about 500 metres off.

They'd set up a temporary checkpoint, and had established sentry posts and fighting holes.

There was a mortar pit in the centre.

Soldiers strung netting over it, too.

Others were setting up razor wire barricades.

Maybe there were other positions like this, around the other side, blocking positions to hem us in.

Or to prepare for a cordon-and-search.

Instead of waiting for us, they'd come looking.

Amarayn was pointing off to the left.

Like her hearing, her eyesight was better than mine.

Two Humvees were approaching the camp, moving up the track towards the tents to join the lone Humvee already there.

It was like an escape-and-evasion exercise back home. As if they knew we were in the hills, waiting to cross the plain, and they were sitting down there, waiting for us to try to get through. A game boys play, only the toys were real this time.

I reasoned we would not be alone in running the American gauntlet. First, Quilty had wanted details of the smugglers' route. That's why he'd sent in Mathilde as far as Kandahar in the hope she'd get it from me and, failing that, to set up her chase squad to do it the hard way. Second, Quilty would not rely on one shootist alone. He'd want to know the way, and he'd want to make sure that if I failed, another team would be ready to step in and have a crack at the target.

Someone had to be tracking us. Someone fit and experienced. Someone who knew how to be invisible, who knew how to use the ground well, how to move. A professional.

My money was on Felix Zotov, with Mathilde in support, feeding him whatever tactical intelligence she could get and with Yannis providing secure communications.

The sun was almost gone. We were in shadow, and night was not far off. With it came the deep cold. I started to count the soldiers. It would give me some idea of what we were up against.

FOURTEEN

Downhill. Slithering, leaning back, jolting on my heels, feeling the impacts in my knees. The pale stones glowed in reflected starlight, but there was always the risk of mines in the dark nothingness between the rocks.

I wouldn't be able to see the de-miners' little red flags planted along the boundaries of the unofficial minefields.

There weren't supposed to be any mines here – after all, important if illicit business was conducted along this unofficial highway – but I could be wrong.

There was always the chance of tripping over unexploded US ordnance.

Washington's aircrews had deliberately attacked everything moving in or out of Kandahar over a period of several weeks, regardless of whether it was civilian or military.

It wasn't worth worrying about because there was nothing we could do. I pushed it out of my mind.

It was like being underwater, too deep to see much.

I went first.

Amarayn was invisible. But I could hear her, somewhere behind me, gravel scattering under her sandals as she descended as quickly as she dared.

We'd eaten. We both carried water. In my Hudson Bay pack I had a little tinned food, some of the goat meat and a few crusts of stale nan, half-rations sufficient to keep us going for up to a week.

The enemy – well, he was the enemy to all intents and

purposes – had set up what appeared to be three positions. Each one of roughly platoon strength: about thirty soldiers. One – the nearest – lay to the north-east in the direction of the village. Another to the north-west, between the hills and Kandahar city. The last was located to the west, at our backs.

They had left the south wide open.

Correction. They had apparently left the south open.

Why? Was it because Quilty had unleashed his blood-hounds, padding along silently behind us, trailing our spoor?

Was that it?

I glanced back.

Nothing.

I had to think like them. Get into the mind of the US commander as he pored over his maps and briefed his patrol leaders.

They had air cover and artillery support on tap, passive night vision, anti-personnel mines, razor wire – and people.

They lacked for nothing.

I thought it likely they were planning the military version of a driven shoot.

They'd have beaters, the shooters would wait in line, and we would be the partridge driven onto the guns if we waited around too long.

We hit bottom in about six minutes. There was a dip in the ground, then a slight rise. I lay on my stomach and wriggled forward to the lip and rested.

Stared off into the blackness.

The drone of aircraft was constant.

The air traffic was focused on Kandahar airport to the north-east, both incoming and outgoing. Choppers taking forces out on operations, C-140s bringing in supplies to the US garrison, yet more aircraft taking al-Qaeda and Taliban sus-pects off to Guantanamo.

The fixed-wing traffic stayed high until the last possible

moment before dropping down fast in a tight, emergency spiral to evade any ground fire.

Amarayn flopped down next to me.

I asked, 'All right?'

She'd fallen a couple of times and grazed her palms and elbows on the way down, but she did not complain. There wasn't any point. I'd bloodied one foot and lost the nail on a big toe. It was nothing, but somehow I couldn't see Aisha doing any of this.

She said, 'We go?'

'No. Wait.'

At low speed Humvees are very quiet. They are squat and hard to see in broken ground. They were going to be hard to locate at all if they did send out patrols, and I couldn't imagine why they wouldn't. I needed to make sure they weren't waiting for us to walk into them.

Amarayn had come to the conclusion that a burka wasn't the most effective garment for a night march; she'd stuffed it in a Pakistani backpack she'd found, along with water and rations, and she wore the Afghan tunic and trousers I'd given her.

I held up my right hand, opened it twice. Ten metres. I pointed. Straight ahead, north by north-east, in the direction of the nearest enemy position.

She knew what to do.

Amarayn made little noise and moved swiftly in the dark. Whatever she might be feeling, there was no hesitation. When she had made the distance she went down flat, facing her front. Waited, counting off the seconds. Then she turned on her side and looked back. She raised her arm.

All clear. Come on.

I leapfrogged ahead another ten paces.

She was a quick learner. In no time we covered 300 metres without mishap, about half the distance between the foothills we had left behind and the first enemy position.

I was gambling on their sentries being more interested in what went on in front of them than in anything that might make a noise behind them.

For a foreign soldier on alien territory and a long way from home, danger is always 'out there'.

The enemy position in front of us resembled an arrow. It pointed down to the left. We lay where the tip would have been. To our right, about 150 metres off on the eastern edge of the arrowhead, was one of their sentry posts. To our left, in a more or less straight line along the western edge of the arrow, were three more. These three were close and parallel to the so-called secondary road that led to Argestan village. Where the arrowhead would have been spliced into its wooden shaft stood the platoon command – tents, aerials, sandbags, wire, vehicles, camouflage nets and mortar pit.

We could see none of it from where we lay.

The enemy showed no lights.

The road passed just behind us, to our left.

Amarayn was on my immediate right. Our shoulders touched, we were so close. We lay in a gully, a shallow and irregular depression formed by a flash flood long before the drought.

It was only a few inches deep, but as long as we stayed flat and kept quiet, they would not see us unless they literally tripped over us.

I started to leopard-crawl forward.

Using my elbows and knees, rifle held with both hands in front of me, hips flat against the dirt.

The depression ended forty paces to the north. By my estimate the platoon headquarters lay directly ahead, and we were behind, and equidistant to, the first outposts on the western and eastern edges of the arrowhead.

In a matter of a few minutes we had moved inside the triangle that formed the enemy position.

The safest place to be.

I touched Amarayn on the shoulder, and pointed left, then right, indicating where I thought the sentry posts were.

Using the edge of my right hand I indicated where I intended to go.

Forward, and over to the left. Due north. Between the platoon HQ and the three posts along the edge of the road.

Amarayn showed me what she was holding. Held out a hand, opened her fingers. When she smiled I could see her teeth.

It was another grenade.

A tent flap moved and a sliver of golden light spilled out across the desert like a flame.

I froze.

Voices.

Too indistinct to make out.

Two people standing outside the tent, but under the camouflage netting.

'Yeah, I do too,' said a confident American voice.

I could smell more than I could see. Tobacco and something sweeter.

The cigarette glowed as its owner raised it to his mouth and drew on it, then flicked it away in a parabola over the sand.

I didn't move.

Something was said in response. Very quietly.

The confident voice again: 'You reckon?'

The figures moved into the open, sidestepping the big stakes keeping the camouflage in place and ducking under the netting. They straightened up. One was tall, the other short.

'It would help enormously,' said the quiet voice.

Female.

And yes, definitely.

British.

'I don't see why not,' said the American.

They were drawing closer. Perhaps a dozen yards separated us.

I went down very slowly onto one knee.

God, don't screw it up for us.

'It wouldn't take long at all,' said the female voice.

It couldn't be anyone else.

The scent I knew all too well.

'And it would be very helpful, colonel.'

Playing the simpering innocent.

'I'm sure we can arrange something.'

She said, 'You're most kind.'

As if it was a foregone conclusion, whatever it was.

'G'night, ma'am.'

'Good night, colonel, and thank you.'

I heard his feet crunch away briskly, heading east. I couldn't see him because he was against the dark shape of the tent and the netting.

Mathilde stood there, not moving. As if in thought.

Remember Me.

I breathed through my mouth, working on slowing my heartbeat.

My right forefinger had taken up the trigger slack.

Mathilde was less than half a kilo of pressure from a bullet in the brain.

If I had to, I would.

No question.

For a queasy moment I thought she'd made us.

The tent flap twitched, the yellow gold poured out into the night once more.

Mathilde was playing the role of a loyal and fragrant ally,

214

charming the Americans out of any local information that might be useful to her team, a team I was sure was already on the move. The notion that the Americans might have anything worth knowing seemed unlikely, but I knew she would use every trick she could come up with to divert the military away from us.

I just didn't want us to end up like the last Afghan wedding party to be gatecrashed by US forces.

The light vanished as the tent flap closed.

She'd gone back inside.

Amazing what a little improvisation can achieve.

Five minutes after Mathilde had disappeared into the tent and we had pushed on into the darkness beyond, there were two loud bangs, moments apart.

We hit the dirt.

The blasts came from behind us, in the Hada hills.

I counted to five before the top of the hills appeared to erupt. The ammunition was going up. I felt the blast on my back, the hot air ruffling my shirt.

The fireworks went on for several seconds, then died to an eerie glow.

Behind us I saw lights, heard shouted orders, running feet, engines revving.

I'd used some fuel oil, and two sacks of ammonium nitrate fertilizer. There was enough of it back there for six truck bombs. A lot better than C4. That, and detonator cord I found with the other stuff in the second tunnel, was all it took to collapse both structures.

I hadn't used a time pencil. I'd used Jameel. My mobile primer. He had waited until after dark, sensibly enough, then gone snooping around, as I knew he would, hobbling out on his one good leg, waving his satphone around to signal his location strong and clear.

He knew too much, that was all it was. There was no enmity involved. It was also a useful misdirect. It gave the US military something to focus on while we slipped through. I'd set the trap just outside the tunnel entrance, a pressure contact involving two pieces of cardboard and foil covered with sand which Jameel would not have noticed when he stepped on the device.

I felt sorry for him.

Jameel and Quilty were cut of the same cloth.

Almost sorry.

I knew exactly what Jess would have said had she seen me at that moment.

She would have laughed heartily.

Jessica was my dear ex-wife and mother of my kids.

You're a bloody fool, Thomas Morgan, you really are.

You never will grow up, will you? Look what a pickle your childish games have got you into now. You look like shite. You've no one to blame but yourself. You won't get any sympathy from me, laddie. So don't come round asking for any.

Some hero. Jesus.

Just look what you've done to your feet . . .

The sight of me would have made her double up with mirth all over again. She would have laughed until the tears came. Then she'd straighten up and give me a different look, and the tears would have been real this time.

I was filthy, covered head to foot in muck and dried blood.

Yes, I was a funny sight all right, or would have been if it had been light enough to see.

I lay on the ground, heels together, facing the way we had come, from the south-west.

Amarayn lay next to me, her feet next to my head, facing the other way, looking north-east.

It was the only rest we were going to get because the noise of machines was tremendous. The wind carried the dust over to us, into my eyes, even between my lips. I could taste it, feel the grit on my teeth.

I dived back into my private world again. I'd shagged Mathilde and Jess had found out. It was as simple as that. Not once or twice. Frequently. In bed, the back of her car, a swimming pool, a phone box, a cinema, under a pin oak in Green Park and, God help us, most uncomfortably under a poncho in the butts at the army shooting range at Strensall in Yorkshire during a thunderstorm. If it had been once or twice, Jess might have learned to forgive and forget. With time she might. But not months. She used to say I looked younger than my age because I was still a kid, had never learned the rule of cause and effect, and was still, at heart, nicking apples from the barrow down the street. Taking what wasn't mine. Loving it all the more for knowing it was wrong.

Addicted to risk.

Jess had said a lot more besides, much of it true and mostly unpublishable.

They were bringing troops in. Hundreds of them.

Just down this road I counted a dozen trucks and six Humvees. Two companies of infantry at least, whipping up a storm of sand and filling the sky with it.

There were more trucks from the north and west.

Jesus, a battalion on the move, maybe two.

Cordon-and-search.

What did Mathilde think she was doing?

There were light armoured vehicles with 20 mm cannon. The Humvees were mounted with anti-tank weapons, mortars and .50 calibre twin machine guns.

Blinking green lights showed the lazy drift of Blackhawks and Apaches across the star-filled sky, shepherding their flocks safely to the start line.

Was it the Sheikh they were after?

Or simply the British terrorist, Bilal?

Back home it would make great television.

Those explosions would have given everybody something to think about. It was our chance to get away unobserved.

I tapped Amarayn's ankle and scrambled to my feet. I pointed the way north. Time to move. At least we were outside the hunters' circle, and had set off something of a red herring, but we had a long way to go before we reached those hills, and we didn't have long before daylight.

We jogged one in front of the other, changing places every so often. Sixty paces were equivalent to a hundred metres. Every sixty steps I moved a pebble from one pocket to another to give me the distance. The stars gave me our bearing. I'd got a fat blood blister on my left heel and the big toe on my right foot felt wet. It had started to bleed again. I'd lost the nail. None of it mattered. Pain could be pushed aside. It was nothing compared to the bother we'd be in if we did not make the Lowrah river before dawn.

Jessica had an explanation.

She had explanations for most things, and I don't mean the astrological signs (though she did like to read that stuff in the papers), the homespun philosophy of *Reader's Digest* or the agony aunts of Sunday supplements. Give her time, and Jess would come up with a convincing analysis. Jess thought about relationships, sought advice from her circle of close women friends and read up all she could find in the local library on the subject of men and women.

It was my childhood, she'd say. No model, see. Nothing to hard-wire anything like a normal male–female relationship into my psyche. My dad was a violent, cowardly lush. My mother was a chain-smoking psychotic depressive. Whatever. Jess had a lot of names for them I didn't understand. Psychobabble, I said it was. She shrugged. Call it what you will, Jess said, you can't escape it. None of us can. We all carry the baggage of childhood. I had learned how to deal with other people on the street, she said, in the playground of our local school. I'd been expelled from playschool for trying to burn the place down. The fascination with arson had not stopped there. As a nine-year-old I used to light matches, then stick them under the lids of matchboxes and toss the improvised incendiary devices into Royal Mail postboxes.

The results were often spectacular: a wonderful whoomf and sudden gusts of smoke and flame.

Brilliant. Just like miniature bombs going off.

If I couldn't beat the other bastards into submission, quite literally, then I manipulated them into doing what I wanted. Coercion first, manipulation the weapon of second choice. I was a predator, and an insecure one. It was a constant rejection–aggression pattern, or so Jess said. Over the years it had worked itself into a highly ornate structure of self-deception. If I couldn't control something by force, I'd try to destroy it, and if I lacked the power to destroy it, I'd work at undermining it by undoing the faith of weaker souls in whatever it was. A project, an idea, an item of equipment, a political party, a religious faith or simply another individual. It didn't matter what. I subverted and rejected what I couldn't subdue or kill. My way of dealing with other people moved from the playground to the army, and from the army to the bedroom.

Wherever.

Jess said I didn't know the meaning of love because I had never been loved myself. I didn't get hugs as a kid, and it never occurred to me that others would like to be shown affection. Didn't I know that women wanted hugs and kisses more than simply sex?

She felt sorry for me, she said.

I told her she was talking through her cakehole.

She said I would say that.

I had convinced myself, she said, that I didn't need other

people. I was frightened of them, so I kept them away. I never let others get close. I used people when I could. I was a mess. Oh, yes. More vulnerable than I knew. Even the army had failed to remake me in its image. With Mathilde the whole edifice had come crashing down. That's how Jess put it. I was one of those blokes who spent half a lifetime striving to keep secrets from the people who loved them.

The deceit. The lies.

I had learned to fuck and fight, sure enough. I was perfect material for special ops, sure. No question. Only I had not learned how to live outside the jungle like a human being.

I didn't know where to start, she said.

Not a bloody clue.

Those tears again. Not laughing any more.

I suspected Jess might have been right, but I'd never admit it.

Not to her. Not to anyone.

Fuck that.

Dawn caught us before we reached our objective.

I cut the rest periods from ten to five minutes every hour. Then I cut the rest out completely. Amarayn kept up, but I could see she was exhausted. I had taken the lead for the past forty minutes. Her face was pinched, her lips so badly chapped they were bleeding. Her legs were wobbly, her pace uneven. She was struggling. Marathon runners call it the 'Wall'. A sensation of utmost effort, but not going anywhere. There was blood on her pants where she'd taken a tumble and cut her knee on a rock. I don't suppose I seemed in any better shape, but I couldn't see myself and that was something to be grateful for.

I saw nothing in front or behind. No figures. No dust.

No movement.

I must be imagining it.

Or else they were just very good.

The greyish-blue hills rose steep and unbroken from the plain just ahead of us. Or so it seemed. They never got any closer. We ran on, our feet scuffing up little puffs of sand, but we seemed to be standing still all the same.

Two-legged animals dragging themselves across a vast sand table towards a refuge that never got any closer.

I knew the way. I remembered it all, every fold in the terrain. It was as if I had never been away.

We passed through a deserted village, the ghostly ruins slowly sliding back into the red dust of which it had been built before the Soviets had knocked it flat.

We didn't see a soul.

Not so much as a goat.

Amarayn wanted water, but I wouldn't let her drink. I tried to explain what it did to the knees, but I don't know if she understood. I sucked a pebble to stimulate the saliva glands. I knew if I drank my knees would stiffen up and become painful. We would be done for. We had to keep going.

The mist saved us. It poured down through the gap of the Lowrah valley. I might not have spotted where it was otherwise. The greyness rolled right over us, chilly and damp, and swallowed us up in its clammy embrace.

We celebrated. Amarayn had already stopped, sinking to her knees and then leaning forward and retching up gouts of bile. When she finished and sat back panting I handed her the bottled water.

'Go on. Drink.'

It ran into her open mouth, down her chin, her neck.

Her hands shook.

She almost choked.

221

'Enough.'

I pulled the bottle away from her. She tried to hang on to it.

'Slowly,' I said.

I took a sip and spat. Another, warming it in my mouth before swallowing. I drank by tipping the bottle, without touching it with my lips.

It tasted a lot better than champagne.

I handed it back to her.

'Careful.'

We couldn't see more than a dozen yards. Better still, no one could see us. Our sweat had turned icy. Moments ago we had been burning. Now we shivered. I wrapped myself in my *potu*. Amarayn tugged out her burka and pulled it on.

I put the half-empty plastic bottle back in my Hudson Bay pack, and retied it.

The mist was moving down into the plain and, as it did so, it began to disperse as the sun rose and the moisture evaporated. It wouldn't be long before we would be visible again.

We had to keep moving.

The stream was dry. It was nothing but stones. The watercourse at the very bottom was a twist of sand, guarded by two majestic sentinels of rock like rough-hewn lions, but their grandeur was made ludicrous by the pathetic stream-that-wasn't, a once quicksilver brook of cold, clean water.

Every sound we made was magnified by the cliffs on either side of the wadi. A cough emerged as a shout, a stumble as a tremor. Our footsteps seemed to be audible for miles.

Neither of us spoke.

The Sheikh and his son Naim were somewhere ahead. How far we didn't know.

We both felt the tension – for very different reasons.

The mist quickly dispersed, leaving a chilly blue sky overhead. We plodded on, northwards, heading up a gentle incline slowly into the hills towards the source of the river. I kept busy by searching for cover, looking for places we could hide should an aircraft appear, or a squad of Humvees roll up over the skyline.

A clump of dried grass, an indentation in the ground, an overhanging boulder – these were the furnishings of the fugitive, the means to survive.

We had gone about a mile upriver when I told myself we had to stop to eat. We'd done well. We'd evaded the searchers. We hadn't been spotted. We deserved a break.

I led the way out of the river bed, climbing the bank at a gentle angle until I reached a rock that covered our backs, shaded our outlines from the front, and gave us a view of the valley floor both ahead and behind.

There was a little shelf in front of it.

I opened up the tinned peaches.

I used the tin lid to dig a cavity in the bank, a hole really, and I made a miniature chimney to draw away the smoke so the fire wouldn't give us away. Amarayn collected wood and dried grass. The goat meat I had carried still looked all okay. There were no worms that I could see. So I cut a slab of about eight ounces into cubes and we roasted them, burning our fingers in our impatience to pull the meat out from the embers of our improvised stove and eat them.

We had a little salt to give it taste.

Noisily sucking our filthy fingers, we looked like a couple of hobos.

There was enough heat left to boil up some water for tea, half a mug each.

The sun warmed our bruised bodies.

We both experienced a strong urge to sleep.

Amarayn lay down on her side, cradling her head on the crook of her elbow, facing away from me. She fell asleep almost at once.

I told myself I'd stay awake while Amarayn rested.

I put my back against the rock and drew my legs up.

I'd give her an hour. Then it would be my turn.

She dug her nails into my arm. Hard. She kept squeezing until the pain woke me.

We had moved closer to each other for warmth without knowing it, while we slept. She lay with her back against my chest. My legs were against hers and my left arm had found its way round her shoulder.

Her hand let my arm go and found its way to my mouth. She pressed my lips.

The message was clear.

Quiet.

Not a sound. Or we're dead.

The sun had gone. The steep little valley was in shadow and it was a lot colder. It was late afternoon already.

She didn't move. Neither did I.

Not a muscle.

I heard voices.

Close.

We dared not raise our heads.

We became part of the landscape.

We'd lost the element of surprise, and I wouldn't be able to get to my rifle quickly enough to make a difference.

There was nothing else we could do.

I held my breath and I think she did, too.

FIFTEEN

It was a man's boot. A desert boot, a type issued by the British armed forces. Worn yellow suede, rubber-soled, ankle high and well used. The laces were parachute string, tied in parallel. It was thirty inches away from my face.

If its owner took a step back he would be standing on my head.

I watched a large brown ant scuttle up to the boot and cautiously test its surface before turning away in disgust.

The marine must have come downhill. If he'd climbed up he would surely have seen us as he drew level with our rock.

My heart was galloping away against Amarayn's back.

This wasn't about the sheikh. It wasn't about my share of $25 million.

It was about staying alive and free.

I could hear the crackle of the radio on his back.

All he had to do was turn his head, look down.

He would see two people under a *potu*. He would see one of them had a rifle under the shawl, but not where I could get at it fast enough.

If we were very lucky we'd be hauled off and interrogated as terrorist suspects.

That would be the ignominious end to it. The Costa Blanca villa and Swiss bank account would remain a fantasy, nothing more, and I'd be back where Quilty wanted me.

Welcome to Her Majesty's Prison Belmarsh.

And it would be my fault.

Not falling asleep – that was bad enough, but I didn't mean that.

I meant Amarayn and the fuckers who'd attacked her.

If only I had ignored it, turned over and gone back to sleep. Or just slipped back to my shawl, pretended I'd seen nothing and left them to it. It had nothing to do with me. It wasn't my affair how Afghans treated one another. It was not my fight. I couldn't change 300 years of what had gone before. It wasn't my task to set the world to rights. I told myself I had had a job to do. I was supposed to be a professional. That was why I'd been hired.

I wasn't supposed to let it get personal.

Feelings had no part in this.

I felt a bloody fool.

Alternatively I could have said she was related to me, kept her close to me. It might have deterred the hash smokers from trying it on.

I was supposed to win Jameel's confidence. That was the idea. I was just too damn thick to have known it at the time. It wasn't in the game plan. Not Jameel's. Not mine, either. It would have taken time, but I would have used my cover as a bona fide Talib commander to help lure the Sheikh into the Hada hills. I would have been a welcome adornment to Jameel's unsavoury gang. And just as Jameel's boys were about to spirit Osama and his mates off down the smuggler's route to a Gabizai-run safe haven in Gulestan across the border, courtesy of Hadi Safar, Nabibullah and others of that ilk, I would have got close enough to the Sheikh to put a bullet in his heart, and somehow get the evidence back home.

To use Mathilde's expression, it was indeed fucked up beyond all recognition.

No wonder they'd rushed in the troops.

I had lost my temper, screwed up.

The radio crackled again.

The boot shifted an inch or two. Another ant just avoided being crushed by a size ten.

'Foxtrot Four.'

'Foxtrot Four.

'Any luck, Foxtrot Four?'

'Foxtrot Four. Negative.'

'Roger that. Out.'

'Foxtrot Four. Out.'

A West Yorkshire accent.

The radio operator's boot vanished.

Cloth scratched against thorn scrub.

I inhaled the bitter-sweet stench of British soldiery.

Sweat, tobacco, soap.

Small stones tumbled down the slope.

Someone was whistling.

'Shut it,' said an angry voice.

The whistling ceased.

They were moving off, going home, moving downhill.

A stick of three or four.

A recce, not a fighting patrol.

Turning south-west, downstream, the way we'd come.

I felt Amarayn relax.

We walked upstream and after an hour rested for a few minutes on a boulder still warm from the sun.

'You know this place, Bilal?'

'Yes. I was here. Before.'

'When?'

'Twenty years back.'

I did recognize it, too. It had been a major pipeline for arms and men fighting the Soviets. It was also the pipeline for drugs heading in the other direction, for kids destined for the Gulf's sex slave industry. I remembered Suleiman's video, and the twenty-seven names.

'Same? It not change?'

'Very little.'

'No water,' Amarayn said. 'Rain finish.'

'Maybe there's some higher up. From the *kerez*.'

The place was called Sweet Spring, after all.

Amarayn looked sceptical.

'We will know soon,' I said. 'Tomorrow.'

'Food finish very soon.'

'Yes, it will.'

'Then? What you do?'

She watched me steadily.

Amarayn was talking at last, and I was curious. I held out my hands, palms down, stuck out my forefingers, putting them together, touching each other, then put my right hand over my heart.

'You,' I said, indicating one forefinger. 'Naim.' I indicated the other finger. 'You love this man – your husband?'

She looked down.

'Children?'

She shook her head.

'What is it?'

The head shook again, still bowed.

We were having our first real conversation in a mixture of broken English and fractured Pashto. Perhaps it took a couple of narrow escapes, a near rape and a number of sleepless nights to get Pashtuns talking.

'Amarayn?'

I put out a hand and raised her chin. She didn't resist.

'What's the matter?'

She pulled away.

'You not understand.'

'Try.'

She didn't respond.

I said, 'Tell me.'

She looked around, as if searching for the words.

'Tell me,' I said again.

For a moment she was undecided.

'I live in Kandahar,' she began. 'With father, mother, uncle, brother, two sister.' She ticked off each close relative on her fingers. 'There is river. Other side of river there is big house. Foreigners live in this house. Many. Many. Al-Qaeda families. Too much. My brother fish in river. He meet Arab boy. His name Naim. Older than brother. Eighteen, nineteen maybe. Understand, Bilal?'

'Sure.'

There she stopped. The tears had returned.

'Yes?'

'Naim see me one day. This last year. He try to talk to me. He tell my brother he like me. My brother say I am already to be married . . .'

'Engaged? Promised?'

'Yes. Promised. Promised to Murad. Murad good man. Student. At university. Murad want to be doctor.'

'What happened?'

'Naim tell his father. His father visit my father. Naim's father Osama bin Laden. My father say no. Amarayn promised to other man, he say.'

Amarayn was finding it hard to continue.

'Go on.'

'Osama bin Laden very angry.'

She paused.

I said, 'You were frightened.'

'For my father, yes. For Murad, also.'

'What happened?'

'Murad go. He must leave Kandahar. He go Pakistan. In night. Quick. Now he go university.'

She used her sleeve to wipe her cheek. The dust and tears left a muddy smear across her face.

'Did you hear from him?'

'No.'

'He didn't write.'

'Write?'

'Send letter.'

I mimicked the scribbling of a letter, folding it and stuffing it in an envelope.

'No. No letter. Too much war.'

'No message?'

'No.' A vigorous shake of the head.

It was choking her up. I waited a beat.

'How was it for your family?'

'Very bad Osama people attack my people. Taliban beat my father and brother in street. They take house.'

'They took your house?'

She nodded. 'Everything they take. House. Car. Everything. Father no job. Bin Laden send man to house. Mullah. Mullah tell father mother she must sign paper. Paper . . .'

Tears splashed down her cheeks and spattered her tunic.

I put a hand on her shoulder, but she shook me off.

'What did the paper say?'

'You are Talib,' she said. 'They your people. Bad people. Bad, bad people.'

'What did it say in the paper?'

She sniffed loudly.

'It say wrong things. Not true. Lies.'

'Okay. But what did it say?'

'It said my mother give Murad milk. When Murad child, my mother give milk to him. You understand?'

She was ashamed to talk about it.

'Suckled him, you mean?'

'Gave milk. Like this.' Amarayn touched her breast. Then cradled her arms as if carrying an infant. 'When Murad baby. But this not true. Not true . . .'

She sniffed and wiped away her tears.

'In Afghan custom, woman cannot marry man who drinks

milk of woman's mother. It means man like girl's brother. Brothers and sisters must not marry. Understand?'

'I understand.'

Custom was law, and law custom.

'It was lie. Everyone know this.'

'So what did you do?'

'They make me marry Naim. He take me away. Make me live in small house in Kandahar. Dirty place. I not love this man. He try make me love him. Force me. You understand, Bilal? I fight. Just like time you come help me. I hit him. I scratch him. He beat me. I fight more. I scream. I tell him I hate him ... He say bad thing about my family. He say I bad woman. He beat me. Many times. I hate him.'

She buried her face in my shoulder.

'Amarayn . . .'

She clung to me, holding my shirt.

I said, 'Did Nabibullah know all this?'

'No.'

I smelled terrible, but she didn't seem to mind.

'Amarayn, why go back to him? To this Naim?'

She had nowhere else to go, that was it.

Her family were refugees in Quetta.

Pakistan could have been Mars as far as Amarayn was concerned. Without money and the right papers, it was truly another world. She belonged to Naim. Like a piece of furniture. A chair, a table, a plate.

There were no jobs for women here in Afghanistan.

Amarayn had no trade, no qualifications.

No free will.

She did not consider the marriage lawful. It had been obtained by extortion. Her family had lost everything – and very nearly their lives – for standing up to the Taliban and al-Qaeda bullies, and in the end they had failed to save her.

Amarayn was my natural ally, but I couldn't tell her.

What would I say? That I wasn't Bilal after all, but a paid assassin seeking the father of her persecutor – at the very moment she had decided she had no option but to submit to bin Laden and his kind?

I was a Talib. The enemy. Along with the Americans, the government – in short, all forms of male authority. Women in Afghanistan formed an underclass, living – if it could be called living – at the whim of others.

By now Naim might well have given her up. He wouldn't be straining at the bit to get her back into the marital bed. He'd be too busy trying to save his own skin.

She was not going to bait the trap I'd hoped for.

We had about an hour before dark. The terrain was becoming increasingly familiar. The Lowrah valley was widening out. It was still bone dry, the clear pools I remember as full of fish that looked like small brown loch trout had long vanished. But as we climbed I did notice that the bottom of what had been the spring-fed river looked damp, the sand darker, moist in places.

The hills around us were rounded, softened. They weren't the towering peaks and savage ridges of eastern Afghanistan. At this time of day the colour of the terrain turned from beige to pink and gold.

A voluptuous landscape.

What I sought was an oasis of green, a tuft of blackberry and oak hidden snug between belly and thigh, a secret place, a sweet and fertile pudendum invisible from below and hopefully insignificant to the spy planes overhead.

While there was light we kept going. The moon came up early and still we walked. I started to push the pace. I was impatient to reach our destination. The incline was gentler, the valley a broad sweep of undulating sand and scrub, devoid of cover.

We couldn't hide, but I thought the relative darkness an advantage.

I had to help an exhausted Amarayn, or rather drag her along.

I took her arm.

'Please,' she said.

'Hurry.'

'I can't, Bilal.'

'You must.'

'I stop now.'

'No. Rest later.'

I slung her arm round my shoulders and half carried her, my left arm around her waist, the rifle in my right hand.

'Stop now.'

'No.'

'Bilal. Stop.'

I gave her a minute or two.

'Look.' Amarayn held up her cupped hands.

'See?'

She was happy, smiling, pleased at her discovery. Where there was water, earth and sunlight there was always life, and that would mean food. We were almost out of bottled drinking water, anyhow.

'Where you go?'

She caught up.

'We watch.' I put my hand up to my eyes to imitate scouring the horizon. 'We must be careful.'

She seemed to agree with this, though she said nothing. It took us another twenty minutes or so of steady climbing to reach the ridge. I helped her. There was no wind. It was not nearly as cold as it had been.

The land on the other side dipped gently, then rose again.

We sat below the crest, side by side.

To our left lay the Lowrah valley and our day's march. To our right, the valley continued on, but narrowed gradually to a gorge. Beyond it, nestling in the arms of the hills, lay the secret oasis. I couldn't see the patch of green, but I knew it was there, in the gathering darkness as the moon slipped away over the whalebacked horizon. It was where we'd lugged the embassy plunder all the way from Kabul back in '96.

We ate all but the last of my bread. We finished the water. Amarayn produced handfuls of dried fruit, mainly sultanas, along with the pine nuts that the Arabs call *snooba*.

There was no sound, no sign of movement.

No lights. No sign anyone was trailing us.

No one waiting ahead.

Not even the sound of aircraft.

It felt like we were the last living things in the world.

We didn't talk until we had wrapped ourselves in our shawls and found places to sleep. I had a large tussock next to me to stop me rolling downhill.

Amarayn was a couple of yards away, her back to a rock.

'Why you help?'

I was on the point of sleep when she spoke.

She repeated the question. 'Why?'

'Why what?'

'Why you help me?'

I looked up at the Plough.

'Not sure,' I said.

That was pretty much the truth of it.

'Who attack Nabibullah house?'

'I don't know,' I said.

That little job had Abdur Rahman's fingerprints all over it. It would have appealed to his sense of humour. I wouldn't have been at all surprised if Aisha was his latest squeeze, and that performance had been laid on deliberately to get Amarayn and myself out of there and on the move – and Aisha out of

234

the obligations of a betrothal that had outlived its usefulness from her point of view.

Or it could have been Mathilde's bright idea, and Abdur Rahman's handiwork with a little help from Felix and Yannis.

That deception operation, those Afghans coming in from an operation at Ghazni: that too smacked of Abdur Rahman moving his chess pieces around the board, using Nabibullah's goons to keep the queen, the rooks and knights away from the black king. Letting him move unobstructed to his doom.

Setting the Sheikh up.

'You are Talib?'

'Yes.'

'Bilal your name?'

'You know it is.'

I punched out a hollow for my hip. I was getting used to sleeping on the ground again, but it was always my hip that got stiff after a few hours unless I made room for it.

One of us should stay awake while the other slept.

'Osama your friend?'

'No.'

'Really?'

'Really.'

'England good?'

'Too much rain.'

'I think England good.'

'Why?'

'Good people.'

'Not all. By no means all.'

'I want go England.'

'You wouldn't be happy, Amarayn.'

'Why not happy?'

'It's cold. It's wet. It's very expensive. People are not very friendly.'

I thought of the refugee detention centres, the Home Office

interrogators and the slow poison of the tabloids' anti-foreigner invective.

There was a pause before she spoke again.

'You good man, Bilal. You not Talib.'

I didn't answer. There were good Taliban and there were bad Taliban, some of them very bad, but mostly they were just ignorant. I fell asleep thinking about it.

I don't think I could have slept for more than an hour. Probably less. It was my gut. It did not feel good. I thought it might go away, but it didn't. Rather the reverse.

It began with uneasiness, a swelling, a mild discomfort. It got worse and worse. When I realized I was not going to be able to hold it, I jumped up, grabbed the AK-74 and ran up and over the crest and down the reverse slope.

I didn't go far. I couldn't. I needed privacy, but I wasn't going to get as far as I would have liked.

All I had were seconds.

I no longer cared who saw or heard.

I flung the rifle down and fumbled with trousers and pants.

Cursing the bloody cord that kept the baggy pants in place.

The surge could not be held back.

My innards exploded.

Venting a flood of evil-smelling brown water.

I thought it would never stop. And just when I thought it was safe to move it started all over again.

It was accompanied by a stabbing gut-ache.

Then the vomiting.

The contractions continued long after there was nothing more to bring up.

During a pause in this digestive cataclysm, I managed to strip off all my clothes. I folded them up and put them on a rock along with the Kalashnikov.

I was bollock naked save for my sandals.

It came in waves.

The army had a euphemism for it.

Winter vomiting.

Both ends in my case, simultaneously.

I recognized what it was. I knew the smell. It was not the first time, but it was the worst. We'd both eaten the same things, but so far at least I was the only one affected.

When a particularly bad upheaval was over, I found a clean patch of ground and lay down on it on my side, my knees drawn up to my chest, and waited for the next attack.

I was sweating heavily. My skin felt prickly. The taste of my own sick burned my tongue.

Every muscle ached.

The next surge hit.

The spasms were seconds apart, contracting my stomach so it bent me like a bow.

If someone had offered me the bullet then I really think I would have taken it.

Gratefully.

Anything to put me out of my misery.

I was sure the operation was well and truly fucked. Or at least my part in it was, but I was too ill to care.

That was when Amarayn found me.

SIXTEEN

She got me close to the water. How she did it I don't know. Amarayn couldn't carry me, but I had no awareness, no memory of it. I do know she covered me up. I would throw off the clothes, and she would patiently cover me up again, wrapping the two *potus* tight around me like swaddling clothes.

So tight I'd struggle for breath, but she talked me down. She spoke to me continuously in Pashto, a soothing monologue, but I understood nothing.

I was out of it.

There were periods of lucidity. I realized I was running a high fever, and my body was giving up the moisture the amoebic dysentery demanded, draining me of fluids, wringing me dry.

I thought I saw the kids. Standing there, looking at me.

Watching us.

Jess was talking to me. Mouth opening and closing, but no sound came out.

A silent movie.

Jess became Mathilde became Amarayn.

Amarayn came close. Her hands were on me, her breasts brushed my arm, her hair touched my cheek.

She made me drink, propping me up and feeding me sips of water. Even opening my mouth to do it, pushing my jaws apart. At first my stomach simply rebelled, throwing it out instantly.

Projectile vomiting.

Showering us both.

'Come on,' she said. 'Come on, Bilal. Come on.'

It was one battle that felt like my last.

When I wasn't shitting or throwing up, I shivered with cold. My teeth rattled in my head. Amarayn piled on clothing and both our shawls and still I shook. She held me close despite my stink. God, I was a mess. Dried vomit. Congealed shit. Moments later I would be pouring with sweat, and I would fight her, thrashing around to be free of her efforts to wrap me in whatever she could find.

It wasn't her. It was Quilty. It was the Sheikh. It was Abdur Rahman and Nabibullah and Felix and Mansour and I was fighting them off, scrapping with fists and feet.

She built a fire. Boiled up water. Pounded something into powder and made me drink it, forcing my teeth open with whatever she used to hold the water, pushing my head back.

Day followed night, night day. I lost time altogether.

I knew what she was trying to do.

She lay curled up at my feet, catnapping whenever she could.

Jess was there with us, too. Telling me how she wanted to forgive me but couldn't.

She'd been had. Violated. Abused. Taken advantage of. The phrases she always hurled at me. She said she'd never forgive any of that. How could she?

Mathilde in my sleeping bag.

Matthew pulling my hand.

Daddy. Wake up, Daddy.

Amarayn again. Shaking me awake, forcing my teeth apart.

I could hear my own groans.

'Drink. Drink, Bilal.'

239

Rehydration was the only way I was going to come out of this alive, but I still couldn't keep anything down.

My skin had changed. When it was pressed with a finger, the hole stayed, and when my skin was pinched, it remained standing. The flesh had no elasticity. I was parched like the landscape, fast turning into a leather bag of bones.

I was dying.

Then there was no more dysentery and we both slept for hours. The brown water had turned to sludge. Suddenly nothing at all. Dry. Nothing left to turn to brown juice. Just massive flatulence and then not even that. Only the gut-ache like red-hot pins driven through to my backbone and the awful, endless dry retching.

'No good,' I said to her. 'No good. Leave me.'

'No. Bilal not die. Bilal live. Bilal drink. Come, Bilal. Drink.' And she would have another cup of some bitter potion to push between my lips, holding my head in her lap, gripping me hard to prevent me from twisting away.

There were times when I hated her for her persistence.

It was some kind of crushed bark. A nasty taste.

It was scalding hot.

She treated me like a child. A wilful child who didn't know what was good for him.

When the fever went and when the contractions stopped, she lifted me up. Got me to my feet, giggling stupidly, and helped me stagger to the spring and bathed me. Helped get my clothes off, sat me in the stream, in the shock of cold water, and rubbed me down, getting rid of the worst of the filth. My nakedness bothered neither of us. She helped me out, then, and used her *potu* to dry me, and dressed me in my one spare set of clean clothing. I was too weak to do up buttons or the draw cord.

She showed me what I looked like.

Amarayn had found a sliver of mirror and held it up.

She smiled when she saw my reaction.

I reared back in surprise.

A wild thing, half man, half beast, stared back at me.

The beast's hair hung down in greasy braids around its predator's narrow face. Its cheeks were shrunken, the cheekbones and jaw pushing out against drum skin darkened by windburn. The beast's eyes had a ferocious look, and the teeth seemed huge in the emaciated face, the mouth a leer of malice. The sinews in the beast's neck stood out.

Thomas Morgan had completely disappeared. There was nothing left of West Pilton.

We sat in the sun and warmed ourselves and for the first time I recognized where we were. The trees, the bushes, the grass, the leaves – the tiny stretch of oasis, green and golden in springtime – was no more than a hundred metres in any direction.

It was beautiful.

So much so I wept.

Chrissakes, Morgan.

Get a fucking grip.

Amarayn reached out and took my hand.

'You better now, Bilal. Very weak. But better.'

I felt better. I felt at peace.

I saw clearly. It was an awareness sharpened by hunger.

The softness of dawn gave way to a hardness of light that drew everything towards me. Distances shrank. The hills, the scrub, the rocks all seemed to edge closer. In a matter of hours the world had been redrawn with a draughtsman's realism.

The air was chill, the sun hot.

Why, in a hostile land where men and women lived so close to the earth, to extremes of weather, where life was short and violent death casual and omnipresent, did I feel so much at ease? Why did I feel release among a people hemmed in by custom and the rigours of a demanding faith? Why was it that

I could so easily make lifelong friends among an impoverished, alien race, whereas back in that other, mad place I came from, I was acquainted with so many, yet knew so few? I missed none of the distractions of 'home'. I didn't miss supermarkets or cinemas, credit cards or television, carpets or central heating, boozers or cash machines, aftershave, cotton sheets, cornflakes or the Sunday joint, lap dancing, cappuccinos or package holidays.

Not even Rangers on a wet Saturday afternoon.

Not really.

If that was civilization, Mr Bush was welcome to it.

With a gannet's eye, without passion, I saw my tawdry life stretch behind me like ragged laundry flapping over a scrap of mud and cinder. Except that it wasn't my own. I had never taken possession of any of it, not really. The episodes in my life were hand-me-downs. I did not even own my feelings. I saw my failed relationships sag on the same backyard washing line. I saw my parents. I saw Jess. I saw my years in the forces, the easy and temporary cures for perpetual unease, from pride in obeying nonsensical orders to pointless punch-ups, from Goose Green to a garrison-town tart face down across a pool table. From a travesty of a home life to the treacherous hedgerows of Ulster's Armagh and Fermanagh.

God, Queen and Country.

My tears were not for the glory, but the sheer waste and hypocrisy of it.

'My rifle . . .'

She guided my hand to it.

It felt so heavy, unfamiliar.

She made tea and shared the last mouldy bread she'd carried in her pack.

'How long have we been here?'

242

She looked at me blankly.

'In this place,' I said, 'how long? A day? Two days?'

'Five days.'

'Five?'

I couldn't believe it.

She counted them off on her fingers.

Five. Nearly a week.

I tried to get up. I did stand, briefly, using the Kalashnikov as a crutch. But the world whirled around me and I fell down again. Toppled over slowly like a drunk losing his balance, seeing the trees over my head and the grass coming up to meet me.

I wondered what if anything she had eaten all that time.

She must be almost starving, I thought.

'Bilal rest,' Amarayn said. 'Bilal sleep.'

She was holding my fingers. She bent over and kissed me on my forehead. I thought I was imagining it.

'Amarayn . . .'

She stroked my back and my head.

What I couldn't figure out was why she bothered.

I slept.

I couldn't walk, but dammit, I could crawl.

It took me a while, but I got my back up against a tree. I checked the AK-74 and placed it across my lap, stretched my legs out in front of me. Every movement was an effort. I hurt all over: my buttocks, calf muscles, my shoulders, even my neck seemed to suffer from bearing the burden of my head. The weight of the rifle was painful on my thighs. But I could see about sixty paces down the path that wound into our hideout of blackberry, alder, willow and twisted oak.

A decent field of fire.

I leaned back, my head resting against the trunk. Better.

Don't sleep.

Whatever might come downhill from the rear wouldn't see me for the thickets of thorn.

I'd surely hear them steal through the brush.

I could put up some kind of defence. Hold them up. The rocks on the high ground would have been much better. But we needed to be near the water and I needed a lot of it, continuously taking small sips from the plastic water bottle Amarayn had kept in her knapsack.

I hated my own weakness.

There was no chance I could complete the mission. Forget it, I told myself. Just give a good account of yourself. Take down as many as you can. Make them pay. Wear them down.

Amarayn had tried to stop me when I dragged myself away from the spring. I swore at her and crawled on. Told her to go to hell. She blocked my path and I scampered around her on hands and knees like a dog. She tried to hold me by the collar of my tunic and I snarled and tried to sink my teeth into her wrist. She shouted at me and I ignored her. I didn't stop. Told her I had a job to do.

I had to be ready.

She wouldn't give me the grenade.

I could not have thrown it anyway. I was too bloody weak. We both knew it. I felt about a hundred years old. Fucking feeble.

But my idea was to rig up a tripwire, or keep hold of it until they reached me, then blow us all to kingdom come.

I kept dropping off, my eyelids like heavy stones refusing to stay open.

Amarayn had one tin left in her knapsack and that evening I ate all of it. She must have saved it, her last reserve of protein. I didn't even ask her if she wanted any.

You really are a shit, Morgan.

Hell, she knew that already.

It was salted beef.

Bully beef. The yellow label said Argentine.

She scraped the fat off the outside, chopped it up into a hash and mixed it with wild herbs and heated it. She fed it to me slowly, morsel by morsel, until there was nothing left.

I kept it all down.

Drank a lot of water. Kept that down, too.

Another small victory Amarayn had paid for.

It was morning. Daylight already.

Voices. A hand supported the back of my head. Amarayn's other hand pushed the plastic between my lips and teeth. Felt the cool water slip over my tongue, down my throat. Felt it go all the way down inside. It felt good.

She bent over me.

I drank more, holding the plastic bottle myself.

My hands shook a little, but I could do it myself.

Those voices.

I thought it was delirium.

If we didn't get something to eat very soon I knew we wouldn't make it.

Living in the open like this I thought we could manage for ten to fifteen days without proper nourishment, but after that we'd weaken fast. We could stay alive for a good three weeks, even longer, provided we found shelter and kept warm, but there was no chance of that.

The voices were closer.

Hair brushed my face.

Finished the water.

Her lips on my ear.

A kiss.

I thought I was already hallucinating.

'Sorry.'

Sorry?

'Sorry, Bilal.'

245

Her shadow lifted. She moved back. Away.

The voices were very close.

Men speaking Pashto.

'Bilal.'

I was up on my feet, hauled upright.

Clasped in a bear hug.

It felt like a dream. I wasn't really there at all.

The voice said, 'My dear brother. Praise be to God.'

A hand slapped me on the back twice. I felt a beard on my neck, the reek of sweat, the heat of another man's lifeblood, the pulse of it in his throat.

My right hand was grasped, pumped vigorously.

'*Salaam.*'

'*Bakhere?*'

'*Singye?*'

'*Kharyet?*'

'*Jurey?*'

Was that my voice I heard in my own ears?

Hands grabbed my upper arms. I was rocked gently back and forth. More back slaps. More hand pumping. More greetings.

I looked uncomprehending into the face of the man who had hold of me. He was staring into my eyes. An intent look. As if he was trying to wake me up, shake me out of my lethargy, get me to say the right things. To understand, not give the game away. To respond in some way I couldn't understand.

I know you.

My brain wouldn't produce his name.

Voices again: orders given, hands reaching out and helping me over to a cushion, a plastic sheet with a floral design spread out on the grass. A glass of sweet tea pressed into my hand, so hot I burned my fingers.

Another cushion pushed into the small of my back.

I looked round, vainly searching for Amarayn.

'We thought you were martyred,' said the voice. 'Thanks be to God, you survived.'

It was a familiar voice. I knew it so well.

Someone helped me drink from the glass because my fingers weren't steady.

The sun was in my face.

They were putting down plates of food. I could smell roast meat. Grilled onions. Freshly sliced tomato. Nan, still warm. It smelled like heaven itself. Saliva filled my mouth.

'She told us what happened. Your woman.'

My woman.

He meant Amarayn.

I was eating. Without thinking. Like an automaton. My hand was shaking. I was rolling up the food in a torn-off slice of bread. Feeding myself with the fingers of my right hand.

Bloody hell, there was even rice.

I couldn't get enough of it.

'Not too quick, Bilal. You don't want to get sick again.'

He was explaining to his companions in Pashto what he'd said in English to me.

This was the famous Bilal with his mouth full. Bilal, who had miraculously escaped the Americans' assault on the Hada hills. With God's help. Before that, the Argendab valley attack. And Oruzgan. So many narrow escapes from death. You should see his wounds. So many battles. And, once again, Bilal had survived a terrible fever.

It was meant to be. God's will. It was written.

Beards and turbans nodded in agreement.

Bull.

I was looking around for Amarayn.

'What's the matter?'

'Where is she?'

'Helping with the food.'

'Has she eaten?'

'Of course. Don't worry.'

'Is she safe?'

'What do you think? Nothing will happen to her.'

I knew this man.

'Don't you know me, Bilal?'

'Of course I do,' I said in Pashto, looking him in the face. 'In God's name, of course I do. You're my very good friend. My very best friend, thanks be to God.'

He smiled at me.

The name.

'My dear brother, Abdur Rahman.'

They were well equipped. They hid their two mules in the undergrowth, and made their headquarters downstream. They used an old mujahedin cave – or maybe it was a mine – on the reverse slope, the same slope where I'd spilled my guts, but considerably further to the south-west. There they stored their weapons, ammunition and food. They were careful to avoid unncessary movement, keeping under cover as much as they could in daylight hours.

I counted twelve, thirteen men with Abdur Rahman. I recognized Khaled among them. By their clothes and their general appearance, it was clear they'd been on the move for some time, evading air patrols and ground forces.

He had set up blocking parties north and south, rotating the men through it every three hours.

Two sentries roamed the flanks, moving about after dusk and before dawn, and lying up and watching in daylight.

Half the party was on guard, half rested.

There was a stand-to at dawn and dusk for everyone.

I said, 'What are you doing here?'

Abdur Rahman was sitting next to me, sharing my tree. He was using a clasp knife to whittle a stick to a sharp point. He had several of them at his feet. He was making a booby trap, the kind the Vietnamese used against their American occupiers. Simple. Environmentally friendly booby traps. They'd dig a hole, plant the stakes in it at an angle, with the points smeared in human faeces, then cover it up with grass.

The stakes would penetrate a boot at the ankle, avoiding the metal plate the Americans used in the soles, making a nasty wound that would become infected very quickly.

'I could ask you the same question, Bilal.'

I said, 'You know why I'm here. I'm asking you what you're doing.'

He stopped whittling for a moment.

He said, 'I meant to say that your friends think you died in the Hada hills. Mr Quilty thinks so. There was shooting and later two big explosions. Don't suppose you'd know anything about that?'

He still hadn't answered my question.

'They've called off their search,' he continued. 'The Americans and British found bodies after the explosions. Unidentifiable, some of them. Badly burned. You wouldn't know anything about that, either, would you?'

He went back to working on the stick.

I didn't answer. I didn't believe him.

Covertly I watched Amarayn. She was collecting water from the spring. She was back in her burka. She had reverted to her traditional role as general dogsbody, manual labourer and kitchen hand. A skivvy. She glanced up and away again. It was as if what had happened between us had never happened. We didn't speak. We couldn't. Neither of us dared to express any kind of familiarity. For her sake.

'So this is the advance party,' I said. 'And you're leading it.'

'Who better, Bilal?'

'None,' I agreed. 'They got the very best.'

He liked that.

'When does the Sheikh get here?'

'Soon.'

'How soon?'

'You know Afghans. Soon, Afghan time.'

'And you will move on to the Hada hills before he gets here with his party. The plan hasn't changed.'

'Something like that.'

'Something like that? Why the caginess, Abdur? Why don't you spit it out and tell me?'

'I suppose it's an old habit of mine,' he said. 'You should just concentrate on getting back into shape. Leave the thinking to me for now. Rest. Eat. We can talk business again later.'

'The need to know,' I said.

'That's right, Bilal. The need to know.'

'And I don't have any need, is that it?'

He started work on another stick.

'How does it feel to be back in Afghanistan, Bilal?'

'Just like home, Abdur.'

'Tell me something. What was it that made this place so special for you? Right in the beginning, I mean. Your first trip. What made you come back again and again?'

I thought about it.

'Tell me,' he said. 'I'd really like to know.'

It wasn't easy, but I gave it a try.

'As a child you are taught that men and women are equal,' I said, 'and that human lives have the same value. The Bible teaches us that the camel will find it easier to pass through the eye of a needle than a rich man to enter heaven. I knew it in theory, but I'd never really grasped the reality of it. I'd never lived it. Not until I came here. Understand?'

'Not really – but go on.'

'The very first time I was here about five weeks. There was little to eat. Just bread and green tea. Very occasionally we managed to buy an egg or a scrawny chicken, but those were rare treats. We walked night and day, dodging the Soviets, sleeping an hour under a rock, another hour or two in a sheep pen. Finally I was on my way back. We came across a track. It was like walking on rubber. My feet felt wonderful. It was a rough cart track, but it felt marvellous, magical, like driving down an Autobahn. Then I saw an electric light. It was the first I'd seen for weeks. It seemed a miracle. We came to a village. It had a *chaikhana* and a few shops. It was like seeing the Manhattan skyline for the first time. Exciting. I squatted in the gutter and relieved myself quite unselfconsciously. We slept on the filthy earth floor of one of the hovels. My clothes were rags. I hadn't had a proper wash for a month. I was infested with crab lice and all manner of other bugs, from fleas to cattle ticks. But I was happy. Really happy. Happy to be alive. The next day we crossed the frontier.'

'So?'

'So there's no such thing as luxury. A banana or twenty minutes' sleep can be far more exquisite than a week in a five-star hotel. I learned I really was no different from anyone else. Being British didn't make me better. Being Afghan with a sense of honour and selflessness might well do so. I found the only difference between me and my companions was that I had come from a consumer society. Until then I had lived by assumptions of superiority, based on a contempt for, and fear of, people who were different. Also a disgust for the poor – because, you see, my family was relatively poor and I had always felt shame at not having what other people had. It was the pain of envy. I lost that here. I shed those feelings as easily as I swapped Western clothes for *chalwar kameez*. I got to know myself. I saw myself as I was. Naked. As a man. A human. Stripped of attachments. It felt good. It was like coming home for the first time.'

I hadn't put it very well.

'You talk like a Sufi.'

'That's no bad thing,' I said. 'But all the same, I'm not.'

'No,' Abdur Rahman said. 'Indeed, you are not.'

He still wasn't going to tell me what I wanted to know.

Things were falling into place, but there was still a piece missing from the jigsaw.

I said, 'You're getting greedy in your old age, Abdur. Not content with your five million you want my share as well. Is that it?'

He laughed.

'Now that would be nice.'

SEVENTEEN

MARCH, 2002

I walked.

It started with short walks. Each time I'd amble a little further, take on a steeper gradient. I didn't see much of Amarayn or Abdur Rahman or anyone else I knew. At first I kept to the gully itself, circling around the spring. There was no point in being impatient. I had to use the time available to get myself back into shape. I was slow and short of breath to begin with. But after eating well and sleeping soundly, I felt strong enough to venture out to the sentry posts and back.

On the third day, as I ventured further afield, I saw there were more men, and they were different.

They stayed in or near the cave. They wore turbans – crudely, without a skullcap. Afghans made fun of their countrymen who wound their turbans around their heads without a cap. The newcomers were dressed in *chalwar kameez*, but most wore combat jackets over their tunics. They did not appear to carry a *potu*. Their jackets were plain green or Nato-style disrupted pattern. They kept to themselves, but they were watchful. Whenever I passed by I looked up at the ridge to my left and saw faces turned to observe my progress. AKSU-74 sub-machine guns were in evidence, too. I hadn't seen many of those stubby-nosed weapons with the distinctive bell-shaped muzzle flashes down south. Not among the Taliban.

Not Afghans, I told myself.

Foreign Muslims.

I extended my walks southwards, beyond Abdur Rahman's forward OP, greeting the two sentries with a wave and walking along the bottom of the wadi until I was out of sight. Or thought I was.

My rifle was slung across my back. I had to get used to the weight of it again. It left my hands free to grope my way back uphill. I felt safe enough – Abdur Rahman had spread the myth of the fighter Bilal and his valorous deeds in the face of the infidel enemy.

On that third day after Abdur Rahman's arrival, I climbed the ridge and walked back along it towards our little camp, hoping to be able to see down the slope to the cave on my right, and get a better view of whatever was going on.

I didn't get far.

'La weyn rayeh?'

A challenge.

I answered the gunman in his own tongue.

'Aam itmasha.'

I smiled when I said it. Yes, I was going for a stroll. Yes, I had a weapon. But I was harmless.

Tone is everything.

I was relying on my cover, my reputation as a famed Taliban fighter, a man of some reputation.

Out of breath, I sat down on a rock.

He was tall, his face the colour of walnut. Dark curly hair down to a full beard tinged with grey, eyes that were large, their darkness giving him a soulful air. The accent was quite guttural, even rough. Not melodious enough for an Egyptian. Further west, from the Maghrib.

Algerian, perhaps, or Libyan.

A fighter, certainly. Yet a man who's found whatever he has been looking for, a serenity, an unwavering certainty in his faith. I'd seen that look before, but couldn't recall where.

My smile had no impact.

He carried a pump-action shotgun, useful for close-quarter work. He held it casually in the crook of his arm, like a gentleman farmer on a day's rough shoot.

'You people must stay over the ridge,' he said.

You people.

'You're a polite one.'

He didn't like that.

This was all the confirmation I needed.

There was an outer ring of security provided by Abdur Rahman and his men, and an inner circle of al-Qaeda people around the Sheikh. His personal escort. His praetorian guard.

I got up slowly, took a step back.

Fuck it, this was a recce. I wasn't up for a scrap. Not yet. I needed to know something of the Sheikh's routine, if there was one, and find out his weak points, but I wasn't going to press my luck too far.

Curiosity got the better of him.

'You're not an Arab, but you speak Arabic.'

'No, I'm not Arab. You're not an Afghan, either, but I think you speak some Pashto.'

'Maybe.'

He almost smiled but thought better of it.

I switched from Arabic to Pashto. 'I'm Bilal.'

'The English Talib.'

He'd heard of me from Abdur Rahman.

'If you say so.'

'What do you say, Bilal?'

'I'm from Scotland. Not England.'

He had no idea where that was. Why should he?

He said, 'You're Muslim.'

'Praise be to God, yes.'

'Indeed. Thank God.'

We had something in common after all. He seemed relieved.

I turned to go.
I said, '*Salaam Aleikum.*'
'*Waleikum Salaam.*'
The north African called out after me.
'Go with God.'
I waved.
By now we were almost pals.

Shortly after I got back to our camp there was an air raid alarm, our first.

An iron pipe beaten three times.

Clothing was torn down from branches, *potus* swept up off the grass, cooking pots gathered up. The only fire permitted in the camp was quickly smothered with bucketfuls of sand.

Every gunman took cover, including the sentries.

In seconds the place seemed uninhabited.

On my back, covered by my *potu*, I gazed up through my roof of oak branches and tendrils of blackberry. My hollowed-out thicket was no bigger than a large dog kennel, but I could only glimpse little bits of blue sky here and there.

The Afghans around me were quiet for once.

There was nothing they feared more than what they called the Bow-Bows.

The B-52s were really high.

Heading to Gardez, maybe.

There'd be vapour trails, perhaps the glint of sunlight on a wingtip, and not much else.

At least we weren't the target.

Not today.

I found Abdur Rahman at lunch.

'You've been avoiding me,' he said. He sat cross-legged at a slight angle, half turned towards me. The others took little notice of our talk. Khaled was on the far side, watching. He ate sparingly, his eyes always on one or other of us. He reminded me a major-domo in fancy dress. Attentive, yet slightly disapproving towards his guests, as if we were juveniles who needed a lesson in etiquette. He carried a stiff hauteur about him that, for such a young man, was faintly disturbing.

'Hardly,' I said. 'I haven't been anywhere.'

Abdur Rahman turned his head to look at me.

I said, 'Is this the start of a lovers' tiff?'

I drank some water and watched him eat.

He said, 'I hear you've been walking around.'

'Your spies have been busy. There's no law against it.'

'Depends where you've been.'

I said, 'So he's there – in the cave or whatever it is.'

Grilled chicken and aubergine were on the menu.

He looked up, squinting in the hard sunlight, a handful of rice paused on its way to his mouth.

'You saw him, then?'

'No,' I said.

Abdur Rahman grunted. He went back to his food, tearing off a piece of flesh and chicken skin with a pinch of nan between his fingers. He put the food in his mouth and chewed.

I wasn't going to get a direct answer from him.

'They said you went up there.'

'I was curious.'

'He's there. You're right. But if I were you, I wouldn't try anything – not yet.'

Liar.

'You're not me. Does he ever come out? To take a dump, for example?'

Abdur Rahman picked up a slice of tomato and ate it.

He knew what I was after.

'Let me give you some advice, Bilal. Stay away from there. They're nervous. You can understand why.'

'Sure.'

The conversation was over. For him, maybe, but I needed more information.

'How many men has he got up there?'

We were speaking English now. Our private language.

'Eight.'

'That's all?'

'What did you expect?'

'Thirty, forty . . .'

Abdur shook his head.

'Closer we get to the border the fewer we need to be,' he said. 'Too many and we attract hostile attention.'

I could see that.

We this. We that.

He looked around to see if anyone was listening closely to what we were talking about, but they were too busy filling their bellies. With the exception of Khaled.

'Of course,' he said, his mouth full, 'the fewer we are, and the closer we get to the frontier, the jumpier everyone gets. You understand.'

Naturally. I said, 'Have you paid your respects to the great man? Had a friendly chat, you and he?'

Abdur Rahman didn't respond.

Out of the corner of my eye I could see Amarayn. She was hanging washing up on a branch. I wondered who the clothes belonged to. Washing. Yes, that might provide one way in.

They wouldn't search a female.

I tried again.

I said, 'You've been inside? Talked to him?'

He didn't answer.

I wanted to know the layout, the position of the guards. I needed to know how the Sheikh spent his time and where he sat and where he ate and where he slept. I wanted to probe their relationship. I wanted some indication whether Abdur Rahman really was prepared to work with me on this, or do his own thing as I suspected, and if that was the case, what that thing might be.

I had a pretty good idea.

I repeated the question.

'Have you talked to him?'

'You're not eating,' Abdur Rahman said. 'You need to get your strength back.' He pricked up a plate of grilled aubergine and put it in front of me. 'Eat, Bilal.'

'You're not my bloody mother,' I told him.

I dreamed.

They say it's only for a few seconds.

Sometimes it was so true it wasn't really a dream at all.

'You broke my heart,' she said. 'Haven't you anything to say?'

What was there to say?

Nothing.

She was a mess. Her hair was all over the place. A rat's nest. Tendrils plastered to her neck and shoulders. The rain was running down her face. It dripped off the end of her nose.

She was barefoot.

Jess said, 'I hate you.'

She was standing out in the rain. It was bitter cold in the yard. I thought it was a stupid thing to do.

'No, you don't hate me,' I said. 'You're just angry. Now come inside. There's no point in making yourself ill.'

I had the crazy idea she was standing in the rain so I wouldn't see her crying. Or to make herself sick so I'd feel guilty.

God knew what the neighbours thought. Not that I gave a damn.

My being calm and sensible only made it worse for her.

'What do you care? I want to know you care. The only way I'll know you do care is if I can hurt you. Truly hurt you. I wish I knew how to really hurt you. I'd want to see you hurting. Then I'd know you did care.'

For a moment I thought she meant hurt as in pain – what it would feel like to have her stick a kitchen knife in me, for example. I knew she had contemplated doing something like that. But what she meant this time was feelings, emotions.

I didn't know too much about them.

'Come in,' I said. 'We can talk about it inside.'

The truth was that I was sick to death of talking about it.

'She's younger than me. And prettier. Taller. More fun. Have you any idea how that feels? Have you, Thomas?'

Her eyeshadow had slid down her face, and off her chin.

It was no good saying Mathilde was nothing like that in reality. Mathilde treated love-making like everything she did. As a challenge. As a means to an end. She was very mannish that way. It had nothing to do with fun, and everything to do with appetite and getting attention and scoring points, but I didn't know how to explain it.

Instead I got Jess a coat from the hall and went out and put it round her shoulders.

I heard whoever it was a long way off.

There was no wind. It helped the night sounds carry across the oasis.

A branch creaked, a twig snapped, a leather sandal scraped the surface of a rock.

I rolled over onto my stomach, tucked the rifle into my shoulder, left forearm extended.

Come on.

Nobody came this way unless they wanted me and knew where I was. I was all but invisible in my hide.

I recognized the silhouette and lowered the rifle.

'Bilal.'

Crouched down, she stumbled over to where I lay. Looking around her in case she was being followed.

Slid down beside me, breathless.

'Take.'

She held out a hand.

Pushing something at me.

The second grenade.

She was offering me the one thing she knew I wanted.

I took it, put it down next to the rifle.

'Soon,' she said. 'Very soon. In the night. They go. Border.'

'And you?'

No answer.

I said, 'Is Naim here?'

I sat up and took both her hands in mine. They were cold.

'No. Not here.'

'Sure?'

'Sure.'

I rubbed her icy fingers.

'Do they know who you are?'

'Abdur Rahman. Your friend. He know.'

'He say anything?'

'To me? No.'

'The others?'

'Amarayn servant woman. Cook. Wash. Clean.'

'I'm sorry.'

'No.' She brushed her fingers across my mouth. She meant I shouldn't speak. 'Listen, Bilal.'

I was listening.

Thinking she could get stuff into the cave for me.

Her mouth was close to my ear.

'They talk. The mujahedin. Abdur Rahman there, too. I hear them talk. They say Bilal English spy. Tell Abdur Rahman it his problem. Big problem. Problem must be . . .'

She searched for the word.

'Solved?'

'Yes. Solved. Before they go.'

'So they're saying it's Abdur Rahman's duty to solve the problem.'

'Yes.'

I put my arms around her, my cheek next to hers.

Hugged her gently. She did not resist.

'Thank you.'

'Bilal . . .'

'What is it?'

'I'm frightened, Bilal. About what happen to you.'

'Nothing will happen. Don't worry.'

She wasn't the only one. I was worried as hell.

Amarayn said, 'You go now. Escape.'

'No.'

'I come with you. We go Pakistan. Then England.'

A simple dream. An impossible one. A fantasy born of a young woman's desperation. How young I didn't know. Younger than Aisha, for sure. Early twenties, maybe.

'No, Amarayn.'

'Then you must go. I help you.'

'No. I stay. Everything will be okay.'

'They kill you,' she said.

'I don't think so. Not yet.'

'What you do?'

'Make plan.'

She ran both hands across my face, like a blind person.

'What plan?'

I said, 'You'll see. Don't worry.'

'Bilal . . .'

She pressed herself against me, her arms round my neck. I felt her heart beating. I thought I could tell what she was thinking. This foreigner did not know her people. Did not know their cruelty, how easily and thoughtlessly, after twenty-four years of war, they could snuff out a life. How little it mattered.

Desire woke and uncoiled itself in unfamilar territory.

'You went into the cave?'

She nodded.

'They let you?'

'To cave. Not inside.'

'How many people?'

She thought for a moment.

'Maybe three inside. Four, five outside.'

That was about right, I thought.

'Who was there?'

'Men. Men with guns.

'Osama bin Laden? His friend the Egyptian mullah?'

She answered with a shrug.

'I don't know.'

'But you didn't see them?'

'Bin Laden? No, I didn't see him. I didn't see any old man. These were mujahedin.'

'You know what bin Laden looks like?'

'Of course.'

He was her father-in-law, after all.

'You're sure?'

'Yes.'

Something was very wrong.

'So what did they do in there?'

'They talk much. Eat. Drink tea. Talk, talk, talk. Arabic. Too much talk.'

'You were there long?'

'No. Take clothes. For wash. But listen. Until guard send me away.'

'I see.'

'I drop something. You know? On purpose. I go back. Fetch. Listen some more. Guard hit me, chase me. Filipino, not Afghan. Also German man there.'

'That's useful to know.'

'Bilal, we say goodbye now.'

'God be with you, Amarayn.'

She didn't move.

We kissed then. Awkward at first, mouths missing each other, then clumsily joining. What she lacked in style she more than made up for in eagerness. She got the hang of it. When we both came up for air, Amarayn said, 'I go now, Bilal.'

'Go in peace.'

I felt certain I would never speak to her again.

EIGHTEEN

I climbed north-east, out the back door.

I couldn't be sure I wasn't seen.

Travelling light, I took just the rifle, the two magazines. The grenade. Water. Nothing else. I left my *potu*, turban and sandals behing, squirrelled away in my thicket.

Barefoot was a lot quieter.

The idea was reconnaissance. Nothing fancy.

I went uphill fast, taking the contours at an angle and counting off 800 metres at a steady run with my pebbles, stealing over the top and slithering over the crest on my belly, then turned ninety degrees south-east, a right-angled triangle, measuring the distances carefully.

I watched my back, stepping off my line of march, lying down flat in the scrub and waiting quietly for anyone tracking me.

None that I could see or hear above the sound of my own breathing.

Yet I was sure I was being observed.

It was just a feeling.

Come on, Felix.

Show yourself.

The hunter hunted.

I made sure I didn't run into an al-Qaeda outpost I didn't already know about.

I told myself I had taken every precaution. Reason said I was in the clear. It made me feel better, but my gut told me otherwise. I still felt someone or something behind me. It raised the hair on the back of my neck.

Every few yards I stopped to listen, holding my breath.

There was danger, I could feel it. It was increasing all the time, pressing in on me.

It was like a persistent alarm, growing increasingly shrill inside my head.

I got where I wanted to be just in time.

Dawn came in a blush of pink and yellow across the east.

She'd gone back into the cave to double-check.

It was a hell of a risk.

Amarayn told me that she had persuaded the cook and his assistant to let her help serve the food. The guards had tried to stop her, but she'd argued the toss and introduced herself as the Sheikh's daughter-in-law. Naim's wife. She knew it was taking an outside chance on her own life. If he was there, she reasoned, she was gambling on him not knowing the details of the married lives of his several male offspring.

She was female, yes, but she was also family. Because she was female and poor, and her clothes were torn, she would not be seen as a threat in any way. She hoped not. The Sheikh was her father-in-law, after all. It was all perfectly correct and above board.

In the event he wasn't there.

She was sure.

At prayers, perhaps?

She didn't think so.

Had he gone for a walk?

She didn't know.

*

'He wasn't there?

'No.'

'You're quite certain of this?'

'Yes.'

'There's no doubt?'

'No.'

'You're absolutely sure?'

She stretched out her hands, palms up. It was a gesture which said that was all she could say, and it was up to me whether I took her at her word. I looked at the slim, capable fingers, the skin of her palms roughened and hardened.

I was tempted to touch them, but I didn't.

'Really sure?'

'Yes, Bilal. Very sure.'

I had to believe her.

While laying out the dishes, she asked if she could go with the fighters to wherever it was they were headed. She wanted, she said, to be reunited with her husband, the Sheikh's youngest son.

Her own family, she said, was in Pakistan.

She could join them, they said. Yes.

They would leave at night, they told her. She should be ready at short notice.

She counted the men. She counted the weapons. She noted the layout of the cave. It wasn't really a cave, she said. More like an old mineshaft. It wasn't deep because the roof had caved in not twenty paces from the entrance.

The tall one was in charge, she thought.

The African, she called him.

When Abdur Rahman came in and saw her, he became angry and shouted at her to leave.

It was just a ramshackle chamber, the air full of dust, the fighters' weapons and gear stacked up in an untidy pile.

Amarayn was adamant that there was no sign at all of bin Laden, or of him ever having been there.

The region reminded me of an old man's open hand pressed palm down on a beige tablecloth, fingers spread wide, pointing south-west.

The tablecloth was the plain, the nobbly fingers represented the spines that ran along the southern boundary of the Kandahar–Kabul highway, the bony knuckles the high promontories like weathered statues standing guard.

The spring lay between middle and third finger, on the edge of the webbed skin that joined them. Abdur Rahman's camp lay on the rise just above the place where the water pushed its way out of the rock, but it was sited well within the patch of trees and undergrowth between the two knuckles. I had climbed up and crossed over, and now looked down at the slope between middle finger and forefinger. My perch was on the side of the middle knuckle, lying in a depression that was nothing more than a wrinkle in the giant's hand.

Enough, or so I thought, to conceal me from the entrance to the shaft.

The sun was as high as it got when he appeared.

He was tall. A head above the others.

I forgot the sun burning my neck, the stony ground under me, my thirst, the urge to urinate.

He carried an AKSU-74 slung over his right shoulder on a long strap. His sub-machine gun, his favourite, appeared in so many photographs and video clips it had become his trademark.

The sight of him gave me a bad dose of the fever the

shooter gets at the sight of his quarry after a long day's stalk. I forced myself to shut my eyes, slow my breathing and get myself back under control.

I counted up to ten.

Looked away. Looked back.

Steady.

He was still there.

In his left hand he carried a stick.

He appeared to lean on it.

He took just a couple of steps out into the morning air.

I knew him by his beard, his white turban, the fawning respect he prompted in the men around him.

He wore a camouflage waistcoat.

At 300 metres I made out his profile – just – but I couldn't see his expression.

He was saying goodbye. Or maybe giving final orders to three men, who slung their weapons and strode off downhill after the usual bows, hugs and salaams.

Couriers, probably.

In the distance, somewhere out of sight, I heard a motor-cycle cough into life.

Two bikes. The buzzing rising and tailing off.

Al-Qaeda didn't use laptops. It used people. It preferred traditional tradecraft – letter drops, cut-outs, all the tried and trusted Cold War means of running clandestine cells. In the West its activists had used payphones and phone cards when they had to, and when they exploited the Web they had used Internet cafés and false IDs and user names, but never laptops. They moved large sums of money across continents in tiny amounts. Their people wore the local dress, spoke the local language, learned to use the local accent, ate the local food and carried local ID. They fitted in. They were careful. They were patient. They were smart, a whole lot smarter than the people chasing them. I admired that. At the same time I had no illusions about what I was up against.

I was on their ground, not mine.

The reverse slope where the Sheikh stood was still in shadow. I was looking down and across at the cave, the entrance facing away from me.

The target was well within the effective range of my rifle.

They were going to pray.

Someone brought them water for the ritual washing.

Another fighter held a towel out to the Sheikh.

The tall man was squatting down, stick and sub-machine gun beside him.

He cupped his hands to catch the water.

Hands, face, feet, hands again.

The target was in the centre, facing east, looking down the gorge parallel to our own.

Facing Mecca.

Abdur Rahman took up position on Osama's left.

Two gunmen kept watch.

I ratcheted up the rear sight.

They would pray on Abdur's *potu*.

I settled myself down, getting comfortable, toes finding a purchase on the stones behind me, then held the AK-74 tight, placing the foresight where it came level with the V of the rear sight – dead centre on the Sheikh's back.

A neck shot, top of the spine.

Just in case his bulky jacket hid body armour.

Three well-placed 5.45 mm rounds would chop the backbone to pieces, maybe slice an artery and destroy the windpipe.

My forefinger took up the trigger slack.

Gently, now.

I thought about five million bucks.

I remembered what Felix had said that night in Hampshire.

They'll make damn sure we're never in a position to collect.

I moved the barrel a fraction to the left so I was aiming at the back of Abdur Rahman's head.

They seemed to be chatting. Nodding their heads. They were barely three feet apart. Abdur Rahman and the Sheikh, old friends, at their ease. I knew Abdur could deal with the sentries, even without Khaled's help, or mine for that matter. I wasn't surprised, though. I almost felt sorry for him. He was making the cardinal error of our trade. He had grown overconfident. He thought he had everything under control, that he was a lot smarter than everyone else.

His pride would cost him.

I moved the foresight back to the white turban.

The target and his companions went down on their knees.

No, I told myself. Not yet.

Two heads went down, two rumps rose.

I couldn't hear them, but the words of the prayer ran through my mind.

'Glory be to my Lord, the Most High, God is greater than all else.'

There was the matter of physical evidence.

The men sat back, then bent forward again.

The target got to his feet, leaning heavily on his stick.

Abdur Rahman helped him up.

They stood together, talking, warmed by the sun, breathing Afghanistan's clean air.

I was judge, jury and executioner.

Not true.

Quilty was. Thousands of miles away, a man in a suit with an indexed pension and maybe a knighthood to look forward to had been told by the prime minister to organize the taking of a man's life.

In a little while Quilty would be saying farewell to the wife and heading off to his usual seat on the 7.24 from Haslemere to Waterloo, *Daily Telegraph* neatly folded under one arm. While he waited on the platform he'd check the previous day's closing stock prices, or amuse himself with the crossword.

I was just the blunt end of the instrument of his will.

Did I believe the man whose life was in my hands had been responsible for the September 11 attacks?

I really didn't know.

It didn't make any difference. It didn't matter what anyone thought. This was nothing to do with justice or the rule of law. It was nothing to do with defending civilization.

Did they really think I'd do it out of greed, or just to stay out of Belmarsh high-security prison?

Yes, of course they did, and they were right.

But what I thought or felt had never meant anything, not to the Quiltys or Mathildes, not even to me.

It was far harder not to take the shot.

But what if Amarayn was right?

What if it wasn't the Sheikh?

And if it was, cutting him down might spawn a hundred others like him. A thousand would-be bin Ladens would spring from this arid place. Perhaps ten thousand.

The blood sang in my ears, the pulse beat in my throat liked a trapped animal.

I was drenched in sweat. My hands trembled.

I released the trigger, removed my forefinger from the trigger guard and lowered the rifle. I closed my eyes.

I stayed very still.

Breathe steadily, Morgan.

Something wasn't right.

At one hundred metres I could tell if a man was smiling or scowling. At two hundred the features of his face – eyes, nose and mouth – merged into short vertical and horizontal lines, a simple caricature, the target's identity as a distinct human being all but gone.

At three hundred the head was still distinct from torso, but only just, the face a pale blob.

At four hundred a man was little more than a stick.

The turban I recognized as simple cotton.

Not the coils of silk which Afghans preferred.

He was around six-two, maybe six-three.

I could make out the beard reaching to the middle of his chest.

But I couldn't see the face.

Dehumanize that which you intend to destroy.

I'd killed for the first time for twenty-six quid a week, less the usual deductions, and I hadn't seen the face of the man I'd shot.

It hadn't bothered me then.

Now I was the killer who wouldn't kill, the bounty hunter who couldn't hunt, not even for a preposterous sum of cash that was almost impossible to imagine.

On the word of a young Afghan woman.

When I opened my eyes again, I knew I'd had the target in my sights for no more than two minutes, maybe less.

Amarayn had seemed so very sure.

The Sheikh turned and said something to Abdur Rahman, then ducked back into the mouth of the mine.

The enemy – if that was what he was – would live to fight another day.

Would I get another chance – and would I take it?

I had no idea.

Abdur Rahman came and went. The sentries didn't even stop him for the formality of an identity check.

Food – prepared in our camp – was brought up over the crest, and someone from the cave came out and took it back inside. Two gunmen would carry it up, and they'd have to make two or three journeys scrambling up and down the hillside.

In the afternoon, Amarayn took up laundry, neatly folded, but she wasn't allowed in. She was stopped at the entrance.

Surely she would see the Sheikh now from where she stood?

Two sentries guarded the approaches to the hideout. One to the south-east, below the entrance. The second below and off to my right, above the cave and to the north-west.

The goons were free to move, but had no set pattern. They were on duty for three hours, followed by three off. They could walk or sit. They didn't use binoculars. In the early part of the day they kept moving to stay warm. As the sun rose and warmed the gully, so they tended to stay in one place. One man found himself a large flat rock and settled himself down on it and stared off to the south, smoking one cigarette after another, enjoying the panoramic view across the valley floor towards the Hada hills.

Abdur Rahman vanished into the cave shortly before lunch and didn't emerge until mid-afternoon.

Other al-Qaeda fighters – the off-duty sentries – would join those on watch, emerging from the Sheikh's shelter and sitting with their comrades and talking, or simply dozing among the rocks, enjoying the sunshine.

Every now and then a man would slip away to relieve himself.

The Sheikh did not reappear.

Then, at dusk, the motorcycles returned.

A little later the three men I saw leave in the morning reappeared on foot. I couldn't be absolutely sure, but they seemed to be the same people. They were halted by the guards and then allowed up to the cave entrance.

They attracted quite a crowd. What appeared to be a lively discussion involving several people ensued – characterized by a lot of arm waving – then they ducked down and went inside.

They were getting ready to move.

Night was falling. I had to get back before I was missed.

NINETEEN

I didn't see Amarayn on my return. I didn't see her when I woke, either. I assumed she had been put to work again, washing and cleaning. It was better that we didn't meet.

'Walk?'

Abdur Rahman had finished praying.

'Sure.'

I gulped down the rest of my tea.

'Let's go.'

He turned away. I grabbed my rifle and followed.

For the first few minutes we said nothing.

I said, 'Where's Naim?'

Abdur Rahman smiled at me through his beard.

'You know who I mean,' I said. 'The Sheikh's son – one of them.'

'You needn't worry, Bilal.'

It was a knowing look. Sly.

'Why would I worry?'

'Naim divorced her. She was a bad wife.'

'Bad, how?'

Abdur Rahman shrugged. 'She didn't tell you?'

'No,' I said. 'She didn't. She hardly speaks a word of English. But she did say she'd come here to find him. She had nowhere else to go.'

'She told you that?'

'It was my impression.'

'Ah, but your Pashto is so much better now, Bilal. I'm sure you and she understand each other very well by now.'

'Does the Sheikh know about the divorce?'

He didn't reply.

'Does he?'

'It's best not to meddle in family matters, Bilal.'

We left the sanctuary of green and followed the dry river bed that ran along the bottom of the wadi in a south-westerly direction, the way Amarayn and I had come the previous week. Abdur Rahman called out a greeting to his sentries as we passed them. It was another chill morning with a breeze strengthening from the west. The sentries were wrapped in their *potus* and looked as if they couldn't wait to get off duty, one vigorously picking his aquiline nose.

'I haven't seen Khaled for the last couple of days – has he gone?'

No response.

'And those mules – they weren't there today.'

He didn't reply.

Another five minutes and we were quite alone.

'There's something I've been meaning to ask you,' I said.

We both stopped. He turned to face me. I noticed he carried a Tokarev in a holster under his left shoulder. No rifle.

I said, 'You were in the Khad in the early nineties, in charge of surveillance of foreigners in Kabul. It was a special unit set up by the Taliban for that purpose.'

He waited, impassive.

'It was you who tipped the British off about our little expedition to collect the goods buried in the grounds of the embassy in Kabul. Your job was to get us and the stuff out of the country, using your contacts with the Taliban in Kandahar. You did a good job, there's no doubt about that, but you grassed us up, Abdur.' He opened his mouth to speak, but I held up my hand. 'My question is this – what was in it for you? You had your cut. It was an equal share. You collected, too. So why do it? What did you have to gain from turning us in? But I have a more important question. You know the smugglers' pipeline even better than I do. So why did you ask for me in this operation? Why get me out of the prison hospital in Dhahran? You had the access, the contacts and the route, but you sold Quilty the idea of hiring me on the grounds that I was the only one who knew the way really well. Why?'

He looked around as if taking his bearings.

'How long have you been waiting to ask me?'

I said, 'Ever since I knew it was you who shopped us.'

'And how did you know?'

'I figured it out.'

'All by yourself?'

'Fuck you.'

'You want the truth, English?'

'It would be nice, Abdur. Just this once.'

'You have a theory, though, don't you?'

'Of course I do.'

'I'd like to hear it.'

He wanted to hear how much I thought I knew.

I didn't mind. What the hell, I would humour him. Nothing I said was going to make any difference now.

Abdur Rahman sat down on a smooth, flat stone. Always fastidious, he first brushed the dirt off it with his *potu*. While I talked he drew circular patterns in the sand with a twig. I sat opposite on a tussock of dead grass. I could feel the weight of my rifle across my back, still sensitive where the weapon dug into the scar tissue.

At least we were partly sheltered from the wind.

I did have a theory.

I said Abdur Rahman had been hired at university by either the Security Service, otherwise known as MI5, or alternatively by the Secret Intelligence Service. Whoever it was encouraged him to spy on his fellow students, especially the militant fringes, from the racist retards of the British National Party to the acidhead anarcho-syndicalists on the far left.

Once he'd successfully completed his six-month probation, he was given some training and directed to focus on the Muslim students.

Get deeper, he was told. Throw yourself into it. We'll back you up, pull you out and set you up elsewhere if things go pear-shaped. Don't worry about the costs. Count on us.

The usual promises.

'Right, Abdur?'

He didn't answer. Just smiled his superior smile and kept doodling in the sand.

Conversion, I said, change of name – they told him to go for it.

Regular Koranic studies, prayer meetings. The works.

At first he was simply an agent, and a bloody good one.

He relished the clandestine life. He got into it big time. His new persona appealed to him. I said it was more than simply good cover. He more than lived it.

Abdur Rahman became his double life. He slipped easily from one to the other. He loved it. But he didn't tell his masters at Vauxhall Cross that.

'You kept it to yourself,' I said.

He didn't answer, just drew in the sand, round and round, going nowhere.

I said, 'That way you thought you could control it. It gave you the feeling that you were in charge. That your destiny was in your hands. It was a sense of power, and you loved it.'

That was just the start, I said.

Mir'aj was his creation, or rather it was the brainchild of an unusually creative case officer, and he had done the leg-work, setting it up.

Was it Mathilde?

I didn't think so.

Someone like Quilty, I suggested, for that disturbing combination of suburban idealism and amoral worldliness.

At some point he was promoted to head agent.

It sounded fancy, but it wasn't, not really.

All it meant was that he recruited sub-agents – such as the unfortunate Bilal, aka Tucker – to the Mir'aj network. They thought they were working for Islam.

Fat chance. It was a classic 'false flag' recruitment. The Warriors of God were working for Her Majesty's Government with Abdur as the cut-out between them and the case officer.

Beautiful. A real work of art.

When the suicide bombers seized the domestic US airliners and slammed them into the twin towers and the Pentagon on September 11, Abdur and his Mir'aj network found themselves in the pound seats. No one else had anything like it – certainly not the Central Intelligence Agency, the Pentagon or the National Security Agency.

The same went for the SVR, successors to the KGB.

He'd started as a shabby copper's nark, I suggested, and almost overnight he had become a star performer.

Money was no longer an issue.

Abdur Rahman and his Mir'aj network were flavour of the month. The Americans wanted the product. The British could play coy and sit above the salt at all the top tables in Washington. The special relationship really meant something again.

Abdur Rahman was one hell of an asset. No wonder Quilty's people took him to London and installed him in the Savoy and gave him his own car and driver-cum-bodyguard. Washington could spend more than the other eighteen NATO member states put together on defence, but they had nothing like Abdur Rahman. He and his people were all there was in 'humint' or human intelligence in Afghanistan, and they reached into the heart of the Taliban and their al-Qaeda allies.

The converse was also true: thanks to Abdur Rahman, al-Qaeda reached into the heart of the Western counter-terror effort.

I had just one other question.

He snapped the twig in two and looked up.

I said, 'Whose side are you really on? Or don't you know yourself any more?'

TWENTY

The big Tokarev was in Abdur's hand.

Not a thing of beauty, but effective.

He was pointing it at me.

'You see, Bilal, I have made my peace with these people. I have decided to live here. I've come down off the fence. This is my home now.'

I said it was good of him to be so honest. I wasn't quite sure at what point it had all fallen into place, but I had realized a long time ago that he'd tipped off London about the embassy job because he needed to appease his British masters. He had to keep Quilty and others of his ilk sweet. He must have known by then that he could pretty well get away with anything by playing both sides off against each other, and by feeding his rival paymasters with titbits from time to time.

There were more than two sides, in fact.

As for me, my cover had been my protection – until this moment. Bilal's reputation, constructed so carefully, even by Abdur Rahman himself, couldn't be undone publicly. He'd had to bring me out here to do the deed himself.

My demise had been part of his plan all along.

I said, 'You're never going back?'

Abdur Rahman shook his head.

I said, 'Captain Jameel told me before he died you worked for ISI. He genuinely believed you were their agent. He was disappointed but not surprised to learn you were also working for London, and that you'd long since given your allegiance –

such as it is – to al-Qaeda. No doubt you thought you could play them all off against one another indefinitely.'

'Which is what I have done, English.'

'And the reward money?'

I couldn't help but like him. We were of a kind, Abdur and I. We were both men of violence and larceny. It was nothing to be proud of, but neither of us was the stuff of corporate theft or state-sanctioned mass murder, dressed up in the rituals of West Point or the claptrap of the International Monetary Fund.

'I knew you of all people would ask that.'

He got to his feet, the 7.62 mm automatic trained on my chest. He held it with both hands, a double-fisted grip, the way he had been taught.

'I will have both,' he said. 'Why not? This – my adopted home – and the money. I could do so much good with it here.'

'What about the evidence you need – still alive and kicking up there in the cave?'

I glanced back up the valley.

'The evidence, as you put it, is in Saudi, or at least in Saudi airspace. The Sheikh was never here, English. I'm really sorry to disappoint you and your friends.' Abdur didn't look sorry at all. His expression and his tone were nothing short of triumphant. 'He crossed into the North West Frontier Province three days ago. From Khost. Our Zadran friends took him across. The Afridis looked after him until the Saudi ambassador's plane flew him out. Both Mr Quilty and Captain Jameel obliged us by looking the wrong way.'

It was all clear to me now.

'He's retiring, is he?'

Abdur Rahman didn't like my tone.

I said, 'You persuaded Jameel you were bringing the Sheikh out this way. You didn't trust the Pakistanis not to change their minds while he was still here in Afghanistan. You couldn't be sure Washington wouldn't find out and twist

Islamabad's arm. So you waited until Khaled sent word the Sheikh was safe on the other side and the Saudi plane was right there on the tarmac at Peshawar airport. That's what all that coming and going was about yesterday. Right?'

He dropped his left hand from the pistol and put forefinger and thumb up to his lips and blew two short, sharp whistles.

The north African stood up from behind a rock.

'You remember our friend? I believe you've already met.'

'How could I forget?'

'Hamid is Tunisian, not Algerian as you thought. But as you see, he is tall, and the white turban he's wearing along with his beard, the sub-machine gun and the camouflage smock give him a superficial resemblance to the Sheikh – especially for the high-resolution cameras the Americans have on their spy planes and satellites. Hamid is our decoy, English. He prays in the open every day and drinks tea in the sunshine. It's not a bad way to fight a war, but it's dangerous work.'

I thought of Hamid kneeling to pray while I took aim at the back of his neck.

How close Hamid had been to martyrdom.

Abdur said, 'Look, you can call it a convergence of interest. The Americans and you British want the Sheikh dead. They don't care how. They don't care about you. Or me. They want him destroyed. That's their main aim. For our part, we want to provide the impression of martyrdom, to create the legend that will outlive all of us. You see?'

I saw.

Abdur Rahman said, 'I think urine and blood samples should do the trick, don't you?'

He was smiling, sure of himself.

'The Sheikh's agreed to this?'

'He's done more than that, English. We're about to send our friends in London and Washington a video clip of the body. His body. It will look very authentic. They cannot take martyrdom away from Muslims no matter how hard the

Sharons and Rumsfelds might try. And of course we'll distribute plenty of copies for al-Jazeera, CNN and the BBC. I'm sorry you won't be there to see it.'

It made sense. It would create the myth while bin Laden himself lived out his natural life in comfortable obscurity. Osama would never die in the imaginations of millions of Muslims. Not really. He would be with us always. He was to Islam what Mao and Che were to the Left. He would be everywhere, his adherents multiplying wherever America and its allies continued to criminalize the poor, outlaw the dispossessed and strip the weak of their rights.

For bin Laden, eternity was a two-minute video clip.

Unless he changed his mind later on and did a Lazarus, timing his rise from the dead to coincide with the start of George W. Bush's re-election campaign.

In the meantime, armed with the Sheikh's body fluids, Abdur Rahman would claim his share of the reward. If it really existed.

He might even inherit whatever was left of al-Qaeda's empire in south Asia and use the reward money to resurrect its clandestine cells.

It would be quite a coup if he could pull it off.

As for me, I was merely the stalking horse and mock executioner. A walk-on part with few lines.

Hamid was advancing towards us. He didn't know he owed his life to me and he wouldn't have cared if he had. Neither he nor Abdur Rahman knew I'd crouched above them on the ridge, my AK-74 pointed at the back of their heads.

Hamid was holding something in front of him. Whatever it was, it was struggling, trying to break free.

I played for time. It was all I could do.

'So what was my role in your game?'

'Don't underestimate yourself, English. You led us all to the Sheikh and you will fall in battle, in the final shoot-out. At least, that's how it will be seen. You were the one foreigner who knew the way, who could use the ground and live among the Afghans. You were the one who did the deed. That's how it will look. You will die a hero, English, bringing down America's most wanted man. Who knows? The Queen might give you the George Cross. Maybe Mr Bush will put up a statue in your honour. Posthumously, of course. You will both die heroic deaths. Except yours will be real. You are part of the legend I have created for Osama. Look on the positive side. You have a place in history.'

He was savouring every moment and that was fine by me.

'One more thing, Abdur.'

I daren't look at what Hamid was doing. I knew if I did, I'd overreact. I had to pretend I didn't care what they did to Amarayn. I had to show I didn't care at all, that I was indifferent, that she didn't matter any more to me than she did to them, or they'd kill her right away for the pleasure of seeing me squirm.

I said, 'How long have you been doubled? Working for al-Qaeda, I mean?'

Abdur Rahman smiled.

'It's not something that happens overnight,' he said. 'Not that I'd expect you to understand. But then you're an unbeliever. A mercenary. There was a time when I thought perhaps I could persuade you to join us . . .'

Fat fucking chance.

'When was it that you finally saw the light? Was it the September 11 attacks?'

I never did get an answer.

Amarayn cried out. Hamid had forced her to her knees. She fell hard. He had hold of her hair in one hand, his AK-47 in the other. He had pushed her ahead of him like something unpleasant, distasteful, and now she was on the ground and he was dragging her, stopping occasionally to give her a vicious kick.

Abdur Rahman said, 'The woman's been helping you, English. She's your spy. Don't deny it. You were seen. A Muslim woman with a non-Muslim, out of wedlock. She told you who was in the mine and who wasn't. She told you the Sheikh wasn't with us. What did you promise her – a British visa? Money? You think the Sheikh doesn't know who she is – or that she's been divorced by his son? Of course he knows.'

Hamid let go and took a step back.

I saw what they meant to do.

Abdur Rahman gestured with the Tokarev. 'On your knees, English. Hands on the back of your head.'

I slid forward. Slowly.

'You're making a mistake, Abdur. I'd really have another think about this if I were you, pal.'

'You would say that. I know I would.'

Hamid was on my right, Abdur Rahman on my left.

Amarayn was on the ground in the middle.

She crawled over to Abdur. She whimpered and clutched at his feet. She too was playing for time, looking for an opportunity to spoil his aim. He pulled back. He didn't want to be touched.

I tried again.

'Listen to me,' I said. 'Don't do it. Do you really think they haven't thought this through? Do you imagine they would let you, or me, or anyone else go off the rails at this stage? You've met Quilty. You know him. He's planned for every eventuality – even your defection. Don't you think he knows what you're up to? So I'm to be shot to keep you on board with the Sheikh and you come out smelling of roses and collect the reward. It's smart. I'm sure you and Rumsfeld would get along famously. You could bring in Sharon and Saddam to complete the global partnership. Rumsfeld needs people like you to feed his war hysteria and keep the defence industries happy. You need bumbling bullies like him to provide you with an endless stream of eager recruits. Between the two of you, you could keep this up for years. But that's only the half of it. They've known all along we'd be heading to this place. You and your friend Suleiman told me, and I told them. You were there. That's why I was picked, Abdur. I knew the way. You said so. They've tracked us, right from the start, all along the pipeline. You're going down too, don't you see? None of us is indispensable. Not even you. Not any more.'

It wasn't a bad speech, but Abdur Rahman wasn't listening.

I'd lost him.

Amarayn tried to grab his hands, but he pulled his left arm behind him. His right was still extended, the Tokarev pointed at me.

He nodded at Hamid.

Hamid levelled his rifle, the muzzle a few inches from the back of Amarayn's head.

I had run out of things to say.

Amarayn shook violently, anticipating the bullet.

Hamid's left hand cocked the Kalashnikov, slamming a round into the breech in a single movement. I saw the thumb of his right hand push the safety catch on to single fire.

He never did hear what hit him.

Hamid took a little jump.

Both his feet left the ground. He spun round, crashed down on his back.

He was dead before any of us heard the bang.

His eyes stared up at the sky. They bulged a little.

His face was permanently spoiled and the white turban lay uncoiled on the ground like a bloodstained bandage.

That was because the top of his skull was missing.

His brains were splashed on the stones behind him.

There was only one weapon that fired a half-inch slug from up to a mile – at such a range that the victims never heard what it was that killed them.

Instinctively, Abdur Rahman crouched down, looking for the source of the shot.

Not so easy at 1,200 yards.

There wasn't time to go for the AK-74 across my back. I dug my toes into the sand and bent my knees and flew at him, my right arm drawn back.

I struck him as hard as I could at the base of the nose with the ball of my palm. It could have killed him, but it didn't.

He dropped the Tokarev and was on his hands and knees, shaking his head, quite dazed.

Abdur Rahman tried to speak but couldn't.

He made a growling sound in his throat.

I bent and picked up the pistol. I tossed it well out of reach.

Then I kicked him hard in the ribs and I heard them crack. He fell heavily on his side, blood gushing out of his broken nose. He seemed to be looking at me, but his eyes weren't focused on anything very much.

'That's for Amarayn,' I said. 'And for being such a smug, double-dealing shit. If only you'd listened.'

Abdur Rahman wasn't going anywhere.

He lay quite still.

That's when I looked up and saw the planes.

TWENTY-ONE

The world filled with relentless noise.

Two special ops C-130s came out of the north-east. One its own length behind the other. The heavy-bellied planes flew parallel to the gorge. They were dark grey and about 3,000 metres away to the west.

I grabbed Amarayn's hand.

We had half a minute to get clear.

'Come on.'

We ran south, along the floor of the Lowrah valley, back the way we'd come ten days earlier. I dragged Amarayn after me. We zigzagged along the sand, dodging the boulders, swerving in and out of the long-dry pools.

'Bilal, Bilal . . .'

No time to explain.

No time at all.

The C-130s' rear doors were open. When the cargo extraction parachutes popped out like some weird embryos, I knew for sure what would come after.

They would obliterate everything. There would be no evidence. There would be no sign any of us – Amarayn, Abdur Rahman, me – had ever been here.

'This way . . .'

I turned right. We ran out of the river bed, uphill, scrabbling, falling and getting up again, grazing our knees, clawing with our hands at the scrub and thorn, throats burning from gasping for air.

JOHN FULLERTON

I needed to get to the high ground if we were to have any chance at all of survival.

I saw the first two bombs.

Like huge barrels, painted a cheery orange.

BLU-82Bs were too big to be dropped by conventional means. Instead they had to be rolled out the back.

I knew what they contained, too: ammonium nitrate, aluminium powder and polystyrene.

A cheap, soapy and highly combustible slurry.

Two more followed, rolling out and falling.

In Vietnam they were used to clear jungle quickly.

In Desert Storm they cleared Iraqi conscripts off the face of the desert and those they didn't kill, they terrified.

At 15,000 pounds apiece, they were the biggest conventional bombs in existence.

Four of them were heading our way.

Courtesy of Quilty and Mathilde of Vauxhall Cross and 10th US Special Forces Group from Fort Campbell, Kentucky.

The second set of stabilization parachutes flipped open.

Hamid's height, his white cotton turban, his brief perambulations and ablutions, had done the trick. Or maybe Felix had talked them in on to the target.

Zotov had been right after all. We'd never be in a position to collect. Not unless we sprouted wings ourselves and got away in time.

The barrel-like objects started to drift towards us, the silky fabric bobbing gently like huge party balloons.

Rocking, unhurried.

So harmless. So jolly.

The breeze out of the west would carry them across, two to our gully and two to the gorge where the Sheikh and his gunmen were supposed to have been.

Deserted now, empty.

The bombs would detonate just above the surface. Producing 1,000 pounds per square inch of overpressure.

290

The killing ground for each had a radius of 900 feet.

No craters.

Just instant oblivion for anything anywhere on the food chain, anything that crawled, squirmed or ran, from bugs and snakes to men and women.

Daisy Cutters, the Americans called them.

I looked up at the crest. Felix Zotov was holding my Barrett rifle over his head. He was shouting, but I couldn't hear anything he was saying.

Yannis was next to him, jumping up and down and waving.

An air superiority fighter barrelled overhead.

Instinctively we all ducked.

The F-15 Eagle banked, straightened up. The pilot pulled on the stick and climbed, leaving us with a brief view of the twin suns of his afterburn receding into the cloudless sky.

He'd be gobbling burgers, fries and beer within the hour somewhere out on the Arabian Sea.

The planes were gone. We were left with the parachutes and the Daisy Cutters swinging over our heads in bright sunshine.

Silence.

I started to climb.

I could hear them shouting.

The AK-74 and Hudson Bay pack were in the way and I got rid of them, flinging both aside.

I grabbed Amarayn's left hand in my right and held tight.

The BLUs were big brutes, measuring just under twelve feet. There were 2,700 feet from the point of delivery to the point of detonation.

I was no mathematician, but it did not look good. I made it twenty-five seconds in a three-knot wind; something that was very carefully calculated with the help of onboard computers.

I dug into the clay soil, kicking toeholds, the fingers of my left hand grappling for something to hold on to, snatching at a root, a stump. Anything.

Amarayn followed.

I couldn't get enough oxygen into my lungs. My chest ached with the effort, sucking at the air.

So this was it. I had been set loose by Quilty to scuttle along the Kandahar–Quetta pipeline. That was all I had ever been expected to do. Quilty was a user of men, and he had used me to run a course I knew best. There were no high-tech gizmos to screw things up. Just an old smugglers' path through the arid hills with Felix on my heels. The stuff about getting close and killing the Sheikh and bringing something back for identification – none of that really mattered to Quilty. It never had. He and his kind hadn't thought it feasible. The money was simply the carrot and here was the stick to beat all sticks.

Abdur Rahman had been a step ahead, but they hadn't known that in the Pentagon or Vauxhall Cross. The lad from Brixton Hill had outfoxed us all, me included.

We'd all understimated him.

But even he didn't count for anything any more.

None of us did. Not to the likes of Quilty.

Just a couple of feet to go before an overhang.

'Bilal . . . no good.'

She was slipping and I couldn't hold her.

'I can't,' she said.

She lost her footing and just for a moment hung in space.

I felt her hand slither out of mine.

It was as if she'd just let go, given up.

She tumbled almost all the way down, a small avalanche of stones and muck rolling with her.

The pressure fuse would crack the canisters open ten feet or so above the floor of the gully. A second detonation would ignite the aerosol spray.

The aircrews knew exactly what they were doing.

'Get up, for Christ's sake. Morgan, get up . . .'

They were cheering me on from the touchline.

Gerber was there, too, on his knees, yelling at the top of his voice. Quilty's people must have organized his reappearance just in time for the final act.

They'd formed a three-man stick to track us, vectored in on the valley by Mathilde and her US forward air controllers.

I stopped. Looked down.

Amarayn wasn't going to get away with dying.

Felix's voice rang out above the din.

'Christ on the cross, Morgan, get a fucking move on.'

Fuck it.

I lowered myself back down again.

I told myself it wasn't far. It wouldn't take a moment. I watched where I put my feet. Up on the ridge they weren't shouting any more.

I moved steadily, carefully.

I stood next to her. I bent, put my left arm under her back, the other under her knees, and lifted. I held her against my chest.

I started the climb back.

I was as unsteady as a Glaswegian on a Saturday night.

Paused right below the overhang.

Felix's frown was only inches away.

Yannis, too, peered down at us.

Like a weightlifter, I pushed her up over my head, using both hands.

Yannis took Amarayn from me. I felt her weight go, the load lighten. They had her by both arms, and were dragging her up.

I didn't let go until I saw the soles of her feet vanish.

My turn.

Six hands reached down and grasped my clothing, my wrists.

I was trying to help, kicking myself higher with my feet. They were pulling me, the world seeming to slow down, time telescoping out, the parachute silk flapping in that ever-so-blue sky, then my arms were over the lip and they were rolling me over, turning me, grabbing my legs, drawing me back from the edge and holding me down.

The first blast wave hit, a stinging blow of hot air. The cliff rocked like blancmange.

We were thrown together, tossed back in a heap, a tangle of limbs and equipment. Dirt clogged mouth and nose. I was spitting and coughing and there was a stench of burning. The sky went dark like someone turning off the power.

We were going to make it. Of course we were. An immense roaring started in my ears. It grew steadily louder, but it wasn't in the least frightening. Perhaps it should have been.

I hugged Felix. You saved us, Russian. I was shouting, but he couldn't hear me. You took the shot. One hell of a shot. You saw a tall man in a white cotton turban and you did it. Felix needn't know who the target really was. It was better that way. Only Amarayn and I knew what had really happened in the valley. Tough about the money, but I was certain that as long as we kept what we knew to ourselves and never spoke of it to anyone, we'd be safe. All of us.

No one need ever know.

Not now, not ever.